The yellowbacks... classics of popular fiction

The yellowjackets or yellowbacks were a great series of bestselling adventure and crime thrillers that had its origins in the mid to late 19th century following on from the 'penny dreadfuls'. They virtually began the mass market revolution of the early 20th century with a clear standard format and imprint/series livery (what would today be called branding). Hodder & Stoughton published the yellowjackets in two main series with series run dates of: 1923-1939 and later 1949-1957.

As the tagline ('where thrillers really began') on the back cover implies, the imprint and series focused on thrillers that were the bestsellers of their time. This current reissue or retro revival if you will, brings back many of these masterpieces, now classics in their own way and extends it further by including key titles from that period that were either great crime or thriller or even general commercial fiction (including sub-genres of noir, horror, gothic, romance, westerns, etc.) influences of their time. There are some perennial favourites and many rarities either lost or not easily available being revived in the current series. Writers and characters ranged from adventure heroes like Bulldog Drummond, Allan Quatermain, Richard Hannay or the Saint through thriller grandmasters Edgar Wallace and E. Phillips Oppenheim, crime and mystery maestros like Patricia Wentworth, GK Chesterton, Agatha Christie and the Detection club, to western and swashbucklers like Zane Grey, Max Brand, Captain Blood and even romance or general fiction classics like Hermina Black, Denise Robins, Marie Corelli or Stella Morton. These were books that had storytelling at their heart and always entertained.

The yellowbacks had both hardback (with varying design elements) and paperback (which built the series look) versions with the latter still carrying the imprint 'yellowjacket'. The current reissues pay tribute to both and use an amalgam of elements from both editions while retaining the complete yellow (or 'mustard-plaster') livery with the author's name in blue beveled type with a 'simulated emboss' effect and a white outer 'outline', and the book title in black. These reissues retain the distinctive size of the original mass market paperback and follow the three main category variations—the thrillers (crime, westerns, mystery, adventure) had blue lettering for the author's name, while Romance and softer general fiction had red; and other categories like humour had green.

For more detail and a full list of titles visit https://www.hachetteindia.com/home/yellowbacks

ZADIG AND VATHEK

ZADIG AND VATHEK

Voltaire François-Marie Arouet (1694–1778) was a French Enlightenment writer, historian and philosopher. Known by his nom de plume M. de Voltaire, he was famous for his wit, and his criticism of Christianity – especially of the Roman Catholic Church – and of slavery. Voltaire was an advocate of freedom of speech, freedom of religion, and separation of church and state.

Voltaire was a versatile and prolific writer, producing works in almost every literary form, including plays, poems, novels, essays, histories and scientific expositions.

William Thomas Beckford (1760–1844) was an English novelist, art collector, patron of decorative art, critic, travel writer, plantation owner and a politician for some time. Beckford is remembered for a Gothic novel, *Vathek* (1786); for building the lost Fonthill Abbey in Wiltshire and Lansdown Tower ("Beckford's Tower") in Bath; and for his art collection.

He was reputed at one stage to be England's richest commoner. The son of William Beckford and Maria Hamilton, daughter of the Hon. George Hamilton, he served as a Member of Parliament for Wells in 1784–1790 and Hindon in 1790–1795 and 1806–1820. As a writer, Beckford is remembered for Vathek, and for his travel memoir, *Italy: With Some Sketches of Spain and Portugal.* He followed *Vathek* with two parodies of current cultural fashions, the formulaic sentimental novel, in *Modern Novel Writing,* or, *The Elegant Enthusiast* (1796) and *Azemia,* a satire on the Minerva Press novels, written as "Jacquetta Agneta Mariana Jenks, of Belgrove Priory in Wales"; and also published *Biographical Memoirs of Extraordinary Painters* (1780), a literary prank burlesquing serious biographical encyclopaedias.

ZADIG

by Voltaire

AND

VATHEK

by William Beckford, Esq.

HODDER AND STOUGHTON
YELLOW JACKET
hachette

Zadig and Vathek
Zadig was first published in 1747;
Vathek was written in French beginning in 1782, and then translated into English by Reverend Samuel Henley and first published in 1786 by J. Johnson.

1

The texts in these editions in most cases have been reprinted as is, with minimal editorial changes and by and large no bowdlerizing for political correctness; though in some editions, a few words and phrases considered archaic, or those considered offensive now, along with archaic punctuation may have been modified in places to make the text more accessible to today's readers. The narratives, language, beliefs, social mores and/or cultural depictions, in these volumes are a reflection of their times and must be viewed as such. They may also contain certain cultural, racial and gender prejudices and stereotypes that may be outdated or clearly wrong then and wrong today; but their removal would be tantamount to claiming these prejudices never existed. The Publisher does not endorse or support those depictions or stereotypes; and these books have been made available for a discerning audience that will read it for entertainment value and a chronicle/record of popular fiction of past times.

Cover design by Priya Singh adapted from the original classic yellowjacket by Hodder & Stoughton.

Cover illustration by Ishan Trivedi.

Series note: Some of the books in the series (unless otherwise credited) may have cover or inside illustrations from the original yellowbacks or early editions, and while full restoration has been attempted, some images may be grainy or faded due to the condition of the original material. The end notes or bonus material or blurb details may have been sourced from the public domain or free use publications such as Wikipedia and attribution is hereby made also allowing similar free use reproduction from here. Sources requiring further specific attribution may write in and further detailing and/or corrections shall be made in subsequent printings/editions.

Reprint specifications may be subject to change including but not limited to finishes, paper, colour sections.

ISBN: 978-93-5731-214-1

Hachette Book Publishing India Pvt. Ltd.
4th & 5th Floors, Corporate Centre,
Plot No. 94, Sector 44, Gurugram - 122 003, India

Typeset in Electra LT STD 10/12.5 pt by Manipal Technologies Limited, Manipal

Printed and bound in India by Manipal Technologies Limited, Manipal

MIX
Paper from
responsible sources
FSC™ C043100

CONTENTS

Zadig

CONTENTS

The Dedication to the

SULTANA SHERAA

By

SADI

I

THE BLIND EYE

In the reign of king *Moabdar*, there was a young man, a native of *Babylon*, by name *Zadig*; who was not only endowed by nature with an uncommon genius, but born of illustrious parents, who bestowed on him an education no ways inferior to his birth. Tho' rich and young, he knew how to give a check to his passions; he was no ways self-conceited; he didn't always act up to the strictest rules of reason himself, and knew how to look on the foibles of others, with an eye of indulgence. Every one was surpriz'd to find, that notwithstanding he had such a fund of wit, he never insulted; nay, never so much as rallied any of his companions, for that tittle tattle, which was so vague and empty, so noisy and confus'd; for those rash reflections, those illiterate conclusions, and those insipid jokes; and, in short, for that flow of unmeaning words, which was call'd polite conversation in *Babylon*. He had learned from the first book of *zoroaster*, that self-love is like a bladder full blown, which when once prick'd, discharges a kind of petty tempest. Zadig, in particular, never boasted of his contempt of the fair sex, or of his facility to make conquests amongst them. He was of a generous spirit; insomuch, that he was not afraid of obliging even an ungrateful man; strictly adhering to that wise maxim of *Zoroaster*. *When you are eating, throw an offal to the dogs that are under the table, lest they should be tempted to bite you.* He was as wise as he could well be wish'd; since he was fond of no company, but such as were distinguish'd for men of sense. As he was well-grounded, in all the sciences of the antient *chaldeans*, he was no stranger to those principles of natural philosophy, which were then known: and understood as much of metaphysics as any one in all ages after him; that is to say, he knew little or nothing of the matter. He was firmly convinc'd, that the year consisted of 365 days and an half, tho' directly repugnant to the new philosophy of the age he liv'd in; and that the sun was situated in the center of the earth; and when the chief magi told him, with an imperious air, that he maintain'd erroneous principles; and that it was an indignity offered to the government under which he liv'd, to imagine the sun should roll round its own axis, and that the year consisted of twelve months, he knew how to sit still and quiet, without shewing the least tokens of resentment or contempt.

As *Zadig* was immensely rich, and had consequently friends without number; and as he was a gentleman of a robust constitution, and remarkably handsome; as he was endowed with a plentiful share of ready and inoffensive wit: and, in a word, as his heart was perfectly sincere and open, he imagin'd himself, in some measure, qualified to be perfectly happy. For which purpose he determin'd to marry a gay young lady (one *semira* by name) whose beauty, birth and fortune, render'd her the most desirable person in all *Babylon*. He had a sincere affection for her, grounded on honour, and *semira* conceiv'd as tender a passion for him. They were just upon the critical minute of a mutual conjunction in the bands of matrimony, when, as they were walking hand in hand together towards one of the gates of *Babylon*, under the shade of a row of palm-trees, that grew on the banks of the river *euphrates*, they were beset by a band of ruffians, arm'd with sabres, bows and arrows. They were the guards, it seems, of young *orcan* (nephew of a certain minister of state) whom the parasites, kept by his uncle, had buoy'd up with a permission to do, with impunity, whatever he thought proper. This young rival, tho' he had none of those internal qualities to boast of that *Zadig* had, yet he imagin'd himself a man of more power; and for that reason, was perfectly outrageous to see the other preferr'd before him. This fit of jealousy, the result of mere vanity, prompted him to think that he was deeply in love with the fair *semira*; and fir'd with that amorous notion, he was determin'd to take her away from *Zadig*, by dint of arms. The ravishers rush'd rudely upon her, and in the transport of their rage, drew the blood of a beauty, the sight of whose charms would have soften'd the very tigers of mount *imaüs*. The injur'd lady rent the very heavens with her exclamations. Where's my dear husband, she cried? they have torn me from the arms of the only man whom I adore. She never reflected on the danger to which she was expos'd; her sole concern was for her beloved *Zadig*. At the same time, he defended her, like a lover, and a man of integrity and courage. With the assistance only of two domestic servants, he put those sons of violence to flight, and conducted *semira*, bloody as she was, and in fainting fits, to her own house. No sooner was she come to her self, but she fix'd her lovely eyes on her dear deliverer. O *Zadig*, said she, I love thee as affectionately, as if I were actually thy bride: I love thee, as the man, to whom I owe my life, and what is dearer to me, the preservation of my honour. No heart sure could be more deeply smitten than that of *semira*. Never did the lips of the fairest creature living utter softer sounds; never did the most enamoured lady breathe such tender sentiments of love and gratitude for his signal service; never, in short, did the most affectionate bride express such transports of joy for the fondest husband. Her wounds, however, were but very superficial, and she was soon recover'd. Zadig receiv'd a wound that was much more dangerous: an unlucky arrow had graz'd one of his eyes, and the orifice was deep.

Semira was incessant in her prayers to the gods that they might restore her *Zadig*. Her eyes were night and day overwhelm'd with tears. She waited with impatience for the happy moment, when those of *Zadig* might dart their fires upon her; but alas! the wounded eye grew so inflam'd and swell'd, that she was terrified to the last degree. She sent as far as *memphis* for *hermes*, the celebrated physician there, who instantly attended his new patient with a numerous retinue. Upon his first visit, he peremptorily declared that *Zadig* would lose his eye; and foretold not only the day, but the very hour when that woeful disaster would befall him. Had it been, said that great man, his right eye, I could have administred an infallible specific; but as it is, his misfortune is beyond the art of man to cure. Tho' all *Babylon* pitied the hard case of *Zadig*, they equally stood astonish'd at the profound penetration of *hermes*. Two days after the imposthume broke, without any application, and *Zadig* soon after was perfectly recover'd. *Hermes* thereupon wrote a very long and elaborate treatise, to prove that his wound ought not to have been heal'd. Zadig, however, never thought it worth his while to peruse his learned lucubrations; but, as soon as ever he could get abroad, determin'd to pay the lady a visit, who had testified such uncommon concern for his welfare, and for whose sake alone he wish'd for the restoration of his sight. *Semira* he found had been out of town for three days; but was inform'd, by the bye, that his intended spouse, having conceived an implacable aversion to a one-ey'd man, was that very night to be married to *orcan*. At this unexpected ill news, poor *Zadig* was perfectly thunder-struck: he laid his disappointment so far to heart, that in a short time he was become a mere skeleton, and was sick almost to death for some months afterwards. At last, however, by dint of reflection, he got the better of his distemper; and the acuteness of the pain he underwent, in some measure, contributed towards his consolation.

Since I have met with such an unexpected repulse, said he, from a capricious court-lady, I am determin'd to marry some substantial citizen's daughter. He pitch'd accordingly upon *azora*, a young gentlewoman extremely well-bred, an excellent economist, and one, whose parents were very rich.

Their nuptials accordingly were soon after solemniz'd, and for a whole month successively, no two turtles were ever more fond of each other. In process of time, however, he perceiv'd she was a little coquettish, and too much inclin'd to think, that the handsomest young fellows were always the most virtuous and the greatest wits.

II

THE NOSE

One day *azora*, as she was just return'd home from taking a short country airing, threw herself into a violent passion, and swell'd with invectives. What, in god's name, my dear, said *Zadig*, has thus ruffled your temper? what can be the meaning of all these warm exclamations? alas! said she, you would have been disgusted as much as I am, had you been an eye-witness of that scene of female falsehood, as I was yesterday. I went, you must know, to visit the disconsolate widow *cosrou*, who has been these two days erecting a monument to the memory of her young deceased husband, near the brook that runs on one side of her meadow. She made the most solemn vow, in the height of her affliction, never to stir from that tomb, as long as ever that rivulet took its usual course—well! and wherein, pray, said *Zadig*, is the good woman so much to blame? Is it not an incontestable mark of her superior merit and conjugal-affection? but, *Zadig*, said *azora*, was you to know how her thoughts were employ'd when I made my visit, you'd never forget or forgive her. Pray, my dearest *azora*, what then was she about? why, the creature, said *azora*, was studying, to be sure, to find out ways and means to turn the current of the river.

Azora, in short, harangu'd so long, and, was so big with her invectives against the young widow, that her too affected, vain shew of virtue, gave *Zadig* a secret disgust.

Zadig had an intimate friend, one *Cador* by name, whose spouse was perfectly honest, and had in reality a greater regard for him, than all mankind besides: this friend *Zadig* made his confident, and bound him to keep a project of his entirely a secret, by a promise of some valuable token of his respect. Azora had been visiting a female companion for two days together in the country, and on the third was returning home: no sooner, however, was she in sight of the house, but the servants ran to meet her with tears in their eyes, and told her, that their master dy'd suddenly the night before; that they durstn't carry her the doleful tidings, but were going to bury *Zadig* in the sepulchre of his ancestors, at the bottom of the garden. She burst into a flood of tears; tore her hair; and vow'd to die by his side. As soon as it was dark, young *Cador* came, and begg'd the favour of being introduc'd to the widow. He was so, and they wept together very cordially. Next day the storm was somewhat abated, and they din'd together; *Cador* inform'd her, that his friend had left him the much greater part of his effects, and gave her to understand, that he should think himself the happiest creature in the world, if she would condescend to be his partner in that demise. The widow wept, sobb'd, and began to melt. More time was spent in supper than at dinner. They discoursed together with a little more freedom. Azora was lavish of her encomiums on *Zadig*; but then, 'twas true, she said, he had some secret infirmities to which *Cador* was a stranger. In the midst of their midnight entertainment, *Cador* all on a sudden complain'd that he was taken with a most violent pleuretic fit, and was ready to swoon away. Our lady being extremely concern'd, and over-officious, flew to her closet of cordials, and brought down every thing she could think of that might be of service on this emergent occasion.

She was extremely sorry that the famous *hermes* was gone from *Babylon*, and condescended to lay her warm hand upon the part affected, in which he felt such an agonizing pain. Pray sir, said she, in a soft, languishing tone, are you subject to this tormenting malady? sometimes, madam, said *Cador*, so strong, that they bring me almost to death's door; and there is but one thing can infallibly cure me; and that is, the application of a dead man's nose to the part affected. An odd remedy truly, said *azora*. Not stranger, madam, said he, than the great **arnon*'s* there was at this time in *Babylon*, a famous doctor, nam'd *arnon*, who both cur'd apoplectic fits, and prevented them from affecting his patients, as was frequently advertiz'd in the gazettes, by a little never-failing purse that he hung round their necks. Infallible apoplectic necklaces.

This assurance of success, together with *Cador*'s personal merit, determin'd *Azora* in his favour. After all, said she, when my husband shall be about to cross the bridge *tchimavar*, from this world of yesterday, to the other, of tomorrow, will the angel *asrael*, think you, make any scruple about his passage, should his nose prove something shorter in the next life than 'twas in this? she would venture, however, and taking up a sharp razor, repair'd to her husband's tomb; water'd it first with her tears, and then intended to perform the innocent operation, as he lay extended breathless, as she thought, in his coffin. Zadig mounted in a moment; secur'd his nose with one hand, and the incision-knife with the other. Madam, said he, never more exclaim against the widow *cosrou*. The scheme for cutting my nose off was much closer laid than hers of throwing the river into a new channel.

III

THE DOG AND THE HORSE

Zadig found, by experience, that the first thirty days of matrimony (as 'tis written in the book of *zend*) is honey-moon; but the second is all wormwood. He was oblig'd, in short, as *Azora* grew such a termagant, to sue out a bill of divorce, and to seek his consolation for the future, in the study of nature. Who is happier, said he, than the philosopher, who peruses with understanding that spacious book, which the supreme being has laid open before his eyes? the truths he discovers there, are of infinite service to him. He thereby cultivates and improves his mind. He lives in peace and tranquility all his days; he is afraid of nobody, and he has no tender, indulgent wife to shorten his nose for him.

Wrapped up in these contemplations, he retir'd to a little country house on the banks of the *Euphrates*; there he never spent his time in calculating how many inches of water run thro' the arch of a bridge in a second of time, or in enquiring if a cube line of rain falls more in the *mouse-month*, than in that of the *ram*. He form'd no projects for making silk gloves and stockings out of spiders webbs, nor of china-ware out of broken glass-bottles; but he pry'd into the nature and properties of animals and plants, and soon, by his strict and repeated enquiries, he was capable of discerning a thousand variations in visible objects, that others, less curious, imagin'd were all alike.

One day, as he was taking a solitary walk by the side of a thicket, he espy'd one of the queen's eunuchs, with several of his attendants, coming towards him, hunting about, in deep concern, both here and there, like persons almost in despair, and seeking, with impatience, for something lost of the utmost importance. Young man, said the queen's chief eunuch, have not you seen, pray, her majesty's dog? *Zadig* very cooly replied, you mean her bitch, I presume. You say very right sir, said the eunuch, 'tis a spaniel-bitch indeed—and very small said *Zadig*: she has had puppies too lately; she's a little lame with her left fore-foot, and has long ears. By your exact description, sir, you must doubtless have seen her, said the eunuch, almost out of breath. But I have not sir, notwithstanding, neither did I know, but by you, that the queen ever had such a favourite bitch.

Just at this critical juncture, so various are the turns of fortune's wheel! the best palfrey in all the king's stable had broke loose from the groom, and got upon the plains of *Babylon*. The head huntsman with all his inferior officers, were in pursuit after him, with as much concern, as the eunuch about the bitch. The head huntsman address'd himself to *Zadig*, and ask'd him, whether he hadn't seen the king's palfrey run by him. No horse, said *Zadig*, ever gallop'd smoother; he is about five foot high, his hoofs are very small; his tail is about three foot six inches long; the studs of his bit are of pure gold, about 23 carats; and his shoes are of silver, about eleven penny weight a-piece. What course did he take, pray, sir? whereabouts is he, said the huntsman? I never sat eyes on him, reply'd *Zadig*, not I, neither did I ever hear before now, that his majesty had such a palfrey.

The head huntsman, as well as the head eunuch, upon his answering their interrogatories so very exactly, not doubting in the least, but that *Zadig* had clandestinely convey'd both the bitch and the horse away, secur'd him, and carried him before the grand desterham, who condemn'd him to the *knout*, and to be confin'd for life in some remote and lonely part of *siberia*. No sooner had the sentence been pronounc'd, but the horse and bitch were both found. The judges were in some perplexity in this odd affair, and yet thought it absolutely necessary, as the man was innocent, to recal their decree. However, they laid a fine upon him of four hundred ounces of gold, for his false declaration of his not having seen, what doubtless he did: and the fine was order'd to be deposited in court accordingly: on the payment whereof, he was permitted to bring his cause on to a hearing before the grand desterham.

On the day appointed for that purpose he open'd the cause himself, in terms to this or the like effect.

Ye bright stars of justice, ye profound abyss of universal knowledge, ye mirrors of equity, who have in you the solidity of lead, the hardness of steel, the lustre of a diamond, and the resemblance of the purest gold! since ye have condescended so far, as to admit of my address to this august assembly, I here, in the most solemn manner, swear to you by *orosmades*, that I never saw the queen's illustrious bitch, nor the sacred palfrey of the king of kings. I'll be ingenuous, however, and declare the truth, and nothing but the truth. As I was walking by the thicket's side, where I met with her majesty's most venerable chief eunuch, and the king's most illustrious chief huntsman, I perceiv'd upon the sand the footsteps of an animal, and I easily inferr'd that it must be a little one. The several small, tho' long ridges of land between the footsteps of the creature, gave me just grounds to imagine it was a bitch whose teats hung down; and for that reason, I concluded she had but lately pupp'd. As I observ'd likewise some other traces, in some degree different, which seem'd to have graz'd all the way upon the surface of the sand, on the side of the fore-feet, I knew well enough she must have had long ears. And forasmuch as I discern'd; with some degree of curiosity, that the sand was every where less hollow'd by one foot in particular, than by the other three, I conceiv'd that the bitch of our most august queen was somewhat lamish, if I may presume to say so.

As to the palfrey of the king of kings, give me leave to inform you, that as I was walking down the lane by the thicket-side, I took particular notice of the prints made upon the sand by a horse's shoes; and found that their distances were in exact proportion; from that observation, I concluded the palfrey gallop'd well. In the next place, the dust of some trees in a narrow lane, which was but seven foot broad, was here and there swept off, both on the right and on the left, about three feet and six inches from the middle of the road. For which reason I pronounc'd the tail of the palfrey to be three foot and a half long, with which he had whisk'd off the dust on both sides as he ran along. Again, I perceiv'd under the trees, which form'd a kind of bower of five feet high, some leaves that had been lately fallen on the ground, and I was sensible the horse must have shook them off; from whence I conjectur'd he was five foot high. As to the bits of his bridle, I knew they must be of gold, and of the value I mention'd; for he had rubb'd the studs upon a certain stone, which I knew to be a touch-stone, by an experiment that I had made of it. To conclude, by the prints which his shoes had left of some flint-stones of another nature, I concluded his shoes were silver, and of eleven penny weight fineness, as I before mention'd.

The whole bench of judges stood astonish'd at the profundity of *Zadig*'s nice discernment. The news was soon carried to the king and the queen. Zadig was not only the whole subject of the court's conversation; but his name was mention'd with the utmost veneration in the king's chambers, and his privy-council. And notwithstanding several of their magi declar'd he ought to be burnt for a sorcerer; yet the king thought proper, that the fine he had deposited in court, should be peremptorily restor'd. The clerk of the court, the tipstaffs, and other petty officers, waited on him in their proper habit, in order to refund the four hundred ounces of gold, pursuant to the king's express order; modestly reserving only three hundred and ninety ounces, part thereof, to defray the fees of the court. And the domesticks swarm'd about him likewise, in hopes of some small consideration.

Zadig, upon winding up of the bottom, was fully convinc'd, that it was very dangerous to be over-wise; and was determin'd to set a watch before the door of his lips for the future.

An opportunity soon offer'd for the trial of his resolution. A prisoner of state had just made his escape, and pass'd under the window of *Zadig*'s house. Zadig was examin'd thereupon, but was absolutely dumb. However, as it was plainly prov'd upon him, that he did look out of the window at the same time, he was sentenc'd to pay five hundred ounces of gold for that misdemeanor; and moreover, was oblig'd to thank the court for their indulgence; a compliment which the magistrates of *Babylon* expect to be paid them. Good god! said he, to himself, have I not substantial reason to complain, that my impropitious stars should direct me to walk by a wood's-side, where the queen's bitch and the king's palfrey should happen to pass by? how dangerous is it to pop one's head out of one's window? and, in a word, how difficult is it for a man to be happy on this side the grave?

IV

THE ENVIOUS MAN

As *Zadig* had met with such a series of misfortunes, he was determin'd to ease the weight of them by the study of philosophy, and the conversation of select friends. He was still possess'd of a little pretty box in the out-parts of *Babylon*, which was furnish'd in a good taste; where every artist was welcome, and wherein he enjoy'd all the rational pleasures that a virtuous man could well wish for. In the morning, his library was always open for the use of the learned; at night his table was fill'd with the most agreeable companions; but he was soon sensible, by experience, how dangerous it was to keep learned men company. A warm dispute arose about a certain law of *zoroaster*; which prohibited the eating of griffins: but to what purpose said some of the company, was that prohibition, since there is no such animal in nature? some again insisted that there must; for otherwise *zoroaster* could never have been so weak as to give his pupils such a caution. Zadig, in order to compromize the matter, said; gentlemen, if there are such creatures in being, let us never touch them; and if there are not, we are well assur'd we can't touch them; so in either case we shall comply with the commandment.

A learned man at the upper end of the table, who had compos'd thirteen volumes, expatiating on every property of the griffin, took this affair in a very serious light, which would greatly have embarrass'd *Zadig*, but for the credit of a magus, who was brother to his friend *Cador*. From that day forward, *Zadig* ever distinguish'd and preferr'd good, before learned company: he associated with the most conversible men, and the most amiable ladies in all *Babylon*; he made elegant entertainments, which were frequently preceded by a concert of musick, and enliven'd by the most facetious conversation, in which, as he had felt the smart of it, he had laid aside all thoughts of shewing his wit, which is not only the surest proof that a man has none, but the most infallible means to spoil all good company.

Neither the choice of his friends, nor that of his dishes, was the result of pride or ostentation. He took delight in appearing to be, what he actually was, and not in seeming to be what he was not; and by that means, got a greater real character than he actually aim'd at.

Directly opposite to his house liv'd *arimazes*, one puff'd up with pride, who not meeting with success in the world, sought his revenge in railing against all mankind. Rich as he was, it was almost more than he could accomplish, to procure ev'n any parasites about him. Tho' the rattling of the chariots which stopp'd at *Zadig*'s door was a perfect nuisance to him; yet the good character which every body gave him was still a higher provocation. He would sometimes intrude himself upon *Zadig*, and set down at his table without any invitation; when there, he would most certainly interrupt the mirth of the company, as harpies, they say, infect the very carrion that they eat.

Arimazes took it in his head one day to invite a young lady to an entertainment; but she, instead of accepting of his offer, spent the evening at *Zadig*'s. Another time, as *Zadig* and he were chatting together at court, a minister of state came up to them, and invited *Zadig* to supper, but took no notice of *arimazes*. The most implacable aversions have frequently no better foundations. This gentleman, who was call'd the *envious man*, would have taken away the life of *Zadig* if he could because most people distinguish'd him by the title of the *happy man*. "An opportunity of doing mischief, says *zoroaster*, offers itself a hundred times a day; but that of doing a friend a good office but once a year."

Arimazes went one day to *Zadig*'s house, when he was walking in his garden with two friends, and a young lady, to whom he said abundance of fine things, with no other design but the innocent pleasure of saying them. Their conversation turn'd on a war that the king had happily put an end to, between him and his vassal, the prince of *hyrcania*. Zadig having signaliz'd himself in that short war, commended his majesty very highly, but was more lavish of his compliments on the lady. He took out his pocket book, and wrote four extempore verses on that occasion, and gave them the lady to read. The gentlemen then present begg'd to be oblig'd with a sight of them, as well as the lady, but either thro' modesty, or rather a self-consciousness that he hadn't happily succeeded, he gave them a flat denial. He was sensible, that a sudden poetic flight must prove insipid to every one but the person in whose favour it is written, whereupon he snapt the table in two whereon the lines were wrote, and threw both pieces into a rose-bush, where they were hunted for, but to no purpose. Soon after it happened to rain, and all the company flew into the house, but *arimazes*. Notwithstanding the shower, he continued in the garden, and never quitted it, till he had found one moiety of the tablet, which was unfortunately broke in such a manner, that even the half lines were good sense, and good metre, tho' very short. But what was still more remarkably unfortunate, they appear'd at first view, to be a severe satyr upon the king: the words were these:

To flagrant crimes
His crown he owes;
To peaceful times
The worst of foes.

This was the first moment that ever *Arimazes* was happy. He had it now in his power to ruin the most virtuous and innocent of men. Big with his execrable joy, he flew to his majesty with this virulent satyr of *Zadig*'s under his own hand. Not only *Zadig*, but his two friends and the lady were immediately close confin'd. His cause was soon over; for the judges turn'd a deaf ear to what he had to say. When sentence of condemnation was pass'd upon him, *arimazes*, still spiteful, was heard to say, as he went out of court, with an air of contempt, that *Zadig*'s lines were treason indeed, but nothing more. Tho' *Zadig* didn't value himself on account of his genius for poetry; yet he was almost distracted to find himself condemn'd for the worst of traitors, and his two friends and the lady lock'd up in a dungeon for a crime, of which he was no ways guilty. He wasn't permitted to speak one word for himself. His pocket-book was sufficient evidence against him. So strict were the laws of *Babylon*! he was carried to the place of execution, through a croud of spectators, who durstn't condole with him, and who flock'd about him, to observe whether his countenance chang'd, or whether he died with a good grace. His relations were the only real mourners; for there was no estate in reversion for them; three parts of his effects were confiscated for the king's use, and the fourth was devoted, as a reward, to the use of the informer.

Just at the time that he was preparing himself for death, the king's parrot flew from her balcony, into *Zadig*'s garden, and alighted on a rose-bush. A peach, that had been blown down, and drove by the wind from an adjacent tree, just under the bush, was glew'd, as it were, to the other moiety of the tablet. Away flew the parrot with her booty, and return'd to the king's lap. The monarch, being somewhat curious, read the words on the broken tablet, which had no meaning in them as he could perceive, but seem'd to be the broken parts of a tetrastick. He was a great admirer of poetry; and the odd adventure of his parrot, put him upon reflection. The queen who recollected full well the lines that were wrote on the fragment of *Zadig*'s tablet, order'd that part of it to be produc'd: both the broken pieces being put together, they answered exactly the indentures; and then the verses which *Zadig* had written, in a flight of loyalty, ran thus,

Tyrants are prone to flagrant crimes;
To clemency his crown he owes;
To concord and to peaceful times,
Love only is the worst of foes.

Upon this the king order'd *Zadig* to be instantly brought before him; and his two friends and the lady to be that moment discharg'd. Zadig, as he stood before the king and queen, fix'd his eyes upon the ground, and begg'd their majesty's pardon for his little worthless, poetical attempt. He spoke, however, with such a becoming grace, and with so much modesty and good sense, that the king and the queen, ordered him to be brought before them once again. He was brought accordingly, and he pleas'd them still more and more. In short, they gave him all the immense estate of *arimazes*, who had so unjustly accus'd him; but *Zadig* generously return'd the wicked informer the whole to a farthing. The envious man, however, was no ways affected, but with the restoration of his effects. Zadig every day grew more and more in favour at court. He was made a party in all the king's pleasures, and nothing was done in the privy-council without him. The queen, from that very hour, shew'd him so much respect, and spoke to him in such soft and endearing terms, that in process of time, it prov'd of fatal consequence to herself, her royal consort, to *Zadig*, and the whole kingdom. Zadig now began to think it was not so difficult a thing to be happy as at first he imagin'd.

V

THE FORCE OF GENEROSITY

The time now drew near for the celebration of a grand festival, which was kept but once in five years. 'Twas a constant custom in *Babylon* at the expiration of the term above-mention'd, to distinguish that citizen from all the rest, in the most solemn manner, who had done the most generous action; and the grandees and magi always sat as judges. The *satrap* inform'd them of every praise-worthy deed that occurr'd within his district. All were put to the vote, and the king himself pronounc'd the definitive sentence. People of all ranks and degrees came from the remotest part of the kingdom to be present at this solemnity. The victor, whoever he was, receiv'd from the king's own hand a golden cup, enrich'd with precious stones, and upon the delivery, the king made use of the following salutation. *Receive this reward of your generosity, and may the gods grant me thousands of such valuable subjects!*

Upon this memorable day, the king appear'd in all the pomp imaginable on his throne of state, surrounded by his grandees, the magi, and the deputies, from all the surrounding nations, of every province that attended these public sports, where honour was to be acquir'd, not by the velocity of the best race-horse, or by bodily strength, but by intrinsic merit. The principal *satrap* proclaim'd, with an audible voice, such actions as would entitle the victor to the inestimable prize; but never mention'd one word of *Zadig*'s greatness of soul, in returning his invidious neighbour all his estate, notwithstanding he would have taken away his life: that was but a trifle, and not worth speaking of.

The first that was set up for the prize, was a judge, that had occasion'd a citizen to lose a very considerable cause, through some mistake, for which he was no ways responsible, and made him restitution out of his private purse.

The next candidate was a youth, that tho' violently in love with one that he intended shortly to make his spouse, yet resign'd her to his friend, who was just expiring at her feet; and moreover, gave her a portion at the same time.

After this appear'd a soldier, who, in the *hyrcanian* war, had done a much more glorious action than the lover. A gang of *hyrcanians* having taken his mistress from him, he fought them bravely, and rescued her out of their hands: soon after, he was inform'd, that another band of the same party had hurried away his mother to a place not far distant; he left his mistress, all drown'd in tears, and ran to his mother's assistance: after that skirmish was over, he returned to his sweet-heart, and found her just expiring. He would fain have plung'd a dagger into his heart that moment; but his mother remonstrated to him, that, should he die, she should be entirely helpless, and upon that account only he had courage to live a little longer.

The judges seem'd very much inclin'd to give their votes for the soldier; but the king prevented them, by saying, that the soldier's action was praise-worthy enough, and so were those of the rest, but none of them give me any surprize. What *Zadig* did yesterday perfectly struck me with astonishment. I'll mention another instance. I had some few days ago, as a testimony of my resentment, banish'd my prime-minister, and favourite *coreb* from the court. I complain'd of his conduct in the warmest terms; and all my sycophants about me, told me that I was too merciful; and loaded him with the sharpest invectives. I ask'd *Zadig* what his opinion was of *coreb*; and he dar'd to give him the best of characters. I must confess, I have read in our publick records, indeed, of instances where restitution have been generally made, for injuries committed by mistake; where a mistress has been resign'd; and where a mother has been preferr'd to a mistress; but I never read of a courtier, that would speak to the advantage of a minister in disgrace, and against whom the sovereign was highly incens'd. I'll give 20,000 pieces of gold to every candidate that has been this day proclaim'd, but i'll give the cup to no one but *Zadig*.

Sire, said *Zadig*, 'tis your majesty alone, that deserves the cup; 'tis you alone who have done an action of generosity, never heard of before; since you, who are king of kings, wasn't exasperated against your slave, when he contradicted you in the heat of your passion. Every body gaz'd with eyes of admiration on the king and *Zadig*. The judge, who had generously made restitution for his error; the lover, who had married his mistress to his friend; the soldier, who had preferr'd the welfare of his mother to that of his mistress; received the promis'd donation from the monarch, and saw their names register'd in the book of *fame*: but *Zadig* had the cup. The king got the universal character of a good prince, which he did not long preserve. This joyful day was solemniz'd with festivals beyond the time by law establish'd. Tragedies were acted there that drew tears from the spectators; and comedies that made them laugh; entertainments, that the *Babylonians* were perfect strangers to: the commemoration of it is still preserv'd in *asia*. Now, said *Zadig*, I am happy at last; but he was grosly mistaken.

VI

THE JUDGMENTS

Young as *Zadig* was, he was constituted chief judge of all the tribunals throughout the empire. He fill'd the place, like one, whom the gods had endow'd with the strictest justice, and the most solid wisdom. It was to him, the nations round about were indebted for that generous maxim; *that 'tis much more prudence to acquit two persons, tho' actually guilty, than to pass sentence of condemnation in one that is virtuous and innocent.* It was his firm opinion, that the laws were intended to be a praise to those who did well, as much as to be a terror to evildoers. It was his peculiar talent to render truth as obvious as possible: whereas most men study to render it intricate and obscure. On the very first day of his entrance into his high office, he exerted this peculiar talent. A rich merchant, and a native of *Babylon*, died in the *indies*. He had made his will, and appointed his two sons joint-heirs of his estate, as soon as they had settled their sister, and married her with their mutual approbation. Moreover, he left a specific legacy of 30,000 pieces of gold to that son, who should, after his decease, be prov'd to love him best. The eldest erected to his memory a very costly monument: the youngest appropriated a considerable part of his bequest to the augmentation of his sister's fortune: every one, without hesitation, gave the preference to the elder, allowing the younger to have the greatest affection for his sister. The legacy therefore was doubtless due to the eldest.

Their cause came before *Zadig*, and he examin'd them apart. To the former, said *Zadig*, your father, sir, is not dead, as is reported, but being happily recover'd, is on his return to *Babylon*. God be praised, said the young man! but I hope the expence I have been at in raising this superb monument will be consider'd. After this, *Zadig* repeated the same story to the younger. God be praised, said he! I will immediately restore all that he has left me; but I hope my father will not recal the little present I have made my sister. You have nothing to restore, sir; you shall have the legacy of the thirty thousand pieces; for 'tis you that have the greatest veneration for your deceased father.

A young lady that was very rich, had entred into a marriage-contract with two *magis*; and having receiv'd instructions from both parties for some months, she prov'd with child. They were both ready and willing to marry her. But, said she, he shall be my husband, that has put me into a capacity of serving my country, by adding one to it. 'Tis I, madam, that have answered that valuable end, said one; but the other insisted 'twas his operation. Well! said she, since this is a moot-point, i'll acknowledge him for the father of the child, that will give him the most liberal education. In a short time after, my lady was brought to bed of a hopeful boy. Each of them insisted on being tutor, and the cause was brought before *Zadig*. The two magi were order'd to appear in court. Pray sir, said *Zadig* to the first, what method of instruction do you propose to pursue for the improvement of your young pupil? he shall first be grounded, said this learned pedagogue, in the eight parts of speech; then i'll teach him logic, astrology, magick, the wide difference between the terms substance and accident, abstract and concrete, *&c. &c.* As for my part, sir, I shall take another course, said the second; i'll do my utmost to make him an honest man, and acceptable to his friends. Upon this, *Zadig* said, you, sir, shall marry the mother, let who will be the father.

There came daily complaints to court against the *itimadoulet* of *media*, whose name was *irax*. He was a person of quality, who was possess'd of a very considerable estate, notwithstanding he had squander'd away a great part of it, by indulging himself in all manner of expensive pleasures. It was but seldom that an inferior was suffer'd to speak to him; but not a soul durst contradict him: no peacock was more gay; no turtle more amorous; and no tortoise more indolent and inactive. He made false glory and false pleasures his sole pursuit.

Zadig, undertaking to cure him, sent him forthwith, as by express order from the king, a musick-master with twelve voices, and 24 violins, as his attendants; a head steward, with six men cooks, and 4 chamberlains, who were never to be out of his sight. The king issued out his writ for the punctual observance of his royal will; and thus the affair proceeded.

The first morning, as soon as the voluptuous *irax* had open'd his eyes, his musick-master, with the voices and violins, entred his apartment. They sang a cantata, that lasted two hours and three minutes. Every three minutes the chorus, or burthen of the song, was to this effect.

Tisn't in words to speak your praise;
What mighty honours are your due!
To worth like yours we altars raise,
No monarch's happier, sir, than you.

After the cantata was over, the chamberlain address'd him in a formal harangue for three quarters of an hour without ceasing; wherein he took occasion to extol every virtue to which he was a perfect stranger; when the oration was over, he was conducted to dinner, where the musicians were all in waiting, and play'd, as soon as he was seated at his table. Dinner lasted three hours before he condescended to speak a word. When he did; you say right, sir, said the chief chamberlain; scarce had he utter'd four words more, but right, sir, said the second. The other two chamberlain's time was taken up in laughing with admiration at *irax*'s smart repartees, or at least such as he ought to have made. After the cloth was taken away, the adulating chorus was repeated.

This first day *irax* was all in raptures; he imagin'd, that this honour done him by the king of kings, was the sole result of his exalted merit. The second wasn't altogether so agreeable; the third prov'd somewhat troublesome; the fourth insupportable; the fifth was tormenting; and at last, he was perfectly outrageous at the continual peal in his ears of no monarch's happier sir, than you, you say right, *&c.* And at being daily harangu'd at the same hour. Whereupon he wrote to court, and begg'd of his majesty to recal his chamberlain, his musick-master, and all his retinue, his head steward and his cooks, and promis'd, in the most submissive manner, to be less vain, and more industrious for the future. Tho' he didn't require so much adulations, nor such grand entertainments, he was much more happy; for, as *sadder* has it, *one continued scene of pleasure, is no pleasure at all.*

Zadig every day gave incontestable proofs of his wondrous penetration, and the goodness of his heart; he was ador'd by the people, and was the darling of the king. The little difficulties that he met with in the first stage of his life, serv'd only to augment his present felicity. Every night, however, he had some unlucky dream or another, that gave him some disturbance. One while, he imagin'd himself extended on a bed of wither'd plants, amongst which there were some that were sharp pointed, and made him very restless and uneasy; another time, he fancied himself repos'd on a bed of roses, out of which rush'd a serpent, that stung him to the heart with his envenom'd tongue. Alas! said he, waking, I was one while upon a bed of hard and nauseous plants, and just this moment repos'd on a bed of roses. But then the serpent.

VII

THE FORCE OF JEALOUSY

The misfortunes that attended *Zadig* proceeded, in a great measure, from his preferment; but more from his intrinsic merit. Every day he had familiar converse with the king, his royal master, and his august consort, *astarte*. And the pleasure arising from thence was greatly enhanc'd from an innate ambition of pleasing, which, in regard to wit, is the same, as dress is to beauty. His youth, and graceful deportment, had a greater influence on *Astarte*, than she was at first aware of. Tho' her affection for him daily encreas'd; yet she was perfectly innocent. Astarte would say, without the least reserve or apprehension of fear, that she was extreamly pleas'd with the company of one, who was, not only a favourite of her husband, but the darling of the whole empire. She was continually speaking in his commendation before the king: he was the subject of her whole discourse amongst her ladies of honour, who were as lavish of their praises as herself. Such repeated discourses, however innocent, made a deeper impression on her heart, than she at that time apprehended. She would every now and then send *Zadig* some little present or another; which he construed as the result of a greater value for him than she intended. She said no more of him, as she thought, than a queen might innocently do, who was perfectly assur'd of his attachment to her husband; sometimes, indeed, she would express her self with an air of tenderness and affection.

Astarte was much handsomer than either his mistress *semira*, who had such a natural antipathy to a one-eyed lord, or *azora*, his late loving spouse, that would innocently have cut his nose off. The freedoms which *Astarte* took, her tender expressions, at which she began to blush, the glances of her eye, which she would turn away, if perceiv'd, and which she fix'd upon his, kindled in the heart of *Zadig* a fire, which struck him with amazement. He did all he could to smother it; he call'd up all the philosophy he was master of to his aid; but all in vain, for no consolation arose from those reflections.

Duty, gratitude, and an injur'd monarch, presented themselves before his eyes, as avenging deities: he bravely struggled; he triumph'd indeed; but this conquest over his passions, which he was oblig'd to check every moment, cost him many a deep sigh and tear. He durst not talk with the queen any more, with that freedom which was too engaging on both sides; his eyes were obnubilated; his discourse was forc'd and unconnected; he turn'd his eyes another way; and when, against his inclination, they met with those of the queen, he found, that tho' drown'd in tears, they darted flames of fire: they seem'd in silence to intimate, that they were afraid of being in love with each other; and that both burn'd with a fire which both condemn'd.

Zadig flew from her presence, like one beside himself, and in despair; his heart was over-charg'd with a burthen, too great for him to bear: in the heat of his conflicts, he disclos'd the secrets of his heart to his trusty friend *Cador*, as one, who, having long groan'd under the weight of an inexpressible anguish of mind, at once makes known the cause of his torments by the groans, as it were, extorted from him, and by the drops of a cold sweat, that trickled down his cheeks.

Cador said to him; 'tis now some considerable time since, I have discover'd that secret passion which you have foster'd in your bosom, and yet endeavour'd to conceal even from your self. The passions carry along with them such strong impressions, that they cannot be conceal'd. Tell me ingenuously *Zadig*; and be your own accuser, whether or no, since I have made this discovery, the king has not shewn some visible marks of his resentment. He has no other foible, but that of being the most jealous mortal breathing. You take more pains to check the violence of your passion, than the queen herself does; because you are a philosopher; because, in short, you are *Zadig*; *Astarte* is but a weak woman; and tho' her eyes speak too visibly, and with too much imprudence; yet she does not think her self blame-worthy. Being conscious of her innocence, to her own misfortune, as well as yours, she is too unguarded. I tremble for her; because I am sensible her conscience acquits her. Were you both agreed, you might conceal your regard for each other from all the world: a rising passion, that is smother'd, breaks out into a flame; love, when once gratified, knows how to conceal itself with art. Zadig shudder'd at the proposition of ungratefully violating the bed of his royal benefactor; and never was there a more loyal subject to a prince, tho' guilty of an involuntary crime. The queen, however, repeated the name of *Zadig* so often, and her cheeks glow'd with such a red, when ever she utter'd it; she was one while so transported, and at another, so dejected, when the discourse turn'd upon him in the king's presence; she was in such a reverie, so confus'd and stupid, when he went out of the presence, that her deportment made the king extremely uneasy. He was convinc'd of every thing he saw, and form'd in his mind an idea of a thousand things he did not see. He observ'd, particularly, that *Astarte*'s sandals were blue; so *Zadig*'s were blue likewise; that as the queen wore yellow ribbands, *Zadig*'s turbet was of the same colour: these were shocking circumstances for a monarch of his cast of mind to reflect on! to a mind, in short, so distemper'd as his was, suspicions were converted into real facts.

All court slaves, and sycophants, are so many spies on kings and queens: they soon discover'd that *Astarte* was fond, and *Moabdar* jealous. *Arimazius*, his envious foe, who was as incorrigible as ever; for flints will never soften; and creatures, that are by nature venemous, forever retain their poison. *Arimazius*, I say, wrote an anonymous letter to *Moabdar*, the infamous recourse of sordid spirits, who are the objects of universal contempt; but in this case, an affair of the last importance; because this letter tallied with the baneful suggestions that monarch had conceiv'd. In short, his thoughts were now wholly bent upon revenge. He determin'd to poison *Astarte* on a certain night, and to have *Zadig* strangled by break of day. Orders for that purpose were expressly given to a merciless, inhuman eunuch, the ready executioner of his vengeance. At that critical conjuncture, there happen'd to be a dwarf, who was dumb, but not deaf, in the king's apartment. Nobody regarded him: he was an eye and ear-witness of all that pass'd, and yet no more suspected than any irrational domestic animal. This little dwarf had conceiv'd a peculiar regard for *Astarte* and *Zadig*: he heard, with equal horror and surprize, the king's orders to destroy them both. But how to prevent those orders from being put into execution, as the time was so short, was all his concern. He could not write, 'tis true, but he had luckily learnt to draw, and take a likeness. He spent a good part of the night in delineating with crayons, on a piece of paper, the imminent danger that thus attended the queen. In one corner, he represented the king highly incens'd, and giving his cruel eunuch the fatal orders; in another, a bowl and a cord upon a table; in the center was the queen, expiring in the arms of her maids of honour, with *Zadig* strangled, and laid dead at her feet. In the horizon was the rising sun, to denote, that this execrable scene was to be exhibited by break of day. No sooner was his design finish'd, but he ran with it to one of *astarte*'s female favourites, then in waiting, call'd her up, and gave her to understand, that she must carry the draught to *Astarte* that very moment.

In the mean time, the queen's attendants, tho' it was dead of night, knock'd at the door of *Zadig*'s apartment, wak'd him, and deliver'd into his hands a billet from the queen. At first he could not well tell whether he was only in a dream or not, but soon read the letter, with a trembling hand, and a heavy heart: words can't express his surprise, and the agonies of despair which he was in upon his perusal of the contents. *Fly*, said she, *dear* Zadig, *this very moment; for your life's in the utmost danger: fly, dear* Zadig, I *conjure you, in the name of that fatal passion, with which I have long struggled, and which I now venture to discover, as I am to make atonement for it, in a few moments, by the loss of my life. Tho' I am conscious to myself of my innocence, I find I am to feel the weight of my husband's resentment, and die the death of a traitor.*

Zadig was scarce able to speak. He order'd his friend *Cador* to be instantly call'd, and gave him the letter the moment he came, without opening his lips. Cador press'd him to regard the contents, and to make the best of his way to *memphis*. If you presume, said he, to have an interview with her majesty first, you inevitably hasten her execution; or if you wait upon the king, the fatal consequence will be the same: i'll prevent her unhappy fate, if possible; you follow but your own: i'll give it out, that you are gone to the *indies*: i'll wait on you as soon as the hurricane is blown over, and i'll let you know all that occurs material in *Babylon*.

Cador, that instant, order'd two of the fleetest dromedaries that could be got, to be in readiness at a private back-door belonging to the court; he help'd *Zadig* to mount his beast, tho' ready to drop into the earth. He had but one trusty servant to attend him, and *Cador*, overwhelm'd with grief, soon lost sight of his dearly beloved friend.

This illustrious fugitive soon reach'd the summit of a little hill, that afforded him a fair prospect of the whole city of *Babylon*: but turning his eyes back towards the queen's palace, he fainted away; and when he had recover'd his senses, he drown'd his eyes in a flood of tears, and with impatience wish'd for death. To conclude, after he had reflected, with horror, on the deplorable fate of the most amiable creature in the universe, and of the most meritorious queen that ever liv'd; he for a moment commanded his passion, and with a sigh, made the following exclamations: what is this mortal life! o virtue, virtue, of what service hast thou been to me! two young ladies, a mistress, and a wife, have prov'd false to me; a third, who is perfectly innocent, and ten thousand times handsomer than either of them, has suffer'd death, 'tis probable, before this, on my account! all the acts of benevolence which I have shewn, have been the foundation of my sorrows, and I have been only rais'd to the highest spoke of fortune's wheel, for no other purpose than to be tumbled down with the greater force. Had I been as abandon'd as some miscreants are, I had like them been happy. His head thus overwhelm'd with these melancholy reflections, his eyes thus sunk in his head, and his meagre cheeks all pale and languid; and, in a word, his very soul thus plung'd in the abyss of deep despair, he pursu'd his journey towards *egypt*.

VIII

THE THRASH'D WIFE

Zadig steer'd his course by the stars that shone over his head. The constellation of orion, and the radiant dog-star directed him towards the pole of canope. He reflected with admiration on those immense globes of light, which appear'd to the naked eye no more than little twinkling lights; whereas the earth he was then traversing, which, in reality, is no more than an imperceptible point in nature, seem'd, according to the selfish idea we generally entertain of it, something very immense, and very magnificent. He then reflected on the whole race of mankind, and look'd upon them, as they are in fact, a parcel of insects, or reptiles, devouring one another on a small atom of clay. This just idea of them greatly alleviated his misfortunes, recollecting the nothingness, if we may be allow'd the expression, of his own being, and even of *Babylon* itself. His capacious soul now soar'd into infinity, and he contemplated, with the same freedom, as if she was disencumber'd from her earthly partner, on the immutable order of the universe. But as soon as she cower'd her wings, and resumed her native seat, he began to consider that *Astarte* might possibly have lost her life for his sake; upon which, his thoughts of the universe vanish'd all at once, and no other objects appear'd before his distemper'd eyes, but his *Astarte* giving up the ghost, and himself overwhelm'd with a sea of troubles: as he gave himself up to this flux and reflux of sublime philosophy and anxiety of mind, he was insensibly arriv'd on the frontiers of *egypt*: and his trusty attendant had, unknown to him, stept into the first village, and sought out for a proper apartment for his master and himself. Zadig in the mean time made the best of his way to the adjacent gardens; where he saw, not far distant from the high-way, a young lady, all drown'd in tears, calling upon heaven and earth for succour in her distress, and a man, fir'd with rage and resentment, in pursuit after her. He had now just overtaken her, and she fell prostrate at his feet imploring his forgiveness. He loaded her with a thousand reproaches; nor did he spare to chastise her in the most outrageous manner. By the *egyptian*'s cruel deportment towards her, he concluded that the man was a jealous husband, and that the lady was an inconstant, and had defil'd his bed: but when he reflected, that the woman was a perfect beauty, and to his thinking something like the unfortunate *astarte*, he perceiv'd his heart yearn with compassion towards the lady, and swell with indignation against her tyrant. For heaven's sake, sir, assist me, said she, to *Zadig*, sobbing as if her heart would break, oh! deliver me out of the hands of this *barbarian*: save, sir, o save my life. Upon these her shocking outcries, *Zadig* threw himself between the injur'd lady and the inexorable brute. And as he had some smattering of the *egyptian* tongue, he expostulated with him in his own dialect, and said: dear sir, if you are endow'd with the least spark of humanity, let me conjure you to have some pity and remorse for so beautiful a creature; have some regard, sir, to the weakness of her sex. How can you treat a lady, who is one of nature's master-pieces, in such a rude and outrageous manner, one who lies weeping at your feet for forgiveness, and one who has no other recourse than her tears for her defence? oh! oh! said the jealous-pated fellow in a fury to *Zadig*, what! you are one of her gallants, I suppose. I'll be reveng'd of thee, thou villain, this moment. No sooner were the words out of his mouth, but he quits hold of the lady, in whose hair he had twisted his fingers before, takes up his lance in a fury, and endeavours to the utmost of his pow'r to plunge it in the stranger's heart: *Zadig*, however, being cool, warded the intended blow with ease. He laid fast hold of his lance towards the point. One strove to recover it, and the other to snatch it away by force. They broke it between them. Whereupon the *egyptian* drew his sword. Zadig drew his: they fought: the former made a hundred rash passes one after another, which the latter parried with the utmost dexterity. The lady sat herself upon a grass-plat, adjusting her head-dress, and looking on the combatants. The *egyptian* was too strong for *Zadig*, but *Zadig* was more nimble and active. The latter fought as a man whose hand was guided by his head; the former as a mad-man who dealt about his blows at random. Zadig took the advantage, made a plunge at him, and disarm'd him. And forasmuch as he found that the *egyptian* was hotter than ever, and endeavour'd all he could to throw him down by dint of strength, *Zadig* laid fast hold of him, flew upon him, and tripp'd up his heels: after that, holding the point of his sword to his breast, like a man of honour, gave him his life. The *egyptian*, fir'd with rage, and having no command of his passion, drew his dagger, and wounded *Zadig* like a coward, whilst the victor generously forgave him. Upon that unexpected action, *Zadig*, being incens'd to the last degree, plung'd his sword deep into his bosom. The *egyptian* fetch'd a hideous groan, and died upon the spot. Zadig then approach'd the lady, and with a kind of concern, in the softest terms told her, that he was oblig'd to kill her insulter, tho' against his inclinations. I have aveng'd your cause, and deliver'd you out of the merciless hands of the most outrageous man I ever saw. Now, madam, let me know your farther will and pleasure with me. You shall die, you villain! you have murder'd my love. Oh! I could tear your heart out. Indeed, madam, said *Zadig*, you had one of the most hot-headed, oddest lovers I ever saw. He beat you most unmercifully, and would have taken away my life because you call'd me in to your assistance. Would to god he was but alive to beat me again, said she, blubbering and roaring; I deserv'd to be beat. I gave him too just occasion to be jealous of me. Would to god that he had beat me, and you had died in his stead! *Zadig* more astonish'd, and more exasperated than ever he was in all his life, said to her: really, madam, you put on such extravagant airs, that you tempt me, pretty as you are, to thresh you most cordially in my turn; but I scorn to concern my self any more about you. Upon this, he remounted his dromedary, and made the best of his way towards the village: but before he had got near a hundred yards, he return'd upon an out-cry that was made by four couriers from *Babylon*. They rode full speed. One of them, spying the young widow, cried out. There she is, that's she. She answers in every respect to the description we had of her. They never took the least notice of her dead gallant, but secur'd her directly. Oh! sir, cried she to *Zadig*, again and again, dear sir, most generous stranger, once more deliver me from a pack of villains. I most humbly beg your pardon for my late conduct and unjust complaint of you. Do but stand my friend, at this critical conjuncture, and i'll be your most obedient vassal till death. Zadig had now no inclination to fight for one so undeserving any more. Find some other to be your fool now, madam; you shan't impose upon me a second time. I'll assure you, madam, I know better things. Besides he was wounded; and bled so fast that he wanted assistance himself: and 'tis very probable, that the sight of the *Babylonian* couriers, who were dispatch'd from king *Moabdar*, might discompose him very much. He made all the haste he could towards the village, not being able to conceive what should be the real cause of the young lady's being secur'd by those *Babylonish* officers, and as much at a loss, at the same time, what to think of such a termagant and a coquet.

IX

THE CAPTIVE

No sooner was *Zadig* arriv'd at the *egyptian* village before-mention'd, but he found himself surrounded by a croud. The people one and all cried out! see! see! there's the man that ran away with the beauteous lady *missouf*, and murder'd *cletofis*. Gentlemen, said he, god forbid that I should ever entertain a thought of running away with the lady you speak of: she is too much of a coquet: and as to *cletofis*, I did not murder him, but kill'd him in my own defence. He endeavour'd all he could to take my life away, because I entreated him to take some pity and compassion on the beauteous *missouf*, whom he beat most unmercifully. I am a stranger, who am fled hither for shelter, and 'tis highly improbable, that upon my first entrance into a country, where I came for safety and protection, I should be guilty of two such enormous crimes, as that of running away with another man's partner, and that of clandestinely murdering him on her account.

The *egyptians* at that time were just and humane. The populace, tis true, hurried *Zadig* to the town-goal; but they took care in the first place to stop the bleeding of his wounds, and afterwards examin'd the suppos'd delinquents apart, in order to discover, if possible, the real truth. They acquitted *Zadig* of the charge of wilful and premeditated murder; but as he had taken a subject's life away, tho' in his own defence, he was sentenc'd to be a slave, as the law directed. His two beasts were sold in open market, for the service of the hamlet; what money he had was distributed amongst the inhabitants; and he and his attendant were expos'd in the market-place to public sale. An *Arabian* merchant, *Setoc* by name, purcha'd them both; but as the valet, or attendant, was a robust man, and better cut out for hard labour than the master, he fetch'd the most money. There was no comparison to be made between them. Zadig therefore was a slave subordinate to his valet; they secur'd them both, however, by a chain upon their legs; and so link'd they accompanied their master home. Zadig, as they were on the road, comforted his fellow-slave, and exhorted him to bear his misfortunes with patience: but, according to custom, he made several reflections on the vicissitudes of human life. I am now sensible, said he, that my impropitious fortune has some malignant influence over thine; every occurrence of my life hitherto has prov'd strangely odd and unaccountable. In the first place, I was sentenc'd to die at *Babylon*, for writing a short panegyrick on the king, my master. In the next, I narrowly escap'd being strangled, for the queen his royal consort's speaking a little too much in my favour; and here I am a joint-slave with thy self; because a turbulent fellow of a gallant would beat his lady. However, comrade, let us march on boldly; let not our courage be cast down; all this may possibly have a happier issue than we expect. 'Tis absolutely necessary that these *Arabian* merchants should have slaves, and why should not you and i, as we are but men, be slaves as thousands of others are? this master of ours may not prove inexorable. He must treat his slaves with some thought and consideration, if he expects them to do his work. This was his discourse to his comrade; but his mind was more attentive to the misfortunes of the queen of *Babylon*.

Two days afterwards *Setoc* set out with his two slaves and his camels, for *arabia deserta*. His tribe liv'd near the desert of *horeb*. The way was long and tedious. *Setoc*, during the journey, paid a much greater regard to *Zadig*'s valet, than to himself; because the former was the most able to load the camels; and therefore what little distinctions were made, they were in his favour. It so happen'd that one of the camels died upon the road: the load which the beast carried was immediately divided, and thrown upon the shoulders of the two slaves; *Zadig* had his share. *Setoc*, couldn't forbear laughing to see his two slaves crouching under their burthen. Zadig took the liberty to explain the reason thereof; and convinc'd him of the laws of the equilibrium. The merchant was a little startled at his philosophical discourse, and look'd upon him with a more favourable eye than at first. Zadig, perceiving he had rais'd his curiosity, redoubled it, by instructing him in several material points, which were in some measure, advantageous to him in his way of business: such as, the specific weight of metals, and other commodities of various kinds, of an equal bulk; the properties of several useful animals, and the best ways and means to make such as were wild, tame by degrees, and fit for service: in short, *Zadig* was look'd upon by his master, as a perfect oracle. Setoc now thought the master the much better man of the two. He us'd him courteously, and had no room to repent of his indulgence towards him.

Being got to their journey's end, the first step that *Setoc* took was to claim a debt of five hundred ounces of silver of a *jew*, who had borrow'd it in the presence of two witnesses; but both of them were dead; and as the *jew* was conscious he couldn't be cast for want of evidence, appropriated the merchant's money to his own use, and thank'd god that it lay in his power for once to bite an *Arabian* with impunity. Setoc discover'd to *Zadig* the unhappy situation of his case, as he was now become his confident. Where was it, pray, said *Zadig*, that you lent this large sum to that ungrateful infidel? upon a large stone, said the merchant, at the foot of mount *horeb*. What sort of a man is your debtor, said *Zadig*? oh! he is as errand a rogue as ever breath'd, reply'd *setoc*. That I take for granted; but, says *Zadig*, is he a lively, active man, or is he a dull heavy-headed fellow? he is one of the worst of pay-masters in the world, but the merriest, most sprightly fellow I ever met with. Very well! said *Zadig*, let me be one of your council when your cause comes to be heard. In short, he summon'd the *jew* to attend the court; where, when the judge was sat, *Zadig* open'd the cause: thou impartial judge of this court of equity, I am come here, in behalf of my master, to demand of the defendant five hundred ounces of silver, which he refuses to pay, and would fain traverse the debt. Have you, friend, your witnesses ready to prove the loan, said the judge? no, they are dead; but there is a large stone still subsisting, on which the money was deposited; and if your excellence, will be pleas'd to order the stone to be brought in court, I don't doubt but the evidence it will give, will be proof sufficient of the fact. I hope your excellence will order, that the *jew* and myself shall be oblig'd to attend the court, till the stone comes, and i'll dispatch a special messenger to fetch it, at my master's expence. Your request is very reasonable, said the judge. Do as you propose; and so call'd another cause.

When the court was ready to break up, well! said the judge to *Zadig*, is your stone come yet? the *jew*, with a sneer, replied, your excellence may wait here till this time tomorrow, before the stone will appear in court; for 'tis above six mile off, and it will require fifteen men to remove it from its place. 'Tis well! replied *Zadig*. I told your excellence that the stone would be a very material evidence. Since the defendant can point out the place where the stone lies, he tacitly confesses, that it was upon that stone the money was deposited. The *jew* thus unexpectedly confuted, was soon oblig'd to acknowledge the debt. The judge order'd that the *jew* should be tied fast to the stone, without victuals or drink, till he should advance the five hundred ounces of silver, which were soon paid accordingly, and the *jew* releas'd. The slave *Zadig*, and this remarkable stone-witness, were in great repute all over *Arabia*.

X

THE FUNERAL PILE

Setoc, transported with his good success, of a slave made *Zadig* his favourite companion and confident; he found him as necessary in the conduct of his affairs, as the king of *Babylon* had before done in the administration of his government; and lucky it was for *Zadig* that *Setoc* had no wife.

He discover'd, that his master was in his temper benevolent, strictly honest, and a man of good natural parts. Zadig was very much concern'd, that one of so much sense should pay divine adoration to a whole host of created, tho' celestial beings, that is to say, the sun, moon, and stars, according to the antient custom of the *Arabians*. He talk'd, at first, to his master, with great precaution on so important a topick. But at last told him, in direct terms, that they were created bodies, as others, tho' of less lustre, and that there was no more adoration due to them, than to a stock or a stone. But, said *setoc*, they are eternal beings to whom we are indebted for all the blessings we enjoy; they animate nature; they regulate the seasons; they are, in a word, at such an infinite distance from us, that it would be downright impious not to adore them. You are more indebted, said *Zadig*, to the waters of the red sea, which transport so many valuable commodities into the *indies*. Why, pray, may not they be deem'd as antient as the stars? and if you are so fond of paying your adoration on account of their vast distance; why don't you adore the land of the *gangarides*, which lies in the utmost extremities of the earth. No, said *setoc*, there is something so surprisingly more brilliant in the stars than what you speak of; that a man must adore them whether he will or not.

At the close of the evening, *Zadig* planted a long range of candles in the front of his tent, where *Setoc* and he were to sup that night: and as soon as he perceiv'd his patron to be at the door, he fell prostrate on his knees before the wax-lights. O ye everlasting, ever-shining luminaries, be always propitious to your votary, said *Zadig*. Having repeated these words so loud as *Setoc* might hear them, he sat down to table, without taking the least notice of *setoc*. What! said *setoc*, somewhat startled at his conduct, art thou at thy prayers before supper? I act just as inconsistently, sir, as you do; I worship these candles; without reflecting on their makers, or yourself, who are my most beneficent patron.

Setoc took the hint, and was conscious of the reproof that was conceal'd so genteely under a vail. The superior wisdom of his slave enlightned his mind; and from that hour he was less lavish than ever he had been, of his incense to those created beings, and for the future, paid his adoration to the eternal god who made them.

At that time there was a most hideous custom in high repute all over *Arabia*, which came originally from *Scythia*; but having met with the sanction of the bigotted brachmans, threatn'd to spread its infection all over the *east*. When a married man happen'd to die, if his dearly beloved widow ever expected to be esteem'd a saint, she must throw herself headlong upon her husband's funeral-pile. This was look'd upon as a solemn festival, and was call'd the widow's sacrifice. That tribe which could boast of the greatest number of burnt-widows, was look'd upon as the most meritorious. An *Arabian*, who was of the tribe of *setoc*, happen'd just at that juncture, to be dead, and his widow (*almona* by name) who was a noted devotee, publish'd the day, nay, the hour, that she propos'd to throw herself (according to custom) on her deceased husband's funeral pile, and be attended by a concert of drums and trumpets. Zadig remonstrated to *setoc*, what a shocking custom this was, and how directly repugnant to human nature; by permitting young widows, almost every day, to become wilful self-murderers; when they might be of service to their country, either by the addition of new subjects, or by the education of such as demanded their maternal indulgence. And, by arguing seriously with *Setoc* for some time, he forc'd from him at last, an ingenuous confession, that the barbarous custom then subsisting, ought, if possible, to be abolish'd. 'Tis now, replied *setoc*, above a thousand years since the widows of *arabia* have been indulg'd with this privilege of dying with their husbands; and how shall any one dare to abrogate a law that has been establish'd time out of mind? Is there any thing more inviolable than even an antient error? but, replied *Zadig*, reason is of more antient date than the custom you plead for. Do you communicate these sentiments to the sovereigns of your tribes, and in the mean while i'll go, and sound the widow's inclinations.

Accordingly he paid her a visit, and having insinuated himself into her favour, by a few compliments on her beauty, after urging what a pity it was, that a young widow, mistress of so many charms, should make away with herself for no other reason but to mingle her ashes with a husband that was dead; he, notwithstanding, applauded her for her heroic constancy and courage. I perceive, madam, said he, you was excessively fond of your deceased spouse. Not I truly, reply'd the young *Arabian* devotee. He was a brute, infected with a groundless jealousy of my virtue; and, in short, a perfect tyrant. But, notwithstanding all this, I am determin'd to comply with our custom. Surely then, madam, there's a sort of secret pleasure in being burnt alive. Alas! with a sigh, cried *almona*, 'tis a shock indeed to nature; but must be complied with for all that. I am a profess'd devotee, and should I shew the least reluctance, my reputation would be lost for ever; all the world would laugh at me, should I not burn myself on this occasion: *Zadig* having forc'd her ingenuously to confess, that she parted with her life more out of regard to what the world would say of her, and out of pride and ostentation, than any real love for the deceas'd, he talk'd to her for some considerable time so rationally, and us'd so many prevailing arguments with her to justify her due regard for the life which she was going to throw away, that she began to wave the thought, and entertain a secret affection for her friendly monitor. Pray, madam, tell me, said *Zadig*, how would you dispose of yourself, upon the supposition, that you could shake off this vain and barbarous notion? why, said dame, with an amorous glance, I think verily I should accept of yourself for a second bed-fellow.

The memory of *Astarte* had made too strong an impression on his mind, to close with this warm declaration: he took his leave, however, that moment, and waited on the chiefs. He communicated to them the substance of their private conversation, and prevailed with them to make it a law for the future, that no widow should be allow'd to fall a victim to a deceased husband, till after she had admitted some young man to converse with her in private for a whole hour together. The law was pass'd accordingly, and not one widow in all *arabia*, from that day to this, ever observ'd the custom. 'Twas to *Zadig* alone that the *Arabian* dames were indebted for the abolition, in one hour, of a custom so very inhuman, that had been practis'd for such a number of ages. Zadig, therefore, with the strictest justice, was look'd upon by all the fair sex in *arabia*, as their most bountiful benefactor.

XI

THE EVENING'S ENTERTAINMENT

Setoc, who would never stir out without his bosom-friend (in whom alone, as he thought, all wisdom center'd) resolv'd to take him with him to *balzora* fair, whither the richest merchants round the whole habitable globe, us'd annually to resort. Zadig was delighted to see such a concourse of substantial tradesmen from all countries, assembled together in one place. It appear'd to him, as if the whole universe was but one large family, and all happily met together at *balzora*. On the second day of the fair, he sat down to table with an *egyptian*, an *indian*, that liv'd on the banks of the river *ganges*, an inhabitant of *cathay*, a *grecian*, a *celt*, and several other foreigners, who by their frequent voyages towards the *Arabian* gulf, were so far conversant with the *arabic* language, as to be able to discourse freely, and be mutually understood. The *egyptian* began to fly into a passion; what a scandalous place is this *balzora*, said he, where they refuse to lend me a thousand ounces of gold, upon the best security that can possibly be offer'd. Pray, said *setoc*, what may the commodity be that you would deposit as a pledge for the sum you mention. Why, the corpse of my deceased aunt, said he, who was one of the finest women in all *egypt*. She was my constant companion; but unhappily died upon the road. I have taken so much care, that no mummy whatever can equal it: and was I in my own country, I could be furnish'd with what sum soever I pleas'd, were I dispos'd to mortgage it. 'Tis a strange thing that nobody here will advance so small a sum upon so valuable a commodity. No sooner had he express'd his resentment, but he was going to cut up a fine boil'd pullet, in order to make a meal on't, when an *indian* laid hold of his hand, and with deep concern, cried out, for god's sake what are you about? why, said the *egyptian*, I design to make a wing of this fowl one part of my supper. Pray, good sir, consider what you are doing, said the *indian*. 'Tis very possible, that the soul of the deceas'd lady may have taken its residence in that fowl. And you wouldn't surely run the risque of eating up your aunt? to boil a fowl is, doubtless, a most shameful outrage done to nature. Pshaw! what a pother you make about the boiling of a fowl, and flying in the face of nature, replied the *egyptian* in a pet; tho' we *egyptians* pay divine adoration to the ox; yet we can make a hearty meal of a piece of roast beef for all that. Is it possible, sir, that your country-men should act so absurdly, as to pay an ox the tribute of divine worship, said the *indian*? absurd as you think it, said the other, the ox has been the principal object of adoration all over *egypt*, for these hundred and thirty five thousand years, and the most abandon'd *egyptian* has never been as yet so impious as to gainsay it. Ay, sir, an hundred thirty five thousand years, say you, surely you must be out a little in your calculation. 'Tis but about fourscore thousand years, since *india* was first inhabited. Sure I am, we are a more antient people than you are, and our *brama* prohibited the eating of beef long before your nation ever erected an altar in honour of the ox, or ever put one upon a spit. What a racket you make about your *brama*! is he able to stand the least in competition with our *apis*, said the *egyptian*? let us hear, pray, what mighty feats have been done by your boasted *brama*? why, replied the *bramin*, he first taught his votaries to write and read; and 'tis to him alone, all the world is indebted for the invention of the noble game of chess. You are quite out, sir, in your notion, said a *chaldean*, who sat within hearing: all these invaluable blessings were deriv'd from the fish *oannés*; and 'tis that alone to which the tribute of divine adoration is justly due. All the world will tell you, that 'twas a divine being whose tail was pure gold, whose head resembled that of a man, tho' indeed the features were much more beautiful; and that he condescended to visit the earth three hours every day, for the instruction of mankind. He had a numerous issue, as is very well known, and all of them were powerful monarchs. I have a picture of it at home, to which, as in duty I ought, I say my prayers at night before I go to bed, and every morning that I rise. There is no harm, sir, as I can conceive, in partaking of a piece of roast beef; but, doubtless, 'tis a mortal sin, a crime of the blackest dye, to touch a piece of fish. Besides, you cannot justly boast of so illustrious an origin, and you are both of you mere moderns, in comparison to us *chaldeans*, you *egyptians* lay claim to no more than 135,000 years, and you *indians*, but of 80,000. Whereas we have almanacks that are dated 4000 centuries backwards. Take my word for it; I speak nothing but truth; renounce your errors, and i'll make each of you a present of a fine portrait of our *oannés*.

A native of *cambalu*, entring into the debate, said, I have a very great veneration, not only for the *egyptians*, *chaldeans*, *greeks*, and *celtæ*; but for *brama*, *apis*, and the *oannés*, but in my humble opinion, the **li*, **the* chinese *term*, li, *signifies, properly speaking, natural light, or reason; and* tien, *the heavens, or the supreme being.*or as 'tis by some call'd, the **tien*, is an object more deserving of divine adoration than any ox, or fish, how much soever you may boast of their respective perfections. All I shall say, in regard to my native country, 'tis of much greater extent, than all *egypt*, *chaldea*, and the *indies* put together. I shall lay no stress on the antiquity of my country; for I imagine 'tis of much greater importance to be the happiest people, than the most antient under the sun. However, since you were talking of the almanacks, I must beg the liberty to tell you, that ours are look'd upon to be the best all over *asia*; and that we had several very correct ones before the art of arithmetick was ever heard of in *chaldea*.

You are all of you a parcel of illiterate, ignorant bigots, cry'd a *grecian*: 'tis plain, you know nothing of the chaos, and that the world, as it now stands, is owing wholly to *matter* and *form*. The *greek* ran on for a considerable time; but was at last interrupted by a *celt*, who having drank deep, during the whole time of this debate, thought himself ten times wiser than any of his antagonists; and wrapping out a great oath, insisted, that all their gods were nothing, if set in competition with the *teutath* or the misletoe on the oak. As for my part, said he, I carry some of it always in my pocket: as to my ancestors, they were *scythians*, and the only men worth talking of in the whole world: 'tis true, indeed, they would now and then make a meal of their country-men, but that ought not to be urg'd as any objection to his country; and, in short, if any one of you, or all of you, shall dare to say any thing disrespectful of *teutath*, i'll defend its cause to the last drop of my blood. The quarrel grew warmer and warmer, and *Setoc* expected that the table would be overset, and that blood-shed would ensue. Zadig, who hadn't once open'd his lips during the whole controversy, at last rose up, and address'd himself to the *celt*, in the first place, as being the most noisy and outrageous. Sir, said he, your notions in this affair are very just: good sir, oblige me with a bit of your misletoe. Then turning about, he expatiated on the eloquence of the *grecian*, and in a word, soften'd in the most artful manner all the contending parties. He said but little indeed to the *cathayian*; because he was more cool, and sedate than any of the others. To conclude, he address'd them all in general terms, to this or the like effect: my dear friends, you have been contesting all this while about an important topick, in which 'tis evident, you are all unanimously agreed. Agreed, quotha! they all cried, in an angry tone, how so, pray? why said he to the hot, testy *celt*, is it not true, that you do not in effect adore this misletoe, but that being who created that misletoe and the oak, to which it is so closely united? doubtless, sir, reply'd the *celt*. And you, sir, said he, to the *egyptian*, you revere, thro' your venerable *apis*, the great author of every ox's being. We do so, said the *egyptian*. The mighty *oannés*, tho' the sovereign of the sea, continued he, must give precedence to that power, who made both the sea, and every fish that dwells therein. We allow it, said the *chaldean*. The *indian*, adds he, and the *cathayan*, acknowledge one supreme being, or first cause, as well as you. As to what that profound worthy gentleman the *grecian* has advanc'd, is, I must own, a little above my weak comprehension, but I am fully persuaded, that he will allow there is a supreme being on whom his favourite matter and form are entirely dependent. The *grecian*, who was look'd upon as a sage amongst them, said, with abundance of gravity, that *Zadig*, had made a very just construction of his meaning. Now, gentlemen, I appeal to you all, said *Zadig*, whether you are not unanimous to a man, in the debate upon the carpet, and whether there are any just grounds for the least divisions or animosities amongst you. The whole company, cool at once, caress'd him; and *setoc*, after he had sold off all his goods and merchandize at a round price, took his friend *Zadig* home with him to the land of *horeb*. Zadig, upon his first arrival was inform'd, that a prosecution had been carried on against him during his absence, and that the sentence pronounc'd against him was, that he should be burnt alive before a slow fire.

XII

THE RENDEZVOUS

Whilst *Zadig* attended his friend *Setoc* to *balzora*, the priests of the stars were determin'd to punish him. As all the costly jewels, and other valuable decorations, in which every young widow that sacrificed her self on her husband's funeral-pile, were their customary fees, 'tis no great wonder, indeed, that they were inclin'd to burn poor *Zadig*, for playing them such a scurvy trick. Zadig therefore, was accus'd of holding heretical and damnable tenets, in regard to the celestial host: they depos'd, and swore point-blank, that he had been heard to aver, that the stars never sat in the sea. This horrid blasphemous declaration thunder-struck all the judges, and they were ready to rend their mantles at the sound of such an impious assertion; and they would have made *Zadig*, had he been a man of substance, paid very severely for his heretical notions. But in the height of their pity and compassion for even such an infidel, they would lay no fine upon him; but content themselves with seeing him roasted alive before a slow fire. *Setoc*, tho' without hopes of success, us'd all the interest he had to save his bosom friend from so shocking a death; but they turn'd a deaf ear to all his remonstrances, and oblig'd him to hold his tongue. The young widow *almona*, who by this time was not only reconcil'd to living a little longer, but had some taste for the pleasures of life, and knew that she was entirely indebted to *Zadig* for it, resolv'd, if possible, to free her benefactor from being burnt, as he had before convinc'd her of the folly of it in her case. She ponder'd upon this weighty affair very seriously; but said nothing to any one whomsoever. Zadig was to be executed the next day; and she had only a few hours left to carry her project into execution. Now the reader shall hear with how much benevolence and discretion this amiable widow behav'd on this emergent occasion.

In the first place, she made use of the most costly perfumes; and drest herself to the utmost advantage to render her charms as conspicuous as possible; and thus gaily attir'd, demanded a private audience of the high priest of the stars. Upon her first admittance into his august and venerable presence, she address'd herself in the following terms. O thou first-born and well-beloved son of the great bear, brother of the bull, and first cousin to the dog, (these you must know were the pontiff's high titles) I come to confess myself before you: my conscience is my accuser, and I am terribly afraid I have been guilty of a mortal sin, by declining the stated custom of burning my self on my husband's funeral-pile? what could tempt me, in short, to a prolongation of my life, I can't imagine, I, who am grown a perfect skeleton, all wrinkled and deform'd. She paus'd, and pulling off, with a negligent but artful air, her long silk gloves; she display'd a soft, plump, naked arm, and white as snow: you see, sir, said she, that all my charms are blasted. Blasted, madam, said the luscious pontiff; no! your charms are still resistless: his eyes, and his mouth, with which he kiss'd her hand, confirm'd their power: such an arm, madam, by the great *orasmades*, I never saw before. Alas! said the widow, with a modest blush; my arm sir, 'tis probable, may have the advantage of any hidden part; but see, good father, what a neck is here; as yellow as saffron, an object not worth regarding. Then she display'd such a snowy, panting bosom, that nature could not mend it. A rose-bud on an ivory apple, would, if set in competition with her spotless whiteness, make no better appearance than common madder upon a shrub; and the whitest wool, just out of the laver, were she but by, would seem but of a light-brown hue.

Her neck, her large black, sparkling eyes, that languishingly roll'd, and seem'd as 'twere, on fire; her lovely cheeks, glowing with white and red, her nose, that was not unlike the tower of mount *lebanon*, her lips, which were like two borders of coral, inclosing two rows of the best pearls in the *Arabian* sea; such a combination, I say, of charms, made the old pontiff judge she was scarce twenty years of age; and in a kind of flutter, to make her a declaration of his tender regard for her. *Almona*, perceiving him enamour'd, begg'd his interest in favour of *Zadig*. Alas! my dear charmer, my interest alone, when you request the favour, would be but a poor compliment; i'll take care his acquittance shall be signed by three more of my brother priests. Do you sign first, however, said *almona*. With all my soul, said the amorous pontiff, provided—you'll be kind, my dearest. You do me too much honour, said *almona*; but should you give your self the trouble to pay me a visit after sunset, and as soon as the star *sheat* twinkles on the horizon, you shall find me, most venerable father, repos'd upon a rosy-colour'd silver sopha, where you shall use your pleasure with your humble servant. With that she made him a low courtesy; took up *Zadig*'s general release as soon as duely sign'd, and left the old doatard all over love, tho' somewhat diffident of his own abilities. The residue of the day he spent in his bagnio; he drank large enlivening draughts of a water distill'd from the cinnamon of *ceilan*, and the costly spices of *tidor* and *ternate*, and waited with the utmost impatience for the up-rising of the brilliant *sheat*.

In the mean time *almona* went to the second pontiff. He assur'd her that the sun, moon, and all the starry host of heav'n, were but languid fires to her bright eyes. He put the question to her, in short, at once, and agreed to sign upon her compliance. She suffer'd herself to be over-persuaded, and made an assignation to meet him at a certain place, as soon as the star *algenib* should make its appearance. From him she repair'd to the third and fourth pontiff, taking care, wherever she went, to see *Zadig*'s acquittance duely sign'd, and made fresh appointments at the rising of star after star.

When she had carried her point thus far, she sent a proper message to the judges of the court, who had condemn'd *Zadig*, requesting that they would come to her house, that she might advise with them upon an affair of the last importance. They waited on her accordingly; she produc'd *Zadig*'s discharge duly sign'd by four several hands, and told them the definitive treaty between all the contracting parties. Each of the pontifical gallants observ'd their summons to a moment. Each was startled at the sight of his rival; but perfectly thunderstruck to see the judges, before whom the widow had laid open her case. Zadig procur'd an absolute pardon, and *Setoc* was so charm'd with the artful address of *almona*, that he married her the next day. Zadig went afterwards to throw himself at the feet of his fair benefactress. Setoc and he took their leave of each other with tears in their eyes, and vowing that an eternal mutual friendship should be preserv'd between them; and, in short, should fortune at any time afterwards prove more propitious than could well be expected to either party; the other should partake of an equal share of his success.

Zadig steer'd his course towards *syria*; forever pondering on the hard fate of the justly-admir'd *astarte*, and reflecting on his own stars that so obstinately darted down their malignant rays, and continu'd daily to torment him. What, said he! to pay four hundred ounces of gold for only seeing a bitch pass by me; to be condemn'd to be beheaded for four witless verses in praise of the king; to be strangled to death, because a queen was pleas'd to look upon me; to be made a prisoner, and sold as a slave for saving a young lady from being sorely abus'd by a brute rather than a man; and to be upon the brink of being roasted alive, for no other offence than saving for the future all the widows in *arabia* from becoming idle burnt-offerings, and mingling their ashes with those of their deceased worthless husbands.

XIII

THE FREE-BOOTER

Zadig, arriving at the frontiers which separate *arabia petrœa* from *syria,* and passing by a very strong castle, several arm'd *Arabian* s rush'd out upon him, and surrounding him, cried out: whatever you have belonging to you is our property, but as for your person, that is entirely at our sovereign's disposal. Zadig, instead of making any reply, drew his sword, and as his attendant was a very couragious fellow, he drew likewise. Those who laid hold on them, first fell a sacrifice to their fury: their numbers redoubled: yet still, both dauntless, determin'd to conquer or to die. When two men defend themselves against a whole gang, the contest, doubtless, cannot last long. The master of the castle, one *arbogad* by name, having been an eye-witness from his window, of the intrepidity and surprising exploits of *Zadig,* took a fancy to him. He ran down therefore in haste, and giving orders himself to his vassals to desist, deliver'd the two travellers out of their hands. Whatever goods or chattels, said he, come upon my territories, are my effects; and whatever I find likewise that is valuable upon the premises of others, is my free booty; but, as you appear, sir, to me to be a gentleman of uncommon courage, you shall prove an exception to my general rule. Upon this, he invited *Zadig* into his magnificent mansion, giving his inferior officers strict orders to use him with all due respect; and at night *arbogad* was desirous of supping with *Zadig*. The lord of the mansion was one of those *Arabian* s, that are call'd *free-booters*; but a man who now and then did good actions amongst a thousand bad ones. He plunder'd without mercy; but was liberal in his benefactions. When in action, intrepid; but in traffick, easy enough; a perfect *epicure* in his eating and drinking, an absolute *debauchee*, but very frank and open. Zadig pleas'd him extremely; his conversation being very lively, prolong'd their repast: at last, *arbogad* said to him; I would advise you, sir, to enlist yourself in my troop; you cannot possibly do a better thing: my profession is none of the worst; and in time, you may become perhaps as great a man as myself. May I presume, sir, to ask you one question; how long may you have follow'd this honourable calling? from my youth upwards, replied his host, I was only a *valet* at first to an *Arabian*, who indeed was courteous enough; but servitude was a state of life I could not brook. It made me stark-mad to see, in a wide world, which ought to be divided fairly between mankind, that fate had reserv'd for me so scanty a portion. I communicated my grievance to an old sage *Arabian* . Son, said he, never despair; once upon a time, there was a grain of sand, that bemoan'd itself, as being nothing more than a worthless *atom* of the deserts. At the expiration, however, of a few years, it became that inestimable diamond, which at this very hour, is the richest, and most admir'd ornament of the *Indian* crown. The old man's discourse fir'd me with some ambition; I was conscious to myself that I was at that time the *atom* he mention'd, but was determin'd, if possible, to become the *diamond*. At my first setting out, I stole two horses; then I got into a gang; where we play'd at small game, and stopp'd the small caravans; thus I gradually lessen'd the wide disproportion, which there was at first between me and the rest of mankind: I enjoy'd not only my full share of the good things of this life, but enjoy'd them with usury. I was look'd upon as a man of consequence, and I procur'd this castle by my military atchievements. The *satrap* of *syria* had thoughts of dispossessing me; but I was then too rich to be any ways afraid of him; I gave the *satrap* a certain sum of money, upon condition that I kept quiet possession of my castle. And, moreover, I aggrandiz'd my domains; for he constituted me, at the same time, treasurer of the imports that *arabia petræa* paid to the king of kings. I executed my trust, in every respect, as I ought, in the capacity of a collector; but I never did, nor never intended to balance my accounts.

The grand *desterham* of *Babylon* sent hither, in the name of the king *Moabdar*, a petty *satrap*, with a commission to strangle me. He and his attendants arriv'd here with his royal warrant. I was appriz'd of the whole affair, and, accordingly, order'd his whole retinue, consisting of four inferior officers, to be strangled before his face, after the same manner as was intended for my execution. After this, I ask'd him what he thought the commission with which he was entrusted, might reasonably be valued at; he answer'd, that he presum'd his premium (had he succeeded) might have amounted to about three hundred pieces of gold. I made him sensible, that it would be for his interest to be a commission'd officer under me; I made him accordingly deputy *free-booter*. He is at this very day not only the best officer, but the richest I have in all my court. If my word may be credited, i'll raise your fortune as I have done his. Never was trade brisker in our way; for *Moabdar*, is knock'd on the head, and all *Babylon* in the utmost confusion. Moabdar kill'd, said you! cry'd *Zadig*, and pray, sir, what is become of his royal consort, *astarte*? I know nothing at all of that affair, replied *arbogad*, all that I have to say, is, that *Moabdar* became a perfect madman, and had his brains beat out; that all the people in *Babylon* are cutting one another's throats, and that the whole empire is laid waste; that there is still an opportunity for making several bold pushes; and let me tell you, sir, I have done my part, and made the most on't. But the queen, sir, said *Zadig*; pray favour me so far, as to inform me, if you know any thing of the queen. I have heard great talk, said he, of a certain prince of *hyrcania*; 'tis very possible, she may have listed herself amongst his concubines, if she had the good fortune to escape the resentment of those popular tumults; but my head, sir, is better turn'd for the highway than for news; I have taken several ladies prisoners in the course of my excursions; I keep none of them for my part; and as to such as are handsomer than ordinary, I make the best market I can of them, without enquiring who they are. Their quality or titles will fetch no price at all; a queen, if she be homely, is worth nothing. 'Tis probable, sir, I have dispos'd of the lady myself; and 'tis possible, likewise, she may be dead; 'tis no concern of mine; and to my thinking, it should be an affair of no manner of importance to you. After this declaration, he drank so hard, and confounded his ideas in such a manner, that *Zadig* was not one whit the wiser. Upon which he was struck dumb, confounded, and stood as motionless as a statue. *Arbogad*, in the mean while, swill'd down whole bumpers, told a hundred merry tales, and swore a thousand times over, that he was the happiest creature upon god's earth; persuading *Zadig* to be as merry, and thoughtless as himself. At last, being gradually overcome by the fumes of his liquor, he fell fast asleep. Zadig spent the remainder of the night in deep contemplation, and in all the uneasiness of mind imaginable. What, said he, the king first became crazy, and then was murder'd. I think I have just grounds for complaint. The whole empire is in confusion, and torn to pieces, and this free-booter is as happy as a king. O fortune! o fate! a highwayman as happy as a monarch! and the most amiable creature that nature ever fram'd has suffer'd perhaps, an ignominious death, or perhaps, is in a state of life a thousand times worse than death itself! o *astarte! astarte!* what art thou become?

As soon as it was break of day he went out, and ask'd every one he saw if they knew any thing of her: but the whole gang were too intent upon other matters, to return him any answer. By virtue of their night's excursions, they had brought in some fresh booty, and were busy in dividing the spoil. All the favour he could procure, in their hurry and tumult, was, to go away without the least examination. He took the advantage of their remissness, and mov'd off the premises, but more overwhelm'd with grief and deep reflection than ever.

Zadig, in his march, was very restless and uneasy. His thoughts were forever rolling on the unfortunate *astarte*, the king of *Babylon*, his bosom-friend *Cador*, the happy *free-booter*, *arbogad*, the fair *coquet*, that was taken prisoner on the confines of *egypt*, by the *Babylonish* courier; in a word, on the various scenes of misfortunes and disappointments, which he had successively met with.

XIV

THE FISHERMAN

When *Zadig* had travelled some few leagues from *arbogad*'s castle, he found himself arriv'd at the banks of a little river; incessantly deploring, as he went along, his unhappy fate, and looking upon himself as the very picture of ill luck. He perceiv'd at a little distance a fisherman, reclin'd on a verdant bank by the river-side, trembling, scarce able to hold his net in his hand, (which he seem'd but little to regard) and with uplift eyes, imploring heaven's assistance. I am, doubtless, said the poor fisherman, the most unhappy wretch that ever liv'd! no merchant in all *Babylon*, it is very well known, was ever so noted for selling cream-cheeses as myself; and yet I am ruin'd to all intents and purposes. No man of my profession ever had a handsomer, more compleat housewife, than my dame was; but I have been treacherously depriv'd of her. I had still left a poor, pitiful cottage, but that I saw plunder'd and destroy'd. I am cubb'd up here in a cell; I have nothing to depend upon but my fishery, and not one single fish have I caught. Thou unfortunate net! i'll never throw thee into the water more: much sooner will I throw myself in. No sooner were the words out of his mouth, but he started up, and ran to the river-side, like one that was resolutely bent to plunge in, and get rid of a miserable life at once. Is it possible, said *Zadig*? Is there then the man in being more wretched than myself? his benevolence, and good will to save the poor man's life, was as quick as the reflection he had just made! he ran to his assistance; he laid hold of him; and ask'd him, with an air of pity and concern, the cause of his rash intention. 'tis an old saying, that a person is less unhappy when he sees himself not singular in misfortune. But if we will credit *zoroaster*, this is not from a principle of malignity, but the effect of a fatal necessity. He was attracted, as it were, to any person in distress, as being one in the same unhappy circumstances. The transport of a happy man, would be a kind of insult; but two persons in bad circumstances, are like two weak shrubs, which, by propping up each other, are fenc'd against a storm. Why are you thus cast down, said *Zadig* to the fisherman? never sink man, under the weight of your burden. I can't help it, said the poor fisherman; I have not the least prospect of redress. I was once, sir, the tip-top man of the whole village of *derlbach*, near *Babylon*, where I liv'd, and with the help of my wife, made the best cream-cheeses that were ever eaten in the *persian* empire. Her majesty, the queen *astarte*, and the famous prime-minister *Zadig* were very fond of them. I serv'd the court with about six hundred of them, I went the other day in hopes of being paid; but before I had well got into the suburbs of *Babylon*, I was inform'd, that not only the queen, but *Zadig* too had privately left the court: whereupon I ran directly to *Zadig*'s house, tho' I never sat eye on the man in all my life. There I found the court-marshals of the grand *desterham*, plundering, by virtue of his majesty's mandate, all his effects, in the most loyal manner. From thence I made the best of my way to the queen's kitchin; where, applying my self to the steward of her household, and his inferior officers; one of them told me she was dead; another, that she was confin'd in prison; a third, indeed, said that she had made her escape by flight; all in general, however, assur'd me for my comfort, that my cheeses would never be paid for. From thence I went, with my wife in my hand, to lord *orcan*'s; who was another of my court-customers; of whom we begg'd for shelter and protection: the favour, I confess, was readily granted to my wife; but as for my own part, I was absolutely rejected. She was fairer, sir, than the fairest cheese I ever sold; from whence I date all my misfortunes; and the red that adorn'd her blushing cheeks was ten times more lively than any *tyrian* scarlet. And between you and i, sir, that was the main cause of my wife's reception, and my disgrace. Whereupon I wrote a doleful letter to my wife, in all the agonies of one in the deepest despair: 'tis very well, said she, to the messenger; I have some little knowledge of the man; I have heard say no one sells better cream-cheeses than he does; desire him, next time he comes, to bring a small parcel with him, and let him know, i'll take care he shall be punctually paid.

In the height of my misfortunes, I determin'd to seek redress in a court of equity: I had but six ounces of gold left: two whereof went for a fee to my counsellor; two to my lawyer, who took my cause in hand, and the other two to the judge's clerk. Notwithstanding what I had done, my cause was not so much as commenc'd; and I had already disburs'd more money than all my cheeses and my wife with them were worth. I return'd therefore to my native habitation, with a full resolution to sell it for the ransom of my wife.

My little cot, with the appurtenances, were worth about threescore ounces of gold: but as the purchasers found I was necessitous, and drove to my last shifts; the first whom I apply'd to, offer'd me thirty ounces; the second, twenty; and the third, but ten: just as I had come to terms of accommodation with one of them, the prince of *hyrcania* came to *Babylon*, and swept all before him. My little cottage, with all its furniture, was first plunder'd of all that was valuable, and at last reduc'd to ashes.

Having thus lost my money, my wife, and my house, I withdrew to this desart, where you see me. I have since endeavour'd to get my bread by fishing; but the fish, as well as all mankind, desert me. I scarce catch one in a day; I am half starv'd; and had it not been for your unexpected benevolence and generosity, I had been at the bottom of the river before this.

This long detail of particulars, however, was not deliver'd without several interruptions; for, said *Zadig*, with abundance of warmth and confusion, have you never heard, sir, of what is become of the queen *astarte*? no sir, not i, said the disconsolate fisherman; but this I know, to my sorrow, that neither the queen, nor *Zadig*, ever paid me the least consideration in the world for my cream cheeses; that my dear spouse is taken from me; and that I am drove to the very brink of despair. I am verily persuaded, said *Zadig*, that you will not lose all your money. I have heard much talk of that same *Zadig*; they say he is very honest, and that if ever he returns to *Babylon*, as 'tis to be hop'd he will, he'll discharge his debts with interest, like a man of honour. But, as for your wife, who appears to me, to be no better than a wag-tail, never take the trouble, if you'll take my advice, to hunt after her any more. Be rul'd, and make the best of your way to *Babylon*. I shall be there before you, as I shall ride, and you will be on foot. Make your applications to the illustrious *Cador*; tell him you met his friend upon the road; and stay there still I come. Observe my orders, and 'tis very probable it may turn out to your advantage.

O puissant *orosmades*, continu'd he, you have made me, 'tis true, an instrument of comfort to this poor man; but what friend will you raise for me, to alleviate my sorrows? having utter'd this short expostulation, he gave the distrest fisherman one full moiety of all the money he brought with him out of *arabia*. The fisherman, thunder-struck, and transported with joy at so unexpected a benefaction, kiss'd the feet of *Cador*'s friend, and cried out, sure you are a messenger of heaven, sent down to be my saviour!

In the mean time, *Zadig* every now and then ask'd him questions, and wept as he ask'd them. What! sir, said the fisherman, can you, who are so bountiful a benefactor, be in distress yourself? alas! said he, friend, I am a hundred times more unhappy than thou art. But pray, sir, said the good man, how can it possibly be, that he, who is so lavish of his favours, should be overwhelm'd with greater misfortunes than the man he so generously relieves? your greatest uneasiness, said he, arose from the narrowness of your circumstances; but mine proceeds from an internal, and much deeper cause. Pray, sir, said the fisherman, has *orcan* robb'd you of your wife? this interrogatory put *Zadig* in a moment upon a retrospection of all his past adventures. He recollected the whole series of his misfortunes; commencing from that of the eunuch and the huntsman, to his arrival at the free-booter's castle. Alas! said he, to the fisherman, *orcan*, 'tis true, deserves severely to be punish'd: but for the generality, we find, such worthless barbarians are the favourites of fortune. Be that, however, as it will, go as I bade you, to my friend *Cador*, and wait there till I come. They took their leave; the fisherman blessing his propitious stars, and *Zadig* cursing, every step he went, the hour he was born.

XV

THE BASILISK

As *Zadig* was traversing a verdant meadow, he perceiv'd several young female *syrians*, intent on searching for something very curious, that lay conceal'd, as they imagin'd, in the grass. He took the freedom to approach one of them, and ask her, in the most courteous manner, if he might have the honour to assist her in her researches. have a care, said she. What we are hunting after, sir, is an animal, that will not suffer itself to be touch'd by a man. 'Tis somewhat surprizing, said *Zadig*. May I be so bold, pray, as to ask you what you are in pursuit after, that shuns the touch of any thing but the hands of the fair sex. 'Tis, sir, said she, the *basilisk*: a *basilisk*, madam, said he! and pray, if you will be so good as to inform me, with what view, are you searching after a creature so very difficult to be met with? 'tis, sir, said she, for our lord and master *ogul*, whose castle, you see, situate on the river-side, at the bottom of the meadow. We are all his vassals. *Ogul*, you must know, is in a very bad state of health, and his first physician has order'd him, as a specific, to eat a *basilisk*, boil'd in rose water: and as that animal is very hard to be catch'd, and will suffer nothing to approach it, but one of our sex, our dying sovereign *ogul* has promis'd to honour her, that shall be so happy as to catch it for him, so far as to make her his consort. The case, being thus circumstantiated, sir, I hope you will not interrupt me any longer, lest my rivals here in the field should happen to circumvent me.

Zadig withdrew, and left the *syrian* ladies in quest of their imaginary booty, in order to pursue his intended journey. But as he came to the banks of a rivulet, at the remotest part of the meadow, he perceiv'd another young lady, reclin'd on the grass, and entirely disengag'd. Her stature seem'd majestic, but her face was cover'd with a vail; and her eyes were fixt, as one at her looking-glass, on the river. Every now and then a sigh burst out, as if her heart were breaking. In her hand she held a little wand or rod, with which she was tracing out some characters on the dry sand, that lay between the flow'ry bank she sat on, and the purling current. Zadig's curiosity induc'd him, unperceiv'd, to observe her operations at some distance. But approaching nearer, and perceiving very distinctly the first character to be an *z*. The next an *a*. And the third a *d*. He started; but when he saw the additional capitals of I and g. His astonishment was too great for words to express. He stood for some time perfectly thunder-struck, and as motionless as a statue; at last, in a soft, faultring tone, he broke silence: o generous lady, said he, forgive a stranger, one overwhelm'd with sorrows like yourself, if he asks you, by what amazing accident he finds the name of *Zadig* delineated by so angelick a hand. Thus unexpectedly interrupted, and at the sound of those words, she turn'd her head; and with a trembling hand, lifting up her vail, she espy'd *Zadig* himself. Upon which, she shriek'd; and as her heart was flutter'd between the two extreams of transport and surprize, she fainted away, and gently dropp'd into his arms. 'twas, it seems *Astarte* her self; 'twas the queen of *Babylon*; 'twas the very *goddess* whom *Zadig* ador'd; 'twas, in short, the very identical lady, whose hard fate he had so long deplor'd; and for whose sake he had felt so many agonizing pains. For a few minutes he stood speechless, and depriv'd, as it were, of all his senses, whilst his eyes were fixt on his *astarte*, who began to revive; and cast a wishful glance at him, attended with some confusion. O ye immortal powers, cried he, who preside over the destiny of us frail mortals! ye have restor'd me my *astarte*; but alas! at what a conjuncture, in what a place, and in what a state and condition do I view her? he threw himself prostrate on the ground, and kiss'd the dust of her feet. The queen of *Babylon* rais'd him up, and oblig'd him to sit by her on the flow'ry bank whereon she was repos'd. Every now and then she wip'd her eyes, as the tears trickl'd down afresh her lovely cheeks. Twenty times she endeavour'd to renew her discourse; but was interrupted by her sighs; she ask'd him over and over to relate to her the hardships he had ran thro' since their parting, and by what chance he came to traverse that solitary meadow; but prevented him at the same time from returning any answer, by repeating question upon question. At last, she gave him a particular detail of her own misfortunes, and again requested to know his. Both of them, in short, having, in some measure, appeas'd the tumult of their souls; *Zadig*, in a few words, inform'd her of the motives that brought him thither.

But tell me, o unfortunate, tho' ever-venerable queen, how I came to find you out, reclining on this verdant bank, dress'd in this servile habit, accompanied by other female slaves, who, I find, have been all day long in quest after a *basilisk*, which, as I understand, is by order of a celebrated physician, to be dissolv'd in rose-water, as a specific medicine for his dying patient.

Whilst they busy in their fruitless search, said the beauteous *astarte*, i'll tell you the whole series of sorrows which I have undergone since last we parted; and since heav'n has thus unexpectedly blest my eyes once more with the sight of my dear *Zadig*, i'll no longer exclaim against my impropitious stars.

You are not insensible, that the jealous king my spouse, was disgusted to find you the most amiable of all mortals, and that for no other reason he determin'd to strangle you, and poison me. You know very well too, that indulgent heav'n inspir'd, as it were, my little dwarf, with artful means to give me timely notice of the rash resolutions of the king, my cruel husband.

No sooner had the faithful *Cador* oblig'd you to obey my orders, and to fly the court, but he ventur'd to enter my apartment in the dead of night thro' a private door. He snatch'd me up, and convey'd me directly into the temple of *orosmades*, where the holy *magus*, who was his brother, lock'd me up in that august and awful statue, that stands erect upon the pavement of the temple, and *colossus*-like, touches the lofty ceiling with his head. There I lay conceal'd, or rather buried for some time; tho' taken all imaginable care of, and furnish'd with all the necessaries of life by that venerable, and loyal priest. In the mean time, his apothecary enter'd at break of day into my apartment, with a potion in his hand, compos'd of opium, black hellebore, aconite, and other ingredients still more baneful. Whilst this mercenary officer of the king's vengeance was thus employ'd, another as inhuman as himself, went to your lodgings with the silken cord. Both, however, were disappointed, as both of us were fled. Cador, very officious, flew to the king, in order the more artfully to blind him; and in a feign'd passion, rail'd at us both, and charg'd us both as perfidious traitors. As for that villain *Zadig*, said he, he has taken his flight towards *india*; and your false, ungrateful consort, sire, said he, is fled to *memphis*. The guards were order'd that moment to pursue us both.

The couriers, who flew after me, knew nothing of me. I had never expos'd my face unveil'd to any one but your self, and that too in the presence, and by the express order of my royal master. As they had no other marks to distinguish me from others but my stature, as it had been describ'd, a young lady, just of my size, but in all probability much more handsome, presented herself to their view, on the frontiers of *egypt*. She was found alone, and in a very disconsolate condition. This lady must, doubtless, said they to themselves, be the queen of *Babylon*: and without listning to her complaints, convey'd her instantly to my husband *Moabdar* . Their gross blunder at first incens'd his majesty to the last degree; but after he had view'd the lady with an attentive eye, he found she was extremely pretty, and was soon pacify'd. Her name was *missouf*. I have been since inform'd, that her name in the *egyptian* language signifies the *fair coquet*. And in effect, she was so: she had as much art, however, as caprice. For she pleas'd the king of kings: in short, she had such an ascendancy over him, that he didn't scruple in publick to own her as his wife. When she had secur'd him thus far in her toils, she never conceal'd her power, but play'd the part of a perfect humourist. She indulg'd herself in every whim that came in her head, without fear of being brow-beat. In the first place, she insisted that the chief magus, who was old and gouty, should dance a saraband before her; and upon his modest refusal to comply with so preposterous a request, she persecuted him without mercy: nothing would serve her turn, in the next place, but his majesty's grand master of the horse must make her a minc'd-pye. The gentleman took the liberty to let her know, that he was no profess'd cook; a tart, however, he must make for her, and she got him turn'd out of his place for being so monstrously careless, as to burn one *corner* of the crust. Whereupon she gave his post to her favourite dwarf, and made her fop of a page the keeper of his majesty's great seal, and confidence. Thus she reign'd arbitrary, and was the female tyrant of *Babylon*. All the world deplor'd the loss of me their former queen. The king, who never acted the part of a tyrant, till the moment he would have imprison'd me, and strangled you, seem'd to have drown'd all his good qualities in his dotage on that capricious enchantress. He came to the temple on the solemn festival of the sacred fire. I saw him prostrate on the pavement before the statue, wherein I was enclos'd, imploring the gods to show'r down their choicest blessings on his beauteous *missouf.* I, with an audible and distinct, but hollow tone, address'd my self thus, like an oracle, to the king of kings. T*he gods reject the vows of a monarch, that acts the tyrant o'er his subjects; one, who could think of murdering an innocent wife; and admit of a worthless beauty to supply her place. Moabdar* was so startled at this unexpected answer from the god he ador'd, that he was just at the point of distraction. The oracle that I had deliver'd, and the tyrannical proceedings of his new spouse *missouf,* were enough to deprive him of his senses. In short, in a few days he became a perfect mad-man. Her caprice, which seem'd a judgement from above, portended a sudden revolution. His subjects accordingly revolted, and were instantly up in arms. Babylon, that had so long indulg'd herself in indolence and ease, became the seat, or theatre of a bloody civil war. Whereupon I was taken from my magnificent prison, the bowels of his god, and set up at the head of a very powerful party. Your friend *Cador* flew to *memphis* in hopes to find you there, and bring you back to *Babylon.* The prince of *hyrcania,* hearing of these intestine broils, return'd with a powerful army, in order to form a third party, among the *Babylonians.* He attack'd the king, who fled with his fair, but fickle *egyptian* before him. Moabdar, however, was so closely pursu'd, that he dy'd of the wounds he receiv'd in his retreat. M*issouf* became the fair victim of the conqueror. As for my own part, I had the misfortune to be over-power'd likewise, and taken prisoner by an *hyrcanian party,* who brought me into the presence of the young prince, at the very juncture when *missouf* stood before him. You'll smile, doubtless, when I tell you the prince look'd upon me as the most amiable captive of the two; but then, I presume you will be sorry to hear, that my hard fate doom'd me to be a vassal in his seraglio. He told me, in direct terms, that as soon as he had put an happy issue to one military expedition, which would not, he flatter'd himself, be long unexecuted, he would honour me with a visit. Judge the dreadful apprehensions I was under, upon his making such a peremptory declaration. My obligations to *Moabdar* were all cancell'd, and I was free to be the bride of *Zadig*; but instead of that, I fell into the toils of a *barbarian*. I answer'd him with all the resentment becoming one of my high character and unspotted virtue. I had always heard say, that heav'n bestow'd on persons of my rank, such a peculiar mark of majesty and grandeur, that with a bare word, or the glance of an angry eye, they could bring down, and abase the pride of those audacious creatures that durst to thwart their inclinations. I talk'd as big as a queen; but I was treated like the most servile domestic. The saucy *hyrcanian*, without so much as vouchsafing me one single word, turn'd to his black eunuch, and told him that I was very impertinent; but yet he could not help thinking I was very pretty. He gave him therefore particular orders to take care of me, and put me under the same regimen, with respect to my diet, as one of his favourites, in order that I might recover my colour, which was somewhat too languid; in a word, that I might become worthy in a little time of his royal favours, and be duely qualified to receive him, when he should honour me so far as to fix the day. I told him, I would die first: he replied, with a sneer, that young ladies, like me, seldom kill'd themselves, and that they were made for enjoyment; and then turn'd upon his heel, with as careless an air, as a man would part with his paroquet, when he had shut her up close in her gilded cage. What a shocking state was I in for the first queen of the universe! nay, i'll say more, for a heart that was wholly devoted to her *Zadig*!

At these endearing words, *Zadig* threw himself at her feet, and bath'd them with his tears. Astarte immediately rais'd him in the most courteous and engaging manner, and thus continu'd her narration.—i too plainly perceiv'd, that I was subject to the tyranny of a *barbarian*, and the rival of a coquet, that was a slave like myself. She related to me all her past adventures in *egypt*. From the description she gave of her gallant, the time and place, the dromedary he was mounted on, and from every other minute circumstance, I imagin'd it was your self that play'd the hero in her favour. As I made no doubt but that you resided somewhere in *memphis*, I determin'd to go thither my self, but in disguise. Beauteous *missouf*, said i, you are of a much sprightlier disposition than I am; you will be able to amuse the gay young prince of *hyrcania* a thousand times better than I shall. Find out some way therefore for my escape; by which you will be sole lady regent. You will oblige me to the last degree, by your friendly assistance, and at the same time get rid of a rival. M*issouf*, (cajol'd with the hint) came into my measures directly. She took care to send me packing forthwith, with no other attendant than an old *egyptian* slave.

No sooner had I reach'd the borders of *arabia*, but a notorious free-booter, (one *arbogad* by name) pick'd me up, as I was strolling along, and sold me to some merchants, who convey'd me to yonder castle, the magnificent residence of the emir *ogul*. He purchas'd me at all adventures, without enquiring what, or who I was. He is a perfect debauchee; his sole delight lies in good eating, wine, and women; and is one, who imagines, that the almighty sent him into the world for no other purpose but to gratify his unruly appetites. He is excessively fat, and puffs and blows every moment, like one half choak'd. When he has gorg'd himself so unmercifully that he is ready to burst, his chief physician can persuade him to take any thing for his relief; tho' he laughs at him, and despises his advice when he's well and sober. He has intimated to him, that at present his life's in danger, and nothing will restore him but a *basilisk*, boil'd in rose-water. Whereupon the grand *ogul* has promis'd his last favours to that slave, whoever she be, that shall be so fortunate as to catch a *basilisk*, for him, since it seems they are so seldom to be met with. You see I have others to struggle for the honour propos'd, and I never had a less inclination to find out this *basilisk* than at present, since I have once more met with my dearest *Zadig*.

After this declaration, *Astarte* and *Zadig* renew'd with warmth the virtuous affection which they had long conceiv'd for each other; and reciprocally utter'd all the tenderest expressions that love in distress could possibly devise. And the *genii*, who preside over all the soft passions, wafted their mutual vows of eternal constancy and truth to the sphere of *venus*.

The whole train of slaves, after a long fruitless search, attended on *ogul*, to inform him that all their strictest search was fruitless. Zadig desired that he might have the honour to be introduc'd into his presence. Accordingly he was, and his address was to this or the like effect. May immortal health descend from heaven to preserve a life, sir, so precious as yours is. I am a physician by profession. I flew to your palace, on the first news of the dangerous situation you were in, and have brought a *basilisk* with me, distill'd in rose-water. I can have no hopes of the honour of your bed, in case I succeed in my application: all the favour I request, is, the release of one of your *Babylonish* slaves, who has been in your highness's retinue for some time. And I am willing to be your bond-slave in her stead, if I fail of restoring the most illustrious and magnificent *ogul* to his pristine state of health.

The proposition was readily embrac'd. Astarte was instantly discharg'd, and set out for *Babylon*, with a proper attendant, according to *Zadig*'s direction; assuring her that she should hear every day, by a special courier, of his proceedings with his new patient. The farewel which they took of each other, was very affectionate and tender, expressive of the strongest obligations to each other. The moments of meeting, and those of parting, are (as it is written in the sacred book of *zend*) the two most remarkable *epochas* of a lover's life. Zadig's repeated protestations of affection for the queen were perfectly sincere, and the pure dictates of his heart; and the queen's love for *Zadig* had made a deeper impression on hers, than she thought proper to discover.

In the mean time, *Zadig*, again addressing himself to *ogul*, said; my *basilisk*, sir, as others are, is not to be drest or eaten; but all its virtues must penetrate your whole fabrick, thro' your pores; I have inclos'd my never-failing *sudorific* in a bladder, full-blown and carefully cover'd with the softest leather. You must kick this bladder, sir, once a day about your hall for a whole hour together, with all the vigour and activity you possibly can. This medicine must be repeated every morning, and i'll attend the operation: upon your due observance of the regimen I shall put you under, I doubt not, but with the blessing of heav'n on my honest endeavours, I shall give you ample demonstration of my being an adept in physick. *Ogul*, upon making the first experiment, was ready to expire for want of breath, and thought he should die with the fatigue. The second day did not prove altogether so irksome, and he slept much better at night than he had done before. In short, our doctor in about eight days time, perform'd an absolute cure. His patient was as brisk, active and gay, as one in the bloom of his youth.

Now, sir, said *Zadig*, i'll be ingenuous with you, and disclose to you the important secret. You have play'd at foot-ball these eight days successively; and you have liv'd all that time, within the bounds of sobriety and moderation. Know, sir, that there is no such animal in nature as a *basilisk*; that health is to be secur'd by temperance and exercise; and that the art of making health consistent with luxury, is altogether as impracticable, and an art, in all respects, as idle and chimerical, as those of the philosopher's stone, judicial astrology, or any other reveries of the like airy and fantastic nature.

8*ogul*'s head-physician, apprehensive that this unexpected cure, thus wrought by a stranger, through such an anti-medicinal preparation, might possibly not only render himself the object of contempt in the eye of his great master, but cast a kind of slur in general on his whole fraternity, conven'd a set of petty doctors and apothecaries, who were his vassals, and entirely devoted to his interest, to find out some sure ways and means to cut off in private his dreadful rival; but whilst their wicked plot was hatching, *Zadig* receiv'd a courier from the queen *astarte*.

XVI

THE TOURNAMENTS

The queen was receiv'd at *Babylon* with all the transports of joy that could possibly be express'd for the safe return of so illustrious and so beautiful a personage, that had run thro' such a long series of misfortunes. Babylon at that time seem'd to be perfectly serene and quiet. As for the young prince of *hyrcania*, he was slain in battle. The *Babylonians*, who were the victors, declar'd that *Astarte* should marry that candidate for the crown, who should gain it by a fair and impartial election. They were determin'd, that the most valuable post of honour in the world, namely, that of being the royal consort of *astarte*, and the sovereign of *Babylon*, should be the result of merit only; and not be procur'd by any party-factions or court-intrigues. A solemn oath was voluntarily taken by all parties, that he who should distinguish himself by his superior valour and wisdom, should unanimously be acknowledg'd the sovereign-elect.

A spacious *list*, or *circus*, was pitched upon, surrounded with commodious seats, erected in an amphitheatrical manner, and richly embellish'd some few leagues from the city. Thither the combatants, or champions were to repair, compleatly accoutred. Each of them had a distinct apartment to himself behind the *lists*, where no soul could either see them, or know who they were. They were to enter the *lists* four several times.

Those who were so happy as to conquer four competitors, were afterwards to engage each other in single combat; in order that he who should remain master of the field should be proclaim'd the happy victor.

Four days afterwards, they were to meet again, accoutred as before, and to explain all such *ænigmas*, or *riddles*, as the *magi* should think proper to propose. If their queries should prove too intricate and perplext for them to resolve, they were to have recourse to the *lists* again, and after that, to fresh *ænigmas*, before they could be entitled to the election: so that the *tournaments* were to be continu'd till one of the candidates should be twice a victor, and shine as conspicuous, with respect to his internal qualities, as to his dexterity and address in heroic atchievements. The queen, in the mean time, was to be narrowly watch'd, and allow'd only to be a spectator of both their amusements, at some considerable distance; and moreover, to be cover'd with a vail: nor was she indulg'd so far as to speak one single word to any candidate whomsoever, in order to prevent the least jealousy or suspicion either of partiality or injustice.

Astarte took care, by the courier, to inform her lover of all the preliminary articles abovemention'd, not doubting but that he would exert both his courage and understanding for her sake, beyond any of the other competitors.

Zadig accordingly set out for *Babylon*, and besought the goddess *venus*, not only to fortify his courage, but to illuminate his mind with wisdom on this important occasion.

The night before these martial atchievements were to commence, *Zadig* arrived upon the banks of the *euphrates*. He inscrib'd his device amongst the list of combatants; concealing, at the same time, both his person and name, as the laws of the election required; and accordingly, withdrew to the apartment that was provided for him, according to his lot.

Cador, who was just return'd to *Babylon*, having hunted all *egypt* over to no purpose, in hopes to find his friend *Zadig*, brought a compleat set of armour into his lodge, by express orders from the queen: she sent him likewise one of the finest horses in all *persia*. Zadig knew that these presents could come from no-body but his dear *astarte*, which redoubled his vigour and his hopes.

The next morning the queen being seated under a canopy of state, enrich'd with precious stones; and the amphitheatres being crowded with gentlemen and ladies of all ranks and conditions from *Babylon*; the competitors made their personal appearance in the *circus*: each of them went up to the grand *magus*, and laid down his particular *device* at his feet. The *devices* were drawn by lot: that of *Zadig* was the last. The first that advanc'd was a grandee, one *itabod* by name, immensely rich, indeed, and very haughty; but no ways couragious; exceedingly awkward, and a man of no acquir'd parts. The sycophants that hover'd round about him flatter'd him, that a man of his merit couldn't fail of being king: he imperiously replied, one of my merit must be king: whereupon he was arm'd *cap-a-pee*. His armour was made of pure gold, enamell'd with green. The housings of his saddle were green, and his lance embellish'd with green ribbands. Every one was sensible, at first sight, by *itobad*'s manner of managing his horse, that he was not the man whom heav'n had pitch'd upon to sway the *Babylonish* scepter. The first combatant that tilted with him, threw him out of the saddle; the second flung him quite over the crupper, and laid him sprawling on the ground, with his heels quiv'ring in the air. I*tobad*, 'tis true, remounted, but with so ill a grace, that an universal laugh went round the amphitheatre. The third, disdaining to use his lance, made only a feint at him: then catch'd hold of his right leg, and whirling him round, threw him flat upon the sand. The esquires, who were the attendants, ran to his assistance, and with a sneer remounted him. The fourth combatant catch'd hold of his left leg, and unhors'd him again. He was convey'd thro' the hissing multitude to his lodge, where, according to the law in that case provided, he was to pass the night. And as he hobbled along, said he, to the esquires, what a sad misfortune is this to one of my birth and character!

The other champions play'd their parts much better; and all came off with credit. Some conquer'd two of their antagonists, and others were so far successful as to get the better of three. None of them, however, except prince *hottam*, vanquish'd four. Zadig, at last, enter'd the lists, and dismounted all his four opponents, one after the other, with the utmost ease, and with such an air and grace, as gain'd him universal applause. As the case stood thus, *Zadig* and *hottam* were to close the day's entertainment in a single combat. The armour of the latter was of a blue colour mixt with gold, and the housings of his saddle were of the same. Those of the former white as snow. The multitude were divided in their wishes. The knight in blue was the favourite of some of the ladies; and others again were admirers of the cavalier in white. The queen, whose heart was in a perfect palpitation, put up her secret prayers to *venus* to assist her darling hero.

The two champions making their passes and their volta's, with the utmost dexterity and address, and keeping firm in their saddles, gave each other such rebuffs with their lances, that all the spectators (the queen only excepted) wish'd for two kings of *Babylon*. At last, their horses being tired, and both their lances broke, *Zadig* made use of the following stratagem, which his antagonist wasn't any ways appriz'd of. He got artfully behind him, and shooting with a spring on his horses buttocks, grasp'd him close, threw him headlong on the sand, then jump'd into his seat, and wheel'd round prince *hottam*, while he lay sprawling on the ground. All the spectators in general, with loud acclamations, cried out, victory! victory! in favour of the champion in white. H*ottam*, incens'd to the last degree, got up, and drew his sword. Zadig sprang from his horse with his sabre in his hand. Now, behold the two chieftains upon their legs, commencing a new trial of skill! where they seem'd to get the better of each other alternately; for both were strong, and both were active. The feathers of their helmets, the studs of their bracelets, their coats of mail, flew about in pieces, thro' the dry blows which they a thousand times repeated. They struck at each other sometimes with the edge of their swords, at other times they push'd, as occasion offer'd: now on the right, then on the left; now on the head, then at the breast; they retreated; they advanc'd; they kept at a distance; they clos'd again; they grasp'd each other, turning and twisting like two serpents, and engag'd each other as fiercely as two *libyan* lions fighting for their prey: their swords struck fire almost at every blow. At last, *Zadig*, in order to recover his breath, for a moment or two stood still, and afterwards, making a feint at the prince, threw him on his back, and disarm'd him. H*ottam*, thereupon, cried out, o thou knight of the white armour! 'tis you only are destin'd to be the king of *Babylon*. The queen was perfectly transported. The two champions were reconducted to their separate lodges, as the others had been before them, in conformity to the laws prescrib'd. Several mutes were order'd to wait on the champions, and carry them some proper refreshment. We'll leave the reader to judge whether the queen's dwarf was not appointed to wait on *Zadig* on this happy occasion. After supper the mutes withdrew, and left the combatants to rest their wearied limbs till the next morning; at which time the victor was to produce his *device*, before the *grand magus*, in order to confer notes, and discover the hero whoever he might be.

Zadig slept very sound, notwithstanding his amorous regard for the queen, being perfectly fatigu'd. I*tabod*, who lay in the lodge contiguous to his, could not once close his eyes for vexation. He got up therefore in the dead of the night, stole imperceptibly into *Zadig*'s apartment, took his white armour and device away with him, and substituted his green one in its place.

As soon as the day began to dawn, he repair'd, with a seemingly undaunted courage, to the *grand magus*, to inform him, that he was the mighty hero, the happy victor. Without the least hesitation, he gain'd his point, and was proclaim'd victor before *Zadig* was awake. *Astarte*, astonish'd at this unexpected disappointment, return'd with a heart overwhelm'd with despair, to the court of *Babylon*. Almost all the spectators were mov'd off from the amphitheatre before *Zadig* wak'd: he hunted for his arms; but could find nothing but those in green. He was oblig'd, tho' sorely against his will, to put it on, having nothing else in his lodge to appear in: confounded, and big with resentment, he drest himself, and made his personal appearance in that despicable equipage. The populace that were left behind in the *circus*, hiss'd him every step he took, they made a ring about him, and treated him with all the marks of ignominy and contempt. The most cowardly wretch breathing was never sure so sweated, or hunted down as poor *Zadig*! he grew quite out of patience at last, and cut his way thro' the insulting mob, with his rival's sabre; but he did not know what measures to pursue, or how to rectify so gross a mistake. It was not in his power to have a sight of the queen; he could never recover the white armour again which she had sent him; that was the compromise, or the engagement, to which the combatants had all unanimously agreed: thus, as he was on the one hand, plung'd in an abyss of sorrow; so on the other, he was almost drove distracted with vexation and resentment. He withdrew therefore, in a solitary mood, to the banks of the *euphrates*, now fully persuaded, that his impropitious star had shed its most baleful influence on him, and that his misfortunes were irretrievable, revolving in his mind, all his disappointments from his first adventure with the court-coquet, who had entertain'd an utter aversion to a blind eye, down to his late loss of his white armour. See! said he, the fatal consequence of being a sluggard! had I been more vigilant, I had been king of *Babylon*; but what is more, I had been happy in the embraces of my dearest *astarte*. All the knowledge of books or mankind; all the personal valour that I can boast of, has only prov'd an aggravation of my sorrows. He carried the point so far at last, as to murmur at the unequal dispensations of divine providence; and was tempted to believe, that all occurrences were govern'd by a malignant destiny, which never fail'd to oppress the virtuous, and always crown'd the actions of such villains as the green knight, with uncommon success. In one of his frantick fits, he put on the green armour, that had created him such a world of disgrace. A merchant happening to pass by, he sold it to him for a trifle, and took in exchange nothing more than a mantle, and a cap. In this disguise, he took a solitary walk along the banks of the *euphrates*, every minute reflecting in his mind on the partial proceedings of providence, which never ceas'd to torment him.

XVII

THE HERMIT

As *Zadig* was travelling along, he met with a hermit, whose grey and venerable beard descended to his girdle. He had in his hand a little book, on which his eyes were fix'd. Zadig threw himself in his way, and made him a profound bow. The hermit return'd the compliment with such an air of majesty and benevolence, that *Zadig*'s curiosity prompted him to converse with so agreeable a stranger. Pray, sir, said he, what may be the contents of the treatise you are reading with such attention. 'Tis call'd, said the hermit, the *book of fate*; will you please to look at it. He put the book into the hands of *Zadig*, who, tho' he was a perfect master of several languages, couldn't decypher one single character. This rais'd his curiosity still higher. You seem dejected, said the good father to him. Alas! I have cause enough, said *Zadig*. If you'll permit me to accompany you, said the old hermit, perhaps I may be of some service to you. I have sometimes instill'd sentiments of consolation into the minds of the afflicted. Zadig had a secret regard for the air of the old man, for his beard, and his book. He found, by conversing with him, that he was the most learned person he had ever met with. The hermit harangu'd on destiny, justice, morality, the sovereign good, the frailty of nature; on virtue and vice, in such a lively manner, and in such a flow of words, that *Zadig* was attach'd to him by an invincible charm. He begg'd earnestly that he would favour him with his company to *Babylon*. That favour I was going to ask my self, said the old man. Swear to me by *orosmades*, that you won't leave me, for some days at least, let me do what I please. Zadig took the oath requir'd, and both pursu'd their journey.

The two travellers arriv'd that evening at a superb castle. The hermit begg'd for an hospitable reception of himself and his young comrade. The porter, whom any one might have taken for some grandee, let them in, but with a kind of coldness and contempt. However, he conducted them to the head-steward, who went with them thro' every rich apartment of his master's house. They were seated at supper afterwards at the lower end, indeed, of the table, and where they were taken little or no notice of by the host; but they were serv'd with as much delicacy and profusion, as any of the other guests. When they arose from table, they wash'd their hands in a golden bason set with emeralds, and other costly stones. When 'twas time to go to rest, they were conducted into a bed-chamber richly furnish'd; and the next morning two pieces of gold were presented to him for their mutual service, by a valet in waiting; and then they were dismiss'd.

The proprietor of this castle, said *Zadig*, as they were upon the road, seems to me to be a very hospitable gentleman; tho' somewhat too haughty indeed, and too imperious: the words were no sooner out of his mouth, but he perceiv'd that the pocket of his comrade's garment, tho' very large, was swell'd, and greatly extended: he soon saw what was the cause, and that he had clandestinely brought off the golden laver. He durst not immediately take notice of the fact; but was ready to sink at the very thoughts on't. About noon, the hermit rapp'd at a petty cottage with his staff, the beggarly residence of an old, rich miser. He desir'd that he and his companion might refresh themselves there for a few hours. An old, shabby domestick let them in indeed, but with visible reluctance, and carried them into the stable, where all their fare was a few musty olives, and a draught or two of sower small beer. The hermit seem'd as content with his repast, as he was the night before. At last, rising off from his seat, he paid his compliments to the old valet (who had as watchful an eye over them all the time, as if they had been a brace of thieves, and intimated every now and then that he fear'd they would be benighted) and gave him the two pieces of gold, he had but just receiv'd that morning, as a token of his gratitude for his courteous entertainment. He added moreover, I would willingly speak one word with your master before I go. The valet, thunder-struck at his unexpected gratuity, comply'd with his request: most hospitable sir, said the hermit, I couldn't go away without returning you my grateful acknowledgments for the friendly reception we have met with this afternoon. Be pleas'd to accept this golden bason as a small token of my gratitude and esteem. The miser started, and was ready to fall down backwards at the sight of so valuable a present. The hermit gave him no time to recover out of his surprise, but march'd off that moment with his young comrade. Father, said *Zadig*, what is all this that I have seen? you seem to me to act in a quite different manner from the generality of mankind. You plunder one, who entertain'd you with all the pomp and profusion in the world, to enrich a covetous, sordid wretch, who treated you in the most unworthy manner. Son, said the old man, that grandee, who receives visits of strangers, with no other view than to gratify his pride, and to raise their astonishment at the furniture of his palace, will henceforward learn to be wiser; and the miser to be more liberal for the time to come. Don't be surpris'd, but follow me. Zadig was at a stand at present; and couldn't well determine whether his companion was a man of greater wisdom than ordinary, or a mad-man. But the hermit assum'd such an ascendency over him, exclusive of the oath he had taken, that he couldn't tell how to leave him. At night they came to a house very commodiously built, but neat and plain; where nothing was wanting, and yet nothing profuse. The master was a philosopher, that had retir'd from the busy world, in order to live in peace, and form his mind to virtue. He was pleas'd to build this little box for the reception of strangers, in a handsome manner, but without ostentation. He came in person to meet them at the door, and for a time, advis'd them to sit down and rest themselves in a commodious apartment. After some respite, he invited them to a frugal, yet elegant repast; during which, he talk'd very intelligently about the late revolutions in *Babylon*. He seem'd entirely to be in the queen's interest, and heartily wish'd that *Zadig* had entred the lists for the regal prize: but *Babylon*, said he, don't deserve a king of so much merit. A modest blush appear'd in *Zadig*'s face at this unexpected compliment, which innocently aggravated his misfortunes. It was agreed, on all hands, that the affairs of this world took sometimes a quite different turn from what the wisest patriots would wish them. The hermit replied, the ways of providence are often very intricate and obscure, and men were much to blame for casting reflections on the conduct of the whole, upon the bare inspection of the minutest part.

The next topick they entred upon was the passions. Alas! said *Zadig*, how fatal in their consequences! however, said the hermit, they are the winds that swell the sail of the vessel. Sometimes, 'tis true, they overset it; but there is no such thing as sailing without them. Phlegm, indeed, makes men peevish and sick; but then there is no living without it. Tho' every thing here below is dangerous, yet all are necessary.

In the next place, their discourse turn'd on sensual pleasures; and the hermit demonstrated, that they were the gifts of heaven; for, said he, man cannot bestow either sensations or ideas on himself; he receives them all; his pain and pleasure, as well as his being, proceed from a superior cause.

Zadig stood astonish'd, to think how a man that had committed such vile actions, could argue so well on such moral topicks. At the proper hour, after an entertainment, not only instructive, but ev'ry way agreeable, their host conducted them to their bed-chamber, thanking heaven for directing two such polite and virtuous strangers to his house. He offer'd them at the same time some silver, to defray their expences on the road; but with such an air of respect and benevolence, that 'twas impossible to give the least disgust. The hermit, however, refus'd it, and took his leave, as he propos'd to set forward for *Babylon* by break of day. Their parting was very affectionate and friendly; *Zadig*, in particular, express'd a more than common regard for a man of so amiable a behaviour. When the hermit and he were alone, and preparing for bed, they talk'd long in praise of their new host. As soon as day-light appear'd, the old hermit wak'd his young comrade. 'tis time to be gone, said he; but as all the house are fast asleep, i'll leave a token behind me of my respect and affection for the master of it. No sooner were the words out of his mouth, but he struck a light, kindled a torch, and set the building in a flame: *Zadig*, in the utmost confusion, shriek'd out, and would, if possible, have prevented him from being guilty of such a monstrous act of ingratitude. The hermit dragg'd him away, by a superior force. The house was soon in a blaze: when they had got at a convenient distance, the hermit, with an amazing sedateness, turn'd back and survey'd the destructive flames. Behold, said he, our fortunate friend! in the ruins, he will find an immense treasure, that will enable him, from henceforth, to exert his beneficence, and render his virtues more and more conspicuous. Zadig, tho' astonish'd to the last degree, attended him to their last stage, which was to the cottage of a very virtuous and well-dispos'd widow, who had a nephew of about fourteen years of age. He was a hopeful youth, and the darling of her heart. She entertain'd her two guests with the best provisions her little house afforded. In the morning she order'd her nephew to attend them to an adjacent bridge, which, having been broken down some few days before, render'd the passage dangerous to strangers.

The lad, being very attentive to wait on them, went formost. When they were got upon the bridge; come hither, my pretty boy, said the hermit, I must give your aunt some small token of my respect for her last night's favours. Upon that, he twisted his fingers in the hair of his head, and threw him, very calmly, into the river. Down went the little lad; he came up once again to the surface of the water; but was soon lost in the rapid stream. O thou monster! thou worst of villains, cry'd *Zadig*! didn't you promise, said the hermit, to view my conduct with patience? know then, that had that boy liv'd but one year longer, he would have murder'd his foster-mother. Who told you so, you barbarous wretch, said *Zadig*? and when did you read that inhuman event in your *black-book* of *fate*? who gave you permission pray, to drown so innocent a youth, that had never disoblig'd you?

No sooner had our young *Babylonian* ceas'd his severe reflections, but he perceiv'd that the old hermit's long beard grew shorter and shorter; that the furrows in his face began to fill up, and that his cheeks glow'd with a rose-coloured red, as if he had been in the bloom of fifteen. His mantle was vanish'd at once; and on his shoulders, which were before cover'd, appear'd four angelic wings, each refulgent as the sun. O thou messenger of heaven! o thou angelic form! cry'd *Zadig*, and fell prostrate at his feet; thou art descended from the empireum,

I find, to instruct such a poor frail mortal as I am, how to submit to the mysteries of fate. Mankind in general, said the angel *jesrad*, judge of the whole, by only viewing the hither link of the chain. Thou, of all the human race, wast the only man that deserv'd to have thy mind enlighten'd. Zadig, begg'd leave to speak. I am somewhat diffident of myself, 'tis true; but may I presume, sir, to beg the solution of one scruple? would it not have been better to have chastiz'd the lad, and by that means reform'd him, than to have cut him off thus unprepar'd in a moment. *Jesrad*, replied, had he been virtuous, and had he liv'd, 'twas his *fate* not only to be murder'd himself, but his wife, whom he would afterwards have married, and the little infant, that was to have been the pledge of their mutual affection. Is it necessary then, venerable guide, that there should be wickedness and misfortunes in the world, and that those misfortunes should fall with weight on the heads of the righteous? the wicked, replied *jesrad*, are always unhappy. Misfortunes are intended only as a touch-stone, to try a small number of the just, who are thinly scatter'd about this terrestrial globe: besides, there is no evil under the sun, but some good proceeds from it: but, said *Zadig*, suppose the world was all goodness, and there was no such thing in nature as evil. Then, that world of yours, said *jesrad*, would be another world; the chain of events would be another wisdom; and that other order, which would be perfect, must of necessity be the everlasting residence of the supreme being, whom no evil can approach. That great and first cause has created an infinite number of worlds, and no two of them alike. This vast variety is an attribute of his omnipotence. There are not two leaves on the trees throughout the universe, nor any two globes of light amongst the myriad of stars that deck the infinite expanse of heaven, which are perfectly alike. And whatever you see on that small atom of earth, whereof you are a native, must exist in the place, and at the time appointed, according to the immutable decrees of him who comprehends the whole. Mankind imagine, that the lad, whom I plung'd into the river, was drown'd by *chance*; and that our generous benefactor's house was reduc'd to ashes by the same *chance*; but know, there is no such thing as *chance*, all misfortunes are intended, either as severe trials, judgments, or rewards; and are the result of foreknowledge. You remember, sir, the poor fisherman in despair, that thought himself the most unhappy mortal breathing. The great *orasmades*, sent you to amend his situation. Frail mortal! cease to contend with what you ought to adore. But, said *Zadig*—whilst the sound of the word but dwelt upon his tongue, the angel took his flight towards the tenth sphere. Zadig sunk down upon his knees, and acknowledg'd an over-ruling providence with all the marks of the profoundest submission. The angel, as he was soaring towards the clouds, cried out in distinct accents; make thy way towards *Babylon*.

XVIII

THE ÆNIGMAS, OR RIDDLES

Zadig, as one beside himself, and perfectly thunder-struck, beat his march at random. He entred, however, into the city of *Babylon*, on that very day, when those combatants who had been before engag'd in the list or circus, were already assembled in the spacious outer-court of the palace, in order to solve the ænigmas, and give the wisest answers they could to such questions, as the *grand magus* should propose. All the parties concern'd were present, except the knight of the green armour. No sooner had *Zadig* made his appearance in the city, but the populace flock'd round about him: no eye was satisfied with gazing at him: all in general were lavish of their praises, and in their hearts wish'd him their sovereign, except the envious man, who as he pass'd by, fetch'd a deep sigh, and turn'd his head aside. The populace with loud acclamations attended him to the palace-gate. The queen, who had heard of his arrival, was in the utmost agony, between hope and despair. Her vexation had almost brought her to death's door; she couldn't conceive why *Zadig* should appear without his accoutrements, nor imagine which way *itobad* could procure the snow-white armour. At the sight of *Zadig* a confus'd murmur ran thro' the whole place. Every eye was surpriz'd, tho' charm'd at the same time to see him again: but then none were to be admitted into the assembly-room except the knights.

I have fought as successfully as any one of them all, said *Zadig*, tho' another appears clad in my armour; but in the mean time, before I can possibly prove my assertion, I insist upon being admitted into court, in order to give my solutions to such ænigmas as shall be propos'd. 'twas put to the vote. As the reputation of his being a man of the strictest honour and veracity was so strongly imprinted on their minds, the motion of his admittance was carried in the affirmative, without the least opposition.

The first question the *grand magus* propos'd was this: what is the longest and yet the shortest thing in the world; the most swift and the most slow; the most divisible, and the most extended; the least valu'd, and the most regretted; and without which nothing can possibly be done: which, in a word, devours every thing how minute soever, and yet gives life and spirit to every object or being, however great?

I*tobad* had the honour to answer first. His reply was, that a man of his merit had something else to think on, than idle riddles; 'twas enough for him, that he was acknowledg'd the hero of the circus. One said, the solution of the ænigma propos'd was *fortune*; others said the *earth*; and others again the *light*: but *Zadig* pronounced it to be *time*. Nothing, said he, can be longer, since 'tis the measure of eternity; nothing is shorter, since there is time always wanting to accomplish what we aim at. Nothing passes so slowly as time to him who is in expectation; and nothing so swift as time to him who is in the perfect enjoyment of his wishes. It's extent is to infinity, in the whole; and divisible to infinity in part. All men neglect it in the passage; and all regret the loss of it when 'tis past. Nothing can possibly be done without it; it buries in oblivion whatever is unworthy of being transmitted down to posterity;

and it renders all illustrious actions immortal. The assembly agreed unanimously that *Zadig* was in the right.

3the next question that was started, was, what is the thing we receive, without being ever thankful for it; which we enjoy, without knowing how we came by it; which we give away to others, without knowing where 'tis to be found; and which we lose, without being any ways conscious of our misfortune?

Each pass'd his verdict. Zadig was the only person that concluded it was LIFE. He solv'd every ænigma propos'd, with equal facility. *Itobad*, when he heard the explications, always said that nothing in the world was more easy, than to solve such obvious questions; and that he could interpret a thousand of them without the least hesitation, were he inclin'd to trouble his head about such trifles. Other questions were propos'd in regard to justice, the sovereign good, and the art of government. Zadig's answers still carried the greatest weight. What pity 'tis, said some who were present, that one of so comprehensive a genius, should make such a scurvy cavalier?

Most illustrious grandees, said *Zadig*, I was the person that had the honour of being victor at your circus; the white armour, most puissant lords, was mine. That awkward warrior there, lord *itobad*, dress'd himself in it whilst I was asleep. He imagin'd, it is plain, that it would do him more honour than his own green one. Unaccoutred as I am, I am ready, before this august assembly, to give them incontestable proof of my superior skill; to engage with the usurper of the white armour with my sword only in my mantle and bonnet; and to testify that I only was the happy victor of the justly admired *hottam*.

Itobad accepted of the challenge with all the assurance of success imaginable. He did not doubt, but being properly accoutred with his helmet, his cuirass, and his bracelets, he should be able to hue down an antagonist, in his mantle and cap, and nothing to skreen him from his resentment, but a single sabre. Zadig drew his sword, and saluted the queen with it, who view'd him with transport mix'd with fear. I*tobad* drew his, but paid his compliments to nobody. He approach'd *Zadig*, as one, whom he imagin'd incapable of making any considerable resistance. He concluded, 'twas in his power to cut *Zadig* into atoms. Zadig, however, knew how to parry the blow, by dexterously receiving it upon his *fort* (as the swordsmen call it) by which means *itobad*'s sword was snapt in two. With that *Zadig* in an instant clos'd his adversary, and by his superior strength, as well as skill, laid him sprawling on his back. Then holding the point of his sword to the opening of his cuirass, submit to be stripp'd of your borrow'd plumes, or you are a dead man this moment. I*tobad*, always surpriz'd, that any disappointment should attend a man of such exalted merit as himself, very tamely permitted *Zadig* to disrobe him by degrees of his pompous helmet, his superb cuirass, his rich bracelets, his brilliant cuisses, or armour for his thighs, and other martial accoutrements. When *Zadig* had equipp'd himself *cap-a-pee*, in his now recover'd armour, he flew to *astarte*, and threw himself prostrate at her feet. Cador prov'd, without any great difficulty, that the white armour was *Zadig*'s property. He was thereupon acknowledg'd king of *Babylon*, by the unanimous content of the whole court; but more particularly with the approbation of *astarte*, who after such a long series of misfortunes, now tasted the sweets of seeing her darling *Zadig* thought worthy, in the opinion of the whole world, to be the partner of her royal bed. I*tobad* withdrew, and contented himself with being call'd *my lord* within the narrow compass of his own domesticks. Zadig, in short, was elected king, and was as happy as any mortal could be.

Now he began to reflect on what the angel *jesrad* had said to him: nay, he reflected so far back as the story of the *Arabian* atom of dust metamorphosed into a diamond. The queen and he ador'd the divine providence. Zadig permitted *missouf*, the fair coquet, to make her conquests where she could. He sent couriers to bring the free-booter *arbogad* to court, and gave him an honourable military post in his army, with a farther promise of promotion to the highest dignity; but upon this express condition, that he would act for the future as a soldier of honour; but assur'd him at the same time, that he'd make a publick example of him, if he follow'd his profession of free-booting for the future.

Setoc was sent for from the lonely desarts of *arabia*, together with the fair *almonza*, his new bride, to preside over the commercial affairs of *Babylon*. Cador was advanc'd to a post near himself, and was his favourite minister at court, as the just reward of his past services. He was, in short, the king's real friend; and *Zadig* was the only monarch in the universe that could boast of such an attendant. The dwarf, tho' dumb, was not wholly forgotten. The fisherman was put into the possession of a very handsome house; and *orcan* was sentenc'd, not only to pay him a very considerable sum for the injustice done him in detaining his wife; but to resign her likewise to the proper owner: the fisherman, however, grown wise by experience, soften'd the rigour of the sentence, and took the money only in full of all accounts.

He didn't leave so much as *semira* wholly disconsolate, tho' she had such an aversion to a blind eye; nor *Azora* comfortless, notwithstanding her affectionate intention to shorten his nose; for he sooth'd their sorrows by very munificent presents. The envious informer indeed, died with shame and vexation. The empire was glorious abroad, and in the full enjoyment of tranquility, peace and plenty, at home: this, in short, was the true golden age. The whole country was sway'd by love and justice. Every one blest *Zadig*; and *Zadig* blest heav'n for his unexpected success.

Vathek

VATHEK

Vathek, ninth Caliph of the race of the Abassides, was the son of Motassem, and the grandson of Haroun Al Raschid. From an early accession to the throne, and the talents he possessed to adorn it, his subjects were induced to expect that his reign would be long and happy. His figure was pleasing and majestic; but when he was angry, one of his eyes became so terrible that no person could bear to behold it; and the wretch upon whom it was fixed instantly fell backward, and sometimes expired. For fear, however, of depopulating his dominions, and making his palace desolate, he but rarely gave way to his anger.

Being much addicted to women, and the pleasures of the table, he sought by his affability to procure agreeable companions; and he succeeded the better, as his generosity was unbounded and his indulgences unrestrained; for he was by no means scrupulous: nor did he think, with the Caliph Omar Ben Abdalaziz, that it was necessary to make a hell of this world to enjoy Paradise in the next.

He surpassed in magnificence all his predecessors. The palace of Alkoremmi, which his father Motassem had erected on the hill of Pied Horses, and which commanded the whole city of Samarah, was in his idea far too scanty: he added, therefore, five wings, or rather other palaces, which he destined for the particular gratification of each of his senses.

In the first of these were tables continually covered with the most exquisite dainties, which were supplied both by night and by day according to their constant consumption; whilst the most delicious wines, and the choicest cordials, flowed forth from a hundred fountains, that were never exhausted. This palace was called "The Eternal, or Unsatiating Banquet."

The second was styled "The Temple of Melody, or the Nectar of the Soul." It was inhabited by the most skilful musicians and admired poets of the time, who not only displayed their talents within, but dispersing in bands without, caused every surrounding scene to reverberate their songs, which were continually varied in the most delightful succession.

The palace named "The Delight of the Eyes, or the Support of Memory," was one entire enchantment. Rarities collected from every corner of the earth were there found in such profusion as to dazzle and confound, but for the order in which they were arranged. One gallery exhibited the pictures of the celebrated Mani; and statues that seemed to be alive. Here a well-managed perspective attracted the sight; there, the magic of optics agreeably deceived it; whilst the naturalist, on his part, exhibited in their several classes the various gifts that heaven had bestowed on our globe. In a word, Vathek omitted nothing in this particular that might gratify the curiosity of those who resorted to it, although he was not able to satisfy his own; for he was, of all men, the most curious.

"The Palace of Perfumes," which was termed likewise, "The Incentive to Pleasure," consisted of various halls, where the different perfumes which the earth produces were kept perpetually burning in censers of gold. Flambeaus and aromatic lamps were here lighted in open day; but the too powerful effects of this agreeable delirium might be avoided by descending into an immense garden, where an assemblage of every fragrant flower diffused through the air the purest odours.

The fifth palace, denominated "The Retreat of Joy, or the Dangerous," was frequented by troops of young females, beautiful as the Houris, and not less seducing, who never failed to receive with caresses all whom the Caliph allowed to approach them; for he was by no means disposed to be jealous, as his own women were secluded within the palace he inhabited himself.

Notwithstanding the sensuality in which Vathek indulged, he experienced no abatement in the love of his people, who thought that a sovereign immersed in pleasure was not less tolerable to his subjects than one that employed himself in creating them foes. But the unquiet and impetuous disposition of the Caliph would not allow him to rest there: he had studied so much for his amusement in the life-time of his father as to acquire a great deal of knowledge, though not a sufficiency to satisfy himself; for he wished to know everything; even sciences that did not exist. He was fond of engaging in disputes with the learned, but liked them not to push their opposition with warmth. He stopped the mouths of those with presents, whose mouths could be stopped; whilst others, whom his liberality was unable to subdue, he sent to prison to cool their blood; a remedy that often succeeded.

Vathek discovered also a predilection for theological controversy; but it was not with the orthodox that he usually held. By this means he induced the zealots to oppose him, and then persecuted them in return; for he resolved, at any rate, to have reason on his side.

The great prophet Mahomet, whose vicars the Caliphs are, beheld with indignation from his abode in the seventh heaven the irreligious conduct of such a vicegerent.

"Let us leave him to himself," said he to the Genii, who are always ready to receive his commands; "let us see to what lengths his folly and impiety will carry him; if he run into excess we shall know how to chastise him. Assist him, therefore, to complete the tower which, in imitation of Nimrod, he hath begun; not, like that great warrior, to escape being drowned, but from the insolent curiosity of penetrating the secrets of heaven: he will not divine the fate that awaits him."

The Genii obeyed; and when the workmen had raised their structure a cubit in the day time, two cubits more were added in the night. The expedition with which the fabric arose was not a little flattering to the vanity of Vathek. He fancied that even insensible matter showed forwardness to subserve his designs; not considering that the successes of the foolish and wicked form the first rod of their chastisement.

His pride arrived at its height when, having ascended, for the first time, the eleven thousand stairs of his tower, he cast his eyes below and beheld men not larger than pismires; mountains than shells; and cities than bee-hives. The idea which such an elevation inspired of his own grandeur completely bewildered him; he was almost ready to adore himself; till lifting his eyes upwards, he saw the stars as high above him as they appeared when he stood on the surface of the earth. He consoled himself, however, for this transient perception of his littleness with the thought of being great in the eyes of the others, and flattered himself that the light of his mind would extend beyond the reach of his sight, and transfer to the stars the decrees of his destiny.

With this view the inquisitive prince passed most of his nights on the summit of his tower, till he became an adept in the mysteries of astrology, and imagined that the planets had disclosed to him the most marvellous adventures, which were to be accomplished by an extraordinary personage, from a country altogether unknown. Prompted by motives of curiosity, he had always been courteous to strangers; but from this instant he redoubled his attention, and ordered it to be announced by sound of trumpet, through all the streets of Samarah, that no one of his subjects, on peril of his displeasure, should either lodge or detain a traveller, but forthwith bring him to the palace.

Not long after this proclamation, there arrived in his metropolis, a man so hideous that the very guards who arrested him were forced to shut their eyes as they led him along. The Caliph himself appeared startled at so horrible a visage; but joy succeeded to this emotion of terror when the stranger displayed to his view such rarities as he had never before seen, and of which he had no conception.

In reality, nothing was ever so extraordinary as the merchandise this stranger produced. Most of his curiosities, which were not less admirable for their workmanship than their splendour, had besides, their several virtues described on a parchment fastened to each. There were slippers which enabled the feet to walk; knives that cut without the motion of a hand; sabres which dealt the blow at the person they were wished to strike; and the whole enriched with gems that were hitherto unknown.

The sabres, whose blades emitted a dazzling radiance, fixed more than all the Caliph's attention, who promised himself to decipher at his leisure the uncouth characters engraven on their sides. Without, therefore, demanding their price, he ordered all the coined gold to be brought from his treasury, and commanded the merchant to take what he pleased. The stranger complied with modesty and silence.

Vathek, imagining that the merchant's taciturnity was occasioned by the awe which his presence inspired, encouraged him to advance, and asked him, with an air of condescension, "Who he was? whence he came? and where he obtained such beautiful commodities?"

The man, or rather monster, instead of making a reply, thrice rubbed his forehead, which, as well as his body, was blacker than ebony; four times clapped his paunch, the projection of which was enormous; opened wide his huge eyes, which glowed like firebrands; began to laugh with a hideous noise, and discovered his long amber coloured teeth bestreaked with green.

The Caliph, though a little startled, renewed his enquiries, but without being able to procure a reply. At which, beginning to be ruffled, he exclaimed, "knowest thou, varlet, who I am? and at whom thou art aiming thy gibes?" Then addressing his guards, "have ye heard him speak? is he dumb?"

"He hath spoken," they replied, "though but little."

"Let him speak then again," said Vathek, "and tell me who he is, from whence he came, and where he procured these singular curiosities, or I swear, by the ass of Balaam, that I will make him rue his pertinacity."

This menace was accompanied by the Caliph with one of his angry and perilous glances, which the stranger sustained without the slightest emotion, although his eyes were fixed on the terrible eye of the prince.

No words can describe the amazement of the courtiers, when they beheld this rude merchant withstand the encounter unshocked. They all fell prostrate with their faces on the ground, to avoid the risk of their lives, and continued in the same abject posture till the Caliph exclaimed in a furious tone:

"Up, cowards! seize the miscreant! see that he be committed to prison, and guarded by the best of my soldiers! Let him, however, retain the money I gave him; it is not my intent to take from him his property, I only want him to speak."

No sooner had he uttered these words than the stranger was surrounded, pinioned with strong fetters, and hurried away to the prison of the great tower, which was encompassed by seven empalements of iron bars, and armed with spikes in every direction, longer and sharper than spits.

The Caliph, nevertheless, remained in the most violent agitation. He sat down indeed to eat, but of the three hundred covers that were daily placed before him, could taste of no more than thirty-two.

A diet to which he had been so little accustomed, was sufficient of itself to prevent him from sleeping, what then must be its effect when joined to the anxiety that preyed upon his spirits? At the first glimpse of dawn he hastened to the prison, again to importune this intractable stranger; but the rage of Vathek exceeded all bounds on finding the prison empty, the gates burst asunder, and his guards lying lifeless around him. In the paroxysm of his passion he fell furiously on the poor carcases, and kicked them till evening without intermission. His courtiers and viziers exerted their efforts to soothe his extravagance, but finding every expedient ineffectual, they all united in one vociferation:

"The Caliph is gone mad! the Caliph is out of his senses!"

This outcry, which was soon resounded through the streets of Samarah, at length reached the ears of Carathis, his mother: she flew in the utmost consternation to try her ascendency on the mind of her son. Her tears and caresses called off his attention; and he was prevailed upon by her entreaties to be brought back to the palace.

Carathis, apprehensive of leaving Vathek to himself, caused him to be put to bed; and seating herself by him, endeavoured by her conversation to heal and compose him. Nor could any one have attempted it with better success; for the Caliph not only loved her as a mother but respected her as a person of superior genius. It was she who had induced him, being a Greek herself, to adopt all the sciences and systems of her country, which good Mussulmans hold in such thorough abhorrence.

Judicial astrology was one of those systems in which Carathis was a perfect adept. She began, therefore, with reminding her son of the promise which the stars had made him; and intimated an intention of consulting them again.

"Alas!" sighed the Caliph, as soon at he could speak, "what a fool have I been! not for the kicks bestowed on my guards, who so tamely submitted to death, but for never considering that this extraordinary man was the same the planets had foretold; whom, instead of ill-treating, I should have conciliated by all the arts of persuasion."

"The past," said Carathis, "cannot be recalled; but it behoves us to think of the future: perhaps you may again see the object you so much regret: it is possible the inscriptions on the sabres will afford information. Eat, therefore, and take thy repose, my dear son. We will consider tomorrow in what manner to act."

Vathek yielded to her counsel as well as he could, and arose in the morning with a mind more at ease. The sabres he commanded to be instantly brought; and poring upon them through a green glass, that their glittering might not dazzle, he set himself in earnest to decipher the inscriptions; but his reiterated attempts were all of them nugatory: in vain did he beat his head and bite his nails; not a letter of the whole was he able to ascertain. So unlucky a disappointment would have undone him again, had not Carathis, by good fortune, entered the apartment.

"Have patience, son!" said she. "You certainly are possessed of every important science, but the knowledge of languages is a trifle, at best; and the accomplishment of none but a pedant. Issue forth a proclamation that you will confer such rewards as become your greatness upon any one that shall interpret what you do not understand, and what it is beneath you to learn. You will soon find your curiosity gratified."

"That may be," said the Caliph; "but in the mean time I shall be horribly disgusted by a crowd of smatterers, who will come to the trial as much for the pleasure of retailing their jargon as from the hope of gaining the reward. To avoid this evil, it will be proper to add that I will put every candidate to death who shall fail to give satisfaction; for, thank heaven, I have skill enough to distinguish between one that translates and one that invents."

"Of that I have no doubt," replied Carathis, "but to put the ignorant to death is somewhat severe, and may be productive of dangerous effects. Content yourself with commanding their beards to be burnt: beards, in a state, are not quite so essential as men."

The Caliph submitted to the reasons of his mother, and sending for Morakanabad, his prime vizier, said:

"Let the common criers proclaim, not only in Samarah, but throughout every city in my empire, that whosoever will repair hither, and decipher certain characters which appear to be inexplicable, shall experience the liberality for which I am renowned; but that all who fail upon trial shall have their beards burnt off to the last hair. Let them add also, that I will bestow fifty beautiful slaves, and as many jars of apricots from the isle of Kirmith, upon any man that shall bring me intelligence of the stranger."

The subjects of the Caliph, like their sovereign, being great admirers of women, and apricots from Kirmith, felt their mouths water at these promises, but were totally unable to gratify their hankering, for no one knew which way the stranger had gone.

As to the Caliph's other requisition the result was different: the learned, the half-learned, and those who were neither, but fancied themselves equal to both, came boldly to hazard their beards, and all shamefully lost them.

The exaction of these forfeitures, which found sufficient employment for the Eunuchs, gave them such a smell of singed hair as greatly to disgust the ladies of the seraglio, and make it necessary that this new occupation of their guardians should be transferred into other hands.

At length, however, an old man presented himself, whose beard was a cubit-and-a-half longer than any that had appeared before him. The officers of the palace whispered to each other, as they ushered him in:

"What a pity such a beard should be burnt!"

Even the Caliph, when he saw it, concurred with them in opinion; but his concern was entirely needless. This venerable personage read the characters with facility, and explained them verbatim, as follows:

"We were made where everything good is made; we are the least of the wonders of a place where all is wonderful; and deserving the sight of the first potentate on earth."

"You translate admirably!" cried Vathek. "I know to what these marvellous characters allude. Let him receive as many robes of honour, and thousands of sequins of gold, as he hath spoken words. I am in some measure relieved from the perplexity that embarrassed me!"

Vathek invited the old man to dine, and even to remain some days in the palace. Unluckily for him, he accepted the offer; for the Caliph having ordered him next morning to be called, said:

"Read again to me what you have read already; I cannot hear too often the promise that is made me, the completion of which I languish to obtain."

The old man forthwith put on his green spectacles; but they instantly dropped from his nose, on perceiving that the characters he had read the day preceding, had given place to others of different import.

"What ails you?" asked the Caliph; "and why these symptoms of wonder?"

"Sovereign of the world," replied the old man, "these sabres hold another language today, from that they yesterday held."

"How say you?" returned Vathek. "But it matters not! tell me, if you can, what they mean."

"It is this, my lord," rejoined the old man: "'Woe to the rash mortal who seeks to know that of which he should remain ignorant and to undertake that which surpasseth his power!'"

"And woe to thee!" cried the Caliph, in a burst of indignation: "today thou art void of understanding: begone from my presence, they shall burn but the half of thy beard, because thou wert yesterday fortunate in guessing. My gifts I never resume."

The old man, wise enough to perceive he had luckily escaped, considering the folly of disclosing so disgusting a truth, immediately withdrew, and appeared not again.

But it was not long before Vathek discovered abundant reason to regret his precipitation; for though he could not decipher the characters himself, yet, by constantly poring upon them, he plainly perceived that they every day changed; and unfortunately no other candidate offered to explain them. This perplexing occupation inflamed his blood, dazzled his sight, and brought on a giddiness and debility that he could not support. He failed not, however, though in so reduced a condition, to be often carried to his tower, as he flattered himself that he might there read in the stars, which he went to consult, something more congruous to his wishes. But in this his hopes were deluded; for his eyes, dimmed by the vapours of his head, began to subserve his curiosity so ill, that he beheld nothing but a thick dun cloud, which he took for the most direful of omens.

Agitated with so much anxiety, Vathek entirely lost all firmness; a fever seized him and his appetite failed. Instead of being one of the greatest eaters, he became as distinguished for drinking. So insatiable was the thirst which tormented him, that his mouth, like a funnel, was always open to receive the various liquors that might be poured into it and especially cold water, which calmed him more than every other.

This unhappy prince being thus incapacitated for the enjoyment of any pleasure, commanded the palaces of the five senses to be shut up; forebore to appear in public, either to display his magnificence or administer justice; and retired to the inmost apartment of his harem. As he had ever been an indulgent husband, his wives, overwhelmed with grief at his deplorable situation, incessantly offered their prayers for his health, and unremittingly supplied him with water.

In the mean time, the Princess Carathis, whose affliction no words can describe, instead of restraining herself to sobbing and tears, was closeted daily with the Vizier Morakanabad, to find out some cure or mitigation of the Caliph's disease. Under the persuasion that it was caused by enchantment, they turned over together leaf by leaf, all the books of magic that might point out a remedy; and caused the horrible stranger, whom they accused as the enchanter, to be everywhere sought for with the strictest diligence.

At the distance of a few miles from Samarah stood a high mountain, whose sides were swarded with wild thyme and basil, and its summit overspread with so delightful a plain that it might be taken for the Paradise destined for the faithful. Upon it grew a hundred thickets of eglantine and other fragrant shrubs; a hundred arbours of roses, jessamine, and honeysuckle; as many clumps of orange trees, cedar, and citron; whose branches, interwoven with the palm, the pomegranate, and the vine, presented every luxury that could regale the eye or the taste. The ground was strewed with violets, harebells, and pansies; in the midst of which sprung forth tufts of jonquils, hyacinths, and carnations, with every other perfume that impregnates the air. Four fountains, not less clear than deep, and so abundant as to slake the thirst of ten armies, seemed purposely placed here to make the scene more resemble the garden of Eden, which was watered by the four sacred rivers. Here the nightingale sang the birth of the rose, her well-beloved, and at the same time lamented its short-lived beauty; whilst the turtle deplored the loss of more substantial pleasures and the wakeful lark hailed the rising light that reanimates the whole creation. Here, more than anywhere, the mingled melodies of birds expressed the various passions they inspired; as if the exquisite fruits, which they pecked at pleasure, had given them a double energy.

To this mountain Vathek was sometimes brought, for the sake of breathing a purer air; and especially, to drink at will of the four fountains, which were reputed in the highest degree salubrious, and sacred to himself. His attendants were his mother, his wives, and some eunuchs, who assiduously employed themselves in filling capacious bowls of rock crystal, and emulously presenting them to him. But it frequently happened that his avidity exceeded their zeal; insomuch that he would prostrate himself upon the ground to lap up the water, of which he could never have enough.

One day when this unhappy prince had been long lying in so debasing a posture, a voice, hoarse but strong, thus addressed him:

"Why assumest thou the function of a dog, oh Caliph, so proud of thy dignity and power?"

At this apostrophe he raised up his head and beheld the stranger that had caused him so much affliction. Inflamed with anger at the sight, he exclaimed:

"Accursed Giaour! what comest thou hither to do? is it not enough to have transformed a prince, remarkable for his agility, into one of those leather barrels which the Bedouin Arabs carry on their camels when they traverse the deserts? Perceivest thou not that I may perish by drinking to excess, no less than by a total abstinence?"

"Drink then this draught," said the stranger, as he presented to him a phial of a red and yellow mixture; "and to satiate the thirst of thy soul as well as of thy body, know that I am an Indian, but from a region of India which is wholly unknown."

The Caliph, delighted to see his desires accomplished in part, and flattering himself with the hope of obtaining their entire fulfilment, without a moment's hesitation swallowed the potion, and instantaneously found his health restored, his thirst appeased, and his limbs as agile as ever.

In the transports of his joy, Vathek leaped upon the neck of the frightful Indian, and kissed his horrid mouth and hollow cheeks, as though they had been the coral lips, and the lilies and roses of his most beautiful wives; whilst they, less terrified than jealous at the sight, dropped their veils to hide the blush of mortification that suffused their foreheads.

Nor would the scene have closed here, had not Carathis, with all the art of insinuation, a little repressed the raptures of her son. Having prevailed upon him to return to Samarah, she caused a herald to precede him, whom she commanded to proclaim as loudly as possible:

"The wonderful stranger hath appeared again; he hath healed the Caliph; he hath spoken! he hath spoken!"

Forthwith all the inhabitants of this vast city quitted their habitations, and ran together in crowds to see the procession of Vathek and the Indian, whom they now blessed as much as they had before execrated, incessantly shouting,

"He hath healed our sovereign; he hath spoken! he hath spoken!"

Nor were these words forgotten in the public festivals, which were celebrated the same evening to testify the general joy, for the poets applied them as a chorus to all the songs they composed.

The Caliph, in the mean while caused the palaces of the senses to be again set open, and as he found himself prompted to visit that of taste, in preference to the rest, immediately ordered a splendid entertainment, to which his great officers and favourite courtiers were all invited. The Indian, who was placed near the prince, seemed to think that as a proper acknowledgment of so distinguished a privilege, he could neither eat, drink, nor talk too much. The various dainties were no sooner served up than they vanished, to the great mortification of Vathek, who piqued himself on being the greatest eater alive, and at this time in particular had an excellent appetite.

The rest of the company looked round at each other in amazement, but the Indian without appearing to observe it, quaffed large bumpers to the health of each of them: sung in a style altogether extravagant; related stories at which he laughed immoderately; and poured forth extemporaneous verses which would not have been thought bad, but for the strange grimaces with which they were uttered. In a word, his loquacity was equal to that of a hundred astrologers; he ate as much as a hundred porters, and caroused in proportion.

The Caliph, notwithstanding the table had been thirty times covered, found himself incommoded by the voraciousness of his guest, who was now considerably declined in the prince's esteem. Vathek, however, being unwilling to betray the chagrin he could hardly disguise, said in a whisper to Bababalouk, the chief of his eunuchs:

"You see how enormous his performances in every way are; what would be the consequence should he get at my wives? Go! redouble your vigilance, and be sure look well to my Circassians, who would be more to his taste than all of the rest."

The bird of the morning had thrice renewed his song, when the hour of the divan sounded. Vathek, in gratitude to his subjects, having promised to attend, immediately arose from table and repaired thither leaning upon his vizier, who could scarcely support him, so disordered was the poor prince by the wine he had drank, and still more by the extravagant vagaries of his boisterous guest.

The viziers, the officers of the crown, and of the law, arranged themselves in a semi-circle about their sovereign, and preserved a respectful silence, whilst the Indian, who looked as cool as if come from a fast, sat down without ceremony on a step of the throne, laughing in his sleeve at the indignation with which his temerity had filled the spectators.

The Caliph, however, whose ideas were confused and his head embarrassed, went on administering justice at haphazard, till at length the prime vizier perceiving his situation, hit upon a sudden expedient to interrupt the audience, and rescue the honour of his master, to whom he said in a whisper:

"My lord, the princess Carathis, who hath passed the night in consulting the planets, informs you that they portend you evil; and the danger is urgent. Beware, lest this stranger whom you have so lavishly recompensed for his magical gewgaws, should make some attempt on your life: his liquor, which at first had the appearance of effecting your cure, may be no more than a poison of a sudden operation. Slight not this surmise; ask him, at least, of what it was compounded; whence he procured it; and mention the sabres, which you seem to have forgotten."

Vathek, to whom the insolent airs of the stranger became every moment less supportable, intimated to his vizier by a wink of acquiescence, that he would adopt his advice, and at once turning towards the Indian, said:

"Get up and declare in full divan of what drugs the liquor was compounded you enjoined me to take, for it is suspected to be poison; add also the explanation I have so earnestly desired concerning the sabres you sold me, and thus show your gratitude for the favours heaped on you."

Having pronounced these words in as moderate a tone as a Caliph well could, he waited in silent expectation for an answer; but the Indian, still keeping his seat, began to renew his loud shouts of laughter, and exhibit the same horrid grimaces he had shown them before, without vouchsafing a word in reply. Vathek, no longer able to brook such insolence, immediately kicked him from the steps, instantly descending repeated his blow, and persisted with such assiduity, as incited all who were present to follow his example. Every foot was aimed at the Indian, and no sooner had any one given him a kick than he felt himself constrained to reiterate the stroke.

The stranger afforded them no small entertainment; for being both short and plump, he collected himself into a ball and rolled round on all sides at the blows of his assailants, who pressed after him wherever he turned, with an eagerness beyond conception, whilst their numbers were every moment increasing. The ball, indeed, in passing from one apartment to another, drew every person after it that came in its way, insomuch that the whole palace was thrown into confusion, and resounded with a tremendous clamour. The women of the harem, amazed at the uproar, flew to their blinds to discover the cause, but no sooner did they catch a glimpse of the ball than feeling themselves unable to refrain, they broke from the clutches of their eunuchs, who to stop their flight pinched them till they bled, but in vain; whilst themselves, though trembling with terror at the escape of their charge, were as incapable of resisting the attraction.

The Indian, after having traversed the halls, galleries, chambers, kitchens, gardens, and stables of the palace, at last took his course through the courts, whilst the Caliph, pursuing him closer than the rest, bestowed as many kicks as he possibly could, yet not without receiving now and then one, which his competitors, in their eagerness, designed for the ball.

Carathis, Morakanabad, and two or three old viziers whose wisdom had hitherto withstood the attraction, wishing to prevent Vathek from exposing himself in the presence of his subjects, fell down in his way to impede the pursuit, but he, regardless of their obstruction, leaped over their heads, and went on as before. They then ordered the muezzins to call the people to prayers, both for the sake of getting them out of the way, and of endeavouring by their petitions to avert the calamity; but neither of these expedients was a whit more successful. The sight of this fatal ball was alone sufficient to draw after it every beholder. The muezzins themselves, though they saw it but at a distance, hastened down from their minarets and mixed with the crowd, which continued to increase in so surprising a manner, that scarce an inhabitant was left in Samarah, except the aged, the sick confined to their beds, and infants at the breast, whose nurses could run more nimbly without them. Even Carathis, Morakanabad, and the rest, were all become of the party.

The shrill screams of the females who had broken from their apartments, and were unable to extricate themselves from the pressure of the crowd, together with those of the eunuchs jostling after them, terrified lest their charge should escape from their sight, increased by the execrations of husbands urging forward and menacing both, kicks given and received, stumblings and overthrows at every step, in a word, the confusion that universally prevailed, rendered Samarah like a city taken by storm, and devoted to absolute plunder.

At last the cursed Indian, who still preserved his rotundity of figure, after passing through all the streets and public places, and leaving them empty, rolled onwards to the plain of Catoul, and traversed the valley at the foot of the mountain of the four fountains.

As a continual fall of water had excavated an immense gulph in the valley, whose opposite side was closed in by a steep acclivity, the Caliph and his attendants were apprehensive lest the ball should bound into the chasm, and to prevent it, redoubled their efforts, but in vain. The Indian persevered in his onward direction, and as had been apprehended, glancing from the precipice with the rapidity of lightning, was lost in the gulph below.

Vathek would have followed the perfidious Giaour, had not an invisible agency arrested his progress. The multitude that pressed after him were at once checked in the same manner, and a calm instantaneously ensued. They all gazed at each other with an air of astonishment; and notwithstanding that the loss of veils and turbans, together with torn habits, and dust blended with sweat, presented a most laughable spectacle, there was not one smile to be seen; on the contrary, all with looks of confusion and sadness returned in silence to Samarah, and retired to their inmost apartments, without ever reflecting that they had been impelled by an invisible power into the extravagance for which they reproached themselves: for it is but just, that men who so often arrogate to their own merit the good of which they are but instruments, should attribute to themselves the absurdities which they could not prevent.

The Caliph was the only person that refused to leave the valley. He commanded his tents to be pitched there, and stationed himself on the very edge of the precipice, in spite of the representations of Carathis and Morakanabad, who pointed out the hazard of its brink giving way, and the vicinity to the magician that had so severely tormented him. Vathek derided all their remonstrances; and having ordered a thousand flambeaus to be lighted, and directed his attendants to proceed in lighting more, lay down on the slippery margin, and attempted, by the help of this artificial splendour, to look through that gloom which all the fires of the empyrean had been insufficient to pervade. One while he fancied to himself voices arising from the depth of the gulph, at another he seemed to distinguish the accents of the Indian, but all was no more than the hollow murmur of waters, and the din of the cataracts that rushed from steep to steep, down the sides of the mountain.

Having passed the night in this cruel perturbation, the Caliph at day-break retired to his tent, where, without taking the least sustenance, he continued to doze till the dusk of evening began to come on; he then resumed his vigils as before, and persevered in observing them for many nights together. At length, fatigued with so successless an employment, he sought relief from change. To this end he sometimes paced with hasty strides across the plain; and as he wildly gazed at the stars, reproached them with having deceived him; but lo! on a sudden the clear blue sky appeared streaked over with streams of blood, which reached from the valley even to the city of Samarah. As this awful phenomenon seemed to touch his tower, Vathek at first thought of repairing thither to view it more distinctly, but feeling himself unable to advance, and being overcome with apprehension, he muffled up his face in his robe.

Terrifying as these prodigies were, this impression upon him was no more than momentary, and served only to stimulate his love of the marvellous. Instead, therefore, of returning to his palace, he persisted in the resolution of abiding where the Indian vanished from his view. One night, however, while he was walking as usual on the plain, the moon and the stars at once were eclipsed, and a total darkness ensued. The earth trembled beneath him, and a voice came forth, the voice of the Giaour, who in accents more sonorous than thunder, thus addressed him:

"Would'st thou devote thyself to me? adore then the terrestrial influences, and abjure Mahomet. On these conditions I will bring thee to the palace of subterranean fire: there shalt thou behold, in immense depositories, the treasures which the stars have promised thee, and which will be conferred by those intelligences whom thou shalt thus render propitious. It was from thence I brought my sabres; and it is there that Soliman Ben Daoud reposes, surrounded by the talismans that control the world."

The astonished Caliph trembled as he answered, yet in a style that showed him to be no novice in preternatural adventures:

"Where art thou? Be present to my eyes; dissipate the gloom that perplexes me, and of which I deem thee the cause. After the many flambeaus I have burnt to discover thee, thou mayest at least grant a glimpse of thy horrible visage."

"Abjure then Mahomet," replied the Indian, "and promise me full proofs of thy sincerity; otherwise thou shalt never behold me again."

The unhappy Caliph, instigated by insatiable curiosity, lavished his promises in the utmost profusion. The sky immediately brightened; and by the light of the planets, which seemed almost to blaze, Vathek beheld the earth open, and at the extremity of a vast black chasm a portal of ebony, before which stood the Indian, still blacker, holding in his hand a golden key, that caused the lock to resound.

"How," cried Vathek, "can I descend to thee, without the certainty of breaking my neck? Come take me, and instantly open the portal."

"Not so fast," replied the Indian, "impatient Caliph! Know that I am parched with thirst, and cannot open this door till my thirst be thoroughly appeased. I require the blood of fifty of the most beautiful sons of thy viziers and great men, or neither can my thirst nor thy curiosity be satisfied. Return to Samarah; procure for me this necessary libation; come back hither; throw it thyself into this chasm; and then shalt thou see!"

Having thus spoken, the Indian turned his back on the Caliph, who, incited by the suggestion of demons, resolved on the direful sacrifice. He now pretended to have regained his tranquillity, and set out for Samarah amidst the acclamations of a people who still loved him, and forbore not to rejoice when they believed him to have recovered his reason. So successfully did he conceal the emotion of his heart, that even Carathis and Morakanabad were equally deceived with the rest. Nothing was heard of but festivals and rejoicings. The ball, which no tongue had hitherto ventured to mention, was again brought on the tapis. A general laugh went round; though many, still smarting under the hands of the surgeon, from the hurts received in that memorable adventure, had no great reason for mirth.

The prevalence of this gay humour was not a little grateful to Vathek, as perceiving how much it conduced to his project. He put on the appearance of affability to every one; but especially to his viziers, and the grandees of his court, whom he failed not to regale with a sumptuous banquet, during which he insensibly inclined the conversation to the children of his guests. Having asked, with a good-natured air, who of them were blessed with the handsomest boys, every father at once asserted the pretensions of his own; and the contest imperceptibly grew so warm, that nothing could have with-holden them from coming to blows but their profound reverence for the person of the Caliph. Under the pretence, therefore, of reconciling the disputants, Vathek took upon him to decide; and with this view commanded the boys to be brought.

It was not long before a troop of these poor children made their appearance, all equipped by their fond mothers with such ornaments as might give the greatest relief to their beauty, or most advantageously display the graces of their age. But whilst this brilliant assemblage attracted the eyes and hearts of every one besides, the Caliph scrutinized each in his turn with a malignant avidity that passed for attention, and selected from their number the fifty whom he judged the Giaour would prefer.

With an equal show of kindness as before, he proposed to celebrate a festival on the plain, for the entertainment of his young favourites, who he said ought to rejoice still more than all at the restoration of his health, on account of the favours he intended for them.

The Caliph's proposal was received with the greatest delight, and soon published through Samarah. Litters, camels, and horses were prepared. Women and children, old men and young—every one placed himself in the station he chose. The cavalcade set forward, attended by all the confectioners in the city and its precincts. The populace, following on foot, composed an amazing crowd, and occasioned no little noise. All was joy; nor did any one call to mind what most of them had suffered when they first travelled the road they were now passing so gaily.

The evening was serene, the air refreshing, the sky clear, and the flowers exhaled their fragrance. The beams of the declining sun, whose mild splendour reposed on the summit of the mountain, shed a glow of ruddy light over its green declivity, and the white flocks sporting upon it. No sounds were audible, save the murmurs of the four fountains, and the reeds and voices of shepherds, calling to each other from different eminences.

The lovely innocents, proceeding to the destined sacrifice, added not a little to the hilarity of the scene. They approached the plain full of sportiveness; some coursing butterflies, others culling flowers, or picking up the shining little pebbles that attracted their notice. At intervals, they nimbly started from each other, for the sake of being caught again, and mutually imparting a thousand caresses.

The dreadful chasm, at whose bottom the portal of ebony was placed, began to appear at a distance. It looked like a black streak that divided the plain. Morakanabad and his companions took it for some work which the Caliph had ordered. Unhappy men! little did they surmise for what it was destined.

Vathek, not liking that they should examine it too nearly, stopped the procession, and ordered a spacious circle to be formed on this side, at some distance from the accursed chasm. The body-guard of eunuchs was detached, to measure out the lists intended for the games, and prepare ringles for the lines to keep off the crowd. The fifty competitors were soon stripped, and presented to the admiration of the spectators the suppleness and grace of their delicate limbs. Their eyes sparkled with a joy which those of their fond parents reflected. Every one offered wishes for the little candidate nearest his heart, and doubted not of his being victorious. A breathless suspense awaited the contest of these amiable and innocent victims.

The Caliph, availing himself of the first moment to retire from the crowd, advanced towards the chasm, and there heard, yet not without shuddering, the voice of the Indian; who, gnashing his teeth, eagerly demanded:

"Where are they? Where are they? perceivest thou not how my mouth waters?"

"Relentless Giaour!" answered Vathek, with emotion, "can nothing content thee but the massacre of these lovely victims? Ah! wert thou to behold their beauty, it must certainly move thy compassion."

"Perdition on thy compassion, babbler!" cried the Indian. "Give them me! instantly give them, or my portal shall be closed against thee for ever!"

"Not so loudly," replied the Caliph, blushing.

"I understand thee," returned the Giaour, with the grin of an ogre: "thou wantest to summon up more presence of mind. I will for a moment forbear."

During this exquisite dialogue the games went forward with all alacrity, and at length concluded, just as the twilight began to overcast the mountains. Vathek, who was still standing on the edge of the chasm, called out with all his might:

"Let my fifty little favourites approach me, separately; and let them come in the order of their success. To the first I will give my diamond bracelet; to the second my collar of emeralds; to the third my aigret of rubies; to the fourth my girdle of topazes; and to the rest, each a part of my dress, even down to my slippers."

This declaration was received with reiterated acclamations; and all extolled the liberality of a prince who would thus strip himself for the amusement of his subjects and the encouragement of the rising generation.

The Caliph, meanwhile, undressed himself by degrees; and raising his arm as high as he was able, made each of the prizes glitter in the air; but, whilst he delivered it with one hand to the child, who sprang forward to receive it, he with the other pushed the poor innocent into the gulph, where the Giaour, with a sullen muttering, incessantly repeated "More! more!"

This dreadful device was executed with so much dexterity, that the boy who was approaching him remained unconscious of the fate of his forerunner; and as to the spectators, the shades of evening, together with their distance, precluded them from perceiving any object distinctly. Vathek, having in this manner thrown in the last of the fifty, and expecting that the Giaour on receiving him would have presented the key, already fancied himself as great as Soliman, and consequently above being amenable for what he had done; when, to his utter amazement, the chasm closed, and the ground became as entire as the rest of the plain.

No language could express his rage and despair. He execrated the perfidy of the Indian; loaded him with the most infamous invectives; and stamped with his foot as resolving to be heard. He persisted in this demeanour till his strength failed him, and then fell on the earth like one void of sense. His viziers and grandees, who were nearer than the rest, supposed him at first to be sitting on the grass at play with their amiable children; but at length, prompted by doubt, they advanced towards the spot, and found the Caliph alone, who wildly demanded what they wanted.

"Our children! our children!" cried they.

"It is assuredly pleasant," said he, "to make me accountable for accidents. Your children, while at play, fell from the precipice that was here; and I should have experienced their fate had I not been saved by a sudden start back."

At these words, the fathers of the fifty boys cried out aloud: the mothers repeated their exclamations an octave higher; whilst the rest, without knowing the cause, soon drowned the voices of both, with still louder lamentations of their own.

"Our Caliph," said they, and the report soon circulated, "Our Caliph has played us this trick, to gratify his accursed Giaour. Let us punish him for his perfidy! let us avenge ourselves! let us avenge the blood of the innocent! let us throw this cruel Prince into the gulph that is near, and let his name be mentioned no more!"

At this rumour, and these menaces, Carathis, full of consternation, hastened to Morakanabad, and said:

"Vizier, you have lost two beautiful boys, and must necessarily be the most afflicted of fathers; but you are virtuous; save your master!"

"I will brave every hazard," replied the Vizier, "to rescue him from his present danger; but afterwards will abandon him to his fate. Bababalouk," continued he, "put yourself at the head of your Eunuchs, disperse the mob, and if possible bring back this unhappy Prince to his palace."

Bababalouk and his fraternity, felicitating each other in a low voice on their disability of ever being fathers, obeyed the mandate of the Vizier; who, seconding their exertions to the utmost of his power, at length accomplished his generous enterprise, and retired, as he resolved, to lament at his leisure.

No sooner had the Caliph re-entered his palace, than Carathis commanded the doors to be fastened; but perceiving the tumult to be still violent, and hearing the imprecations which resounded from all quarters, she said to her son:

"Whether the populace be right or wrong, it behoves you to provide for your safety: let us retire to your own apartment, and from thence, through the subterranean passage known only to ourselves, into your tower; there, with the assistance of the mutes who never leave it, we may be able to make some resistance. Bababalouk, supposing us to be still in the palace, will guard its avenues for his own sake; and we shall soon find, without the counsels of that blubberer Morakanabad, what expedient may be the best to adopt."

Vathek, without making the least reply, acquiesced in his mother's proposal, and repeated as he went:

"Nefarious Giaour! where art thou? hast thou not yet devoured those poor children? where are thy sabres? thy golden key? thy talismans?"

Carathis, who guessed from these interrogations a part of the truth, had no difficulty to apprehend in getting at the whole, as soon as he should be a little composed in his tower. This Princess was so far from being influenced by scruples that she was as wicked as woman could be, which is not saying a little, for the sex pique themselves on their superiority in every competition. The recital of the Caliph therefore occasioned neither terror nor surprise to his mother; she felt no emotion but from the promises of the Giaour; and said to her son:

"This Giaour, it must be confessed, is somewhat sanguinary in his taste, but the terrestrial powers are always terrible: nevertheless, what the one has promised and the others can confer, will prove a sufficient indemnification. No crimes should be thought too dear for such a reward. Forbear then to revile the Indian: you have not fulfilled the conditions to which his services are annexed. For instance, is not a sacrifice to the subterranean Genii required? and should we not be prepared to offer it as soon as the tumult is subsided? This charge I will take on myself, and have no doubt of succeeding by means of your treasures; which, as there are now so many others in store, may without fear be exhausted."

Accordingly, the Princess, who possessed the most consummate skill in the art of persuasion, went immediately back through the subterranean passage, and presenting herself to the populace from a window of the palace, began to harangue them with all the address of which she was mistress, whilst Bababalouk showered money from both hands amongst the crowd, who by these united means were soon appeased. Every person retired to his home, and Carathis returned to the tower.

Prayer at break of day was announced, when Carathis and Vathek ascended the steps which led to the summit of the tower, where they remained for some time, though the weather was lowering and wet. This impending gloom corresponded with their malignant dispositions; but when the sun began to break through the clouds, they ordered a pavilion to be raised as a screen from the intrusion of his beams. The Caliph, overcome with fatigue, sought refreshment from repose, at the same time hoping that significant dreams might attend on his slumbers; whilst the indefatigable Carathis, followed by a party of her mutes, descended to prepare whatever she judged proper for the oblation of the approaching night.

By secret stairs, known only to herself and her son, she first repaired to the mysterious recesses in which were deposited the mummies that had been brought from the catacombs of the ancient Pharaohs. Of these she ordered several to be taken. From thence she resorted to a gallery, where, under the guard of fifty female negroes, mute, and blind of the right eye, were preserved the oil of the most venomous serpents, rhinoceros' horns, and woods of a subtle and penetrating odour, procured from the interior of the Indies, together with a thousand other horrible rarieties. This collection had been formed for a purpose like the present, by Carathis herself, from a presentiment that she might one day enjoy some intercourse with the infernal powers, to whom she had ever been passionately attached, and to whose taste she was no stranger.

To familiarize herself the better with the horrors in view, the Princess remained in the company of her negresses, who squinted in the most amiable manner from the only eye they had, and leered with exquisite delight at the skulls and skeletons which Carathis had drawn forth from her cabinets, whose key she entrusted to no one; all of them making contortions, and uttering a frightful jargon, but very amusing to the Princess till at last, being stunned by their gibbering, and suffocated by the potency of their exhalations, she was forced to quit the gallery, after stripping it of a part of its treasures.

Whilst she was thus occupied, the Caliph, who instead of the visions he expected, had acquired in these insubstantial regions a voracious appetite, was greatly provoked at the negresses: for, having totally forgotten their deafness, he had impatiently asked them for food; and seeing them regardless of his demand, he began to cuff, pinch, and push them, till Carathis arrived to terminate a scene so indecent, to the great content of these miserable creatures, who having been brought up by her, understood all her signs, and communicated in the same way their thoughts in return.

"Son! what means all this?" said she, panting for breath. "I thought I heard as I came up, the shrieks of a thousand bats, tearing from their crannies in the recesses of a cavern, and it was the outcry only of these poor mutes, whom you were so unmercifully abusing. In truth you but ill deserve the admirable provision I have brought you."

"Give it me instantly!" exclaimed the Caliph: "I am perishing for hunger!"

"As to that," answered she, "you must have an excellent stomach if it can digest what I have been preparing."

"Be quick," replied the Caliph. "But oh, heavens! what horrors! What do you intend?"

"Come, come," returned Carathis, "be not so squeamish, but help me to arrange every thing properly, and you shall see that what you reject with such symptoms of disgust will soon complete your felicity. Let us get ready the pile for the sacrifice of tonight, and think not of eating till that is performed. Know you not that all solemn rites are preceded by a rigorous abstinence?"

The Caliph, not daring to object, abandoned himself to grief, and the wind that ravaged his entrails, whilst his mother went forward with the requisite operations. Phials of serpents' oil, mummies, and bones, were soon set in order on the balustrade of the tower. The pile began to rise; and in three hours was as many cubits high. At length, darkness approached, and Carathis having stripped herself to her inmost garment, clapped her hands in an impulse of ecstasy, and struck light with all her force. The mutes followed her example: but Vathek, extenuated with hunger and impatience, was unable to support himself, and fell down in a swoon. The sparks had already kindled the dry wood; the venomous oil burst into a thousand blue flames; the mummies, dissolving, emitted a thick dun vapour; and the rhinoceros' horns beginning to consume; all together diffused such a stench, that the Caliph, recovering, started from his trance and gazed wildly on the scene in full blaze around him. The oil gushed forth in a plentitude of streams; and the negresses, who supplied it without intermission, united their cries to those of the Princess. At last the fire became so violent, and the flames reflected from the polished marble so dazzling, that the Caliph, unable to withstand the heat and the blaze, effected his escape, and clambered up the imperial standard.

In the meantime, the inhabitants of Samarah, scared at the light which shone over the city, arose in haste, ascended their roofs, beheld the tower on fire, and hurried half-naked to the square. Their love to their sovereign immediately awoke; and apprehending him in danger of perishing in his tower, their whole thoughts were occupied with the means of his safety. Morakanabad flew from his retirement, wiped away his tears, and cried out for water like the rest. Bababalouk, whose olfactory nerves were more familiarized to magical odours, readily conjecturing that Carathis was engaged in her favourite amusements, strenuously exhorted them not to be alarmed. Him, however, they treated as an old poltroon; and forbore not to style him a rascally traitor. The camels and dromedaries were advancing with water, but no one knew by which way to enter the tower. Whilst the populace was obstinate in forcing the doors, a violent east wind drove such a volume of flame against them, as at first forced them off; but afterwards, rekindled their zeal. At the same time, the stench of the horns and mummies increasing, most of the crowd fell backward in a state of suffocation. Those that kept their feet mutually wondered at the cause of the smell, and admonished each other to retire. Morakanabad, more sick than the rest, remained in a piteous condition. Holding his nose with one hand, he persisted in his efforts with the other to burst open the doors, and obtain admission. A hundred and forty of the strongest and most resolute at length accomplished their purpose. Having gained the staircase by their violent exertions, they attained a great height in a quarter of an hour.

Carathis, alarmed at the signs of her mutes, advanced to the staircase, went down a few steps, and heard several voices calling out from below:

"You shall in a moment have water!"

Being rather alert, considering her age, she presently regained the top of the tower, and bade her son suspend the sacrifice for some minutes, adding:

"We shall soon be enabled to render it more grateful. Certain dolts of your subjects, imagining, no doubt, that we were on fire, have been rash enough to break through those doors, which had hitherto remained inviolate, for the sake of bringing up water. They are very kind, you must allow, so soon to forget the wrongs you have done them: but that is of little moment. Let us offer them to the Giaour. Let them come up: our mutes, who neither want strength nor experience, will soon despatch them, exhausted as they are with fatigue."

"Be it so," answered the Caliph, "provided we finish, and I dine."

In fact, these good people, out of breath from ascending eleven thousand stairs in such haste, and chagrined at having spilt, by the way, the water they had taken, were no sooner arrived at the top than the blaze of the flames and the fumes of the mummies at once overpowered their senses. It was a pity! for they beheld not the agreeable smile with which the mutes and the negresses adjusted the cord to their necks: these amiable personages rejoiced, however, no less at the scene. Never before had the ceremony of strangling been performed with so much facility. They all fell without the least resistance or struggle; so that Vathek, in the space of a few moments, found himself surrounded by the dead bodies of his most faithful subjects, all of which were thrown on the top of the pile.

Carathis, whose presence of mind never forsook her, perceiving that she had carcases sufficient to complete her oblation, commanded the chains to be stretched across the staircase, and the iron doors barricaded, that no more might come up.

No sooner were these orders obeyed, than the tower shook; the dead bodies vanished in the flames; which at once changed from a swarthy crimson to a bright rose colour. An ambient vapour emitted the most exquisite fragrance; the marble columns rang with harmonious sounds, and the liquefied horns diffused a delicious perfume. Carathis, in transports, anticipated the success of her enterprise; whilst the mutes and negresses, to whom these sweets had given the cholic, retired to their cells grumbling.

Scarcely were they gone, when, instead of the pile, horns, mummies, and ashes, the Caliph both saw and felt, with a degree of pleasure which he could not express, a table, covered with the most magnificent repast: flaggons of wine, and vases of exquisite sherbet, floating on snow. He availed himself, without scruple, of such an entertainment; and had already laid hands on a lamb stuffed with pistachios, whilst Carathis was privately drawing from a fillagreen urn, a parchment that seemed to be endless; and which had escaped the notice of her son. Totally occupied, in gratifying an importunate appetite, he left her to peruse it, without interruption; which having finished, she said to him, in an authoritative tone,

"Put an end to your gluttony, and hear the splendid promises with which you are favoured!" She then read, as follows:

"Vathek, my well-beloved, thou hast surpassed my hopes: my nostrils have been regaled by the savour of thy mummies, thy horns; and, still more, by the lives devoted on the pile. At the full of the moon, cause the bands of thy musicians, and thy tymbals, to be heard; depart from thy palace surrounded by all the pageants of majesty; thy most faithful slaves, thy best beloved wives; thy most magnificent litters; thy richest loaden camels; and set forward on thy way to Istakar. There await I thy coming. That is the region of wonders. There shalt thou receive the diadem of Gian Ben Gian, the talismans of Soliman, and the treasures of the preadimite Sultans: there shalt thou be solaced with all kinds of delight. But, beware how thou enterest any dwelling on thy route, or thou shalt feel the effects of my anger."

The Caliph, who, notwithstanding his habitual luxury, had never before dined with so much satisfaction, gave full scope to the joy of these golden tidings, and betook himself to drinking anew. Carathis, whose antipathy to wine was by no means insuperable, failed not to supply a reason for every bumper, which they ironically quaffed to the health of Mahomet. This infernal liquor completed their impious temerity, and prompted them to utter a profusion of blasphemies. They gave a loose to their wit, at the expense of the ass of Balaam, the dog of the seven sleepers, and the other animals admitted into the paradise of Mahomet. In this sprightly humour they descended the eleven thousand stairs, diverting themselves as they went at the anxious faces they saw on the square, through the oilets of the tower, and at length arrived at the royal apartments by the subterranean passage. Bababalouk was parading to and fro, and issuing his mandates with great pomp to the eunuchs, who were snuffing the lights and painting the eyes of the Circassians. No sooner did he catch sight of the Caliph and his mother than he exclaimed,

"Hah! you have then, I perceive, escaped from the flames; I was not, however, altogether out of doubt."

"Of what moment is it to us what you thought or think?" cried Carathis "go, speed, tell Morakanabad that we immediately want him; and take care how you stop by the way to make your insipid reflections."

Morakanabad delayed not to obey the summons, and was received by Vathek and his mother with great solemnity. They told him with an air of composure and commiseration that the fire at the top of the tower was extinguished, but that it had cost the lives of the brave people who sought to assist them.

"Still more misfortunes!" cried Morakanabad with a sigh. "Ah, commander of the faithful, our holy prophet is certainly irritated against us! it behoves you to appease him."

"We will appease him hereafter," replied the Caliph, with a smile that augured nothing of good. "You will have leisure sufficient for your supplications during my absence; for this country is the bane of my health. I am disgusted with the mountain of the Four Fountains, and am resolved to go and drink of the stream of Rocnabad. I long to refresh myself in the delightful valleys which it waters. Do you, with the advice of my mother, govern my dominions; and take care to supply whatever her experiments may demand; for you well know that our tower abounds in materials for the advancement of science."

The tower but ill suited Morakanabad's taste. Immense treasures had been lavished upon it, and nothing had he ever seen carried thither but female negroes, mutes, and abominable drugs. Nor did he know well what to think of Carathis, who like a chamelion could assume all possible colours. Her cursed eloquence had often driven the poor Mussulman to his last shifts. He considered, however, that if she possessed but few good qualities, her son had still fewer, and that the alternative, on the whole, would be in her favour. Consoled, therefore, with this reflection, he went in good spirits to soothe the populace, and make the proper arrangements for his master's journey.

Vathek, to conciliate the spirits of the subterranean palace, resolved that his expedition should be uncommonly splendid. With this view he confiscated on all sides the property of his subjects, whilst his worthy mother stripped the seraglios she visited of the gems they contained. She collected all the sempstresses and embroiderers of Samarah, and other cities, to the distance of sixty leagues, to prepare pavilions, palanquins, sofas, canopies, and litters, for the train of the monarch. There was not left in Masulipatan a single piece of chintz; and so much muslin had been bought up to dress out Bababalouk and the other black eunuchs, that there remained not an ell in the whole Irak of Babylon.

During these preparations, Carathis, who never lost sight of her great object, which was to obtain favour with the powers of darkness, made select parties of the fairest and most delicate ladies of the city; but in the midst of their gaiety she contrived to introduce serpents amongst them, and to break pots of scorpions under the table. They all bit to a wonder, and Carathis would have left them to bite, were it not that to fill up the time, she now and then amused herself in curing their wounds with an excellent anodyne of her own invention; for this good princess abhorred being indolent.

Vathek, who was not altogether so active as his mother, devoted his time to the sole gratification of his senses, in the palaces which were severally dedicated to them. He disgusted himself no more with the divan or the mosque. One half of Samarah followed his example, whilst the other lamented the progress of corruption.

In the midst of these transactions, the embassy returned which had been sent in pious times to Mecca. It consisted of the most reverend moullahs, who had fulfilled their commission, and brought back one of those precious besoms which are used to sweep the sacred caaba; a present truly worthy of the greatest potentate on earth!

The Caliph happened at this instant to be engaged in an apartment by no means adapted to the reception of embassies, though adorned with a certain magnificence, not only to render it agreeable, but also because he resorted to it frequently, and staid a considerable time together. Whilst occupied in this retreat, he heard the voice of Bababalouk calling out from between the door and the tapestry that hung before it:

"Here are the excellent Mahomet Ebn Edris al Shafei, and the seraphic Al Mouhadethin, who have brought the besom from Mecca, and with tears of joy entreat they may present it to your majesty in person."

"Let them bring the besom hither, it may be of use," said Vathek, who was still employed, not having quite racked off his wine.

"How!" answered Bababalouk, half aloud and amazed.

"Obey," replied the Caliph, "for it is my sovereign will; go instantly! vanish! for here will I receive the good folk who have thus filled thee with joy."

The eunuch departed muttering, and bade the venerable train attend him. A sacred rapture was diffused amongst these reverend old men. Though fatigued with the length of their expedition, they followed Bababalouk with an alertness almost miraculous, and felt themselves highly flattered as they swept along the stately porticos, that the Caliph would not receive them like ambassadors in ordinary, in his hall of audience. Soon reaching the interior of the harem (where, through blinds of persian they perceived large soft eyes, dark and blue, that went and came like lightning) penetrated with respect and wonder, and full of their celestial mission, they advanced in procession towards the small corridors that appeared to terminate in nothing, but nevertheless led to the cell where the Caliph expected their coming.

"What! is the commander of the faithful sick?" said Ebn Edris al Shafei, in a low voice to his companion.

"I rather think he is in his oratory," answered Al Mouhadethin.

Vathek, who heard the dialogue, cried out "What imports it you how I am employed? approach without delay."

They advanced, and Bababalouk almost sunk with confusion, whilst the Caliph, without showing himself, put forth his hand from behind the tapestry that hung before the door, and demanded of them the besom.

Having prostrated themselves as well as the corridor would permit, and even in a tolerable semi-circle, the venerable Al Shafei, drawing forth the besom from the embroidered and perfumed scarfs in which it had been enveloped, and secured from the profane gaze of vulgar eyes, arose from his associates and advanced with an air of the most awful solemnity towards the supposed oratory; but with what astonishment! with what horror was he seized!

Vathek, bursting out into a villainous laugh, snatched the besom from his trembling hand, and fixing upon it some cobwebs that hung suspended from the ceiling, gravely brushed away till not a single one remained.

The old men, overpowered with amazement, were unable to lift their beards from the ground; for as Vathek had carelessly left the tapestry between them half drawn, they were witnesses to the whole transaction. Their tears gushed forth on the marble. Al Mouhadethin swooned through mortification and fatigue, whilst the Caliph, throwing himself backward on his seat, shouted and clapped his hands without mercy. At last, addressing himself to Bababalouk:

"My dear black," said he, "go, regale these pious poor souls with my good wine from Shiraz; and as they can boast of having seen more of my palace than any one besides, let them also visit my office courts, and lead them out by the back steps that go to my stables." Having said this, he threw the besom in their face, and went to enjoy the laugh with Carathis.

Bababalouk did all in his power to console the ambassadors, but the two most infirm expired on the spot; the rest were carried to their beds, from whence, being heart-broken with sorrow and shame, they never arose.

The succeeding night, Vathek, attended by his mother, ascended the tower to see if everything were ready for his journey, for he had great faith in the influence of the stars. The planets appeared in their most favourable aspects. The Caliph, to enjoy so flattering a sight, supped gaily on the roof, and fancied that he heard, during his repast, loud shouts of laughter resound through the sky, in a manner that inspired the fullest assurance.

All was in motion at the palace; lights were kept burning through the whole of the night; the sound of implements, and of artisans finishing their work; the voices of women and their guardians who sung at their embroidery; all conspired to interrupt the stillness of nature, and infinitely delight the heart of Vathek, who imagined himself going in triumph to sit upon the throne of Soliman.

The people were not less satisfied than himself; all assisted to accelerate the moment which should rescue them from the wayward caprices of so extravagant a master.

The day preceding the departure of this infatuated prince was employed by Carathis in repeating to him the decrees of the mysterious parchment, which she had thoroughly gotten by heart; and in recommending him not to enter the habitation of any one by the way; "for well thou knowest," added she, "how liquorish thy taste is after good dishes and young damsels; let me therefore enjoin thee to be content with thy old cooks, who are the best in the world; and not to forget that in thy ambulatory seraglio there are three dozen pretty faces, which Bababalouk hath not yet unveiled. I, myself, have a great desire to watch over thy conduct, and visit the subterranean palace, which no doubt contains whatever can interest persons like us.

There is nothing so pleasing as retiring to caverns; my taste for dead bodies and everything like mummy is decided; and I am confident thou wilt see the most exquisite of their kind. Forget me not then, but the moment thou art in possession of the talismans which are to open to thee the mineral kingdoms, and the centre of the earth itself, fail not to dispatch some trusty genius to take me and my cabinet, for the oil of the serpents I have pinched to death will be a pretty present to the Giaour, who cannot but be charmed with such dainties."

Scarcely had Carathis ended this edifying discourse, when the sun, setting behind the mountain of the Four Fountains, gave place to the rising moon. This planet being that evening at full, appeared of unusual beauty and magnitude in the eyes of the women, the eunuchs, and the pages, who were all impatient to set forward. The city re-echoed with shouts of joy and flourishing of trumpets. Nothing was visible but plumes nodding on pavilions, and aigrets shining in the mild lustre of the moon. The spacious square resembled an immense parterre, variegated with the most stately tulips of the east.

Arrayed in the robes which were only worn at the most distinguished ceremonials, and supported by his vizier and Bababalouk, the Caliph descended the grand staircase of the tower in the sight of all his people. He could not forbear pausing at intervals to admire the superb appearance which everywhere courted his view, whilst the whole multitude, even to the camels with their sumptuous burdens, knelt down before him. For some time a general stillness prevailed, which nothing happened to disturb, but the shrill screams of some eunuchs in the rear. These vigilant guards having remarked certain cages of the ladies swagging somewhat awry, and discovered that a few adventurous gallants had contrived to get in, soon dislodged the enraptured culprits, and consigned them with good commendations, to the surgeons of the serail. The majesty of so magnificent a spectacle was not, however, violated by incidents like these. Vathek, meanwhile, saluted the moon with an idolatrous air, that neither pleased Morakanabad nor the doctors of the law, any more than the viziers and grandees of his court, who were all assembled to enjoy the last view of their sovereign.

At length the clarions and trumpets from the top of the tower announced the prelude of departure. Though the instruments were in unison with each other, yet a singular dissonance was blended with their sounds. This proceeded from Carathis, who was singing her direful orisons to the Giaour, whilst the negresses and mutes supplied thorough bass without articulating a word. The good Mussulmans fancied that they heard the sullen hum of those nocturnal insects which presage evil, and importuned Vathek to beware how he ventured his sacred person.

On a given signal the great standard of the Califat was displayed; twenty thousand lances shone around it; and the Caliph, treading royally on the cloth of gold which had been spread for his feet, ascended his litter amidst the general awe that possessed his subjects.

The expedition commenced with the utmost order, and so entire a silence, that even the locusts were heard from the thickets on the plain of Catoul. Gaiety and good humour prevailing, six good leagues were past before the dawn; and the morning star was still glittering in the firmament when the whole of this numerous train had halted on the banks of the Tigris, where they encamped to repose for the rest of the day.

The three days that followed were spent in the same manner, but on the fourth the heavens looked angry, lightnings broke forth in frequent flashes, re-echoing peals of thunder succeeded, and the trembling Circassians clung with all their might to their ugly guardians. The Caliph himself was greatly inclined to take shelter in the large town of Gulchissar, the governor of which came forth to meet him, and tendered every kind of refreshment the place could supply. But having examined his tablets, he suffered the rain to soak him almost to the bone, notwithstanding the importunity of his first favourites. Though he began to regret the palace of the senses, yet he lost not sight of his enterprise, and his sanguine expectations confirmed his resolution. His geographers were ordered to attend him, but the weather proved so terrible, that these poor people exhibited a lamentable appearance; and as no long journeys had been undertaken since the time of Haroun al Raschid, their maps of the different countries were in a still worse plight than themselves. Every one was ignorant which way to turn; for Vathek, though well versed in the course of the heavens, no longer knew his situation on earth. He thundered even louder than the elements, and muttered forth certain hints of the bowstring which were not very soothing to literary ears. Disgusted at the toilsome weariness of the way, he determined to cross over the craggy heights, and follow the guidance of a peasant, who undertook to bring him, in four days, to Rocnabad. Remonstrances were all to no purpose, his resolution was fixed, and an invasion commenced on the province of the goats, who sped away in large troops before them. It was curious to view on these half calcined rocks camels richly caparisoned, and pavilions of gold and silk waving on their summits, which till then had never been covered, but with sapless thistles and fern.

The females and eunuchs uttered shrill wailings at the sight of the precipices below them, and the dreary prospects that opened in the vast gorges of the mountains. Before they could reach the ascent of the steepest rock night overtook them, and a boisterous tempest arose, which having rent the awnings of the palanquins and cages, exposed to the raw gusts the poor ladies within, who had never before felt so piercing a cold. The dark clouds that overcast the face of the sky deepened the horrors of this disastrous night, insomuch that nothing could be heard distinctly but the mewling of pages, and lamentations of sultanas.

To increase the general misfortune, the frightful uproar of wild beasts resounded at a distance, and there were soon perceived in the forest they were skirting the glaring of eyes which could belong only to devils or tigers. The pioneers, who as well as they could, had marked out a track, and a part of the advanced guard were devoured before they had been in the least apprised of their danger. The confusion that prevailed was extreme. Wolves, tigers, and other carnivorous animals, invited by the howling of their companions, flocked together from every quarter. The crushing of bones was heard on all sides, and a fearful rush of wings over head, for now vultures also began to be of the party.

The terror at length reached the main body of the troops which surrounded the monarch and his harem, at the distance of two leagues from the scene. Vathek (voluptuously reposed in his capacious litter upon cushions of silk, with two little pages beside him, of complexions more fair than the enamel of Franguestan, who were occupied in keeping off flies) was soundly asleep, and contemplating in his dreams the treasures of Soliman. The shrieks, however, of his wives awoke him with a start, and instead of the Giaour with his key of gold, he beheld Bababalouk full of consternation.

"Sire," exclaimed this good servant of the most potent of monarchs, "misfortune has arrived at its height; wild beasts, who entertain no more reverence for your sacred person than for that of a dead ass, have beset your camels and their drivers: thirty of the richest laden are already become their prey, as well as all your confectioners, your cooks, and purveyors, and unless our holy prophet should protect us, we shall have all eaten our last meal."

At the mention of eating, the Caliph lost all patience. He began to bellow, and even beat himself, for there was no seeing in the dark. The rumour every instant increased, and Bababalouk finding no good could be done with his master stopped both his ears against the hurly-burly of the harem, and called out aloud:

"Come, ladies and brothers! all hands to work! strike light in a moment! never shall it be said that the commander of the faithful served to regale these infidel brutes."

Though there wanted not in this bevy of beauties a sufficient number of capricious and wayward, yet, on the present occasion they were all compliance. Fires were visible in a twinkling in all their cages. Ten thousand torches were lighted at once. The Caliph himself seized a large one of wax; every person followed his example; and by kindling ropes ends dipped in oil and fastened on poles, an amazing blaze was spread. The rocks were covered with the splendour of sunshine. The trails of sparks wafted by the wind, communicated to the dry fern, of which there was plenty. Serpents were observed to crawl forth from their retreats with amazement and hissings, whilst the horses snorted, stamped the ground, tossed their noses in the air, and plunged about without mercy.

One of the forests of cedar that bordered their way took fire, and the branches that overhung the path extending their flames to the muslins and chintzes which covered the cages of the ladies, obliged them to jump out at the peril of their necks. Vathek, who vented on the occasion a thousand blasphemies, was himself compelled to touch with his sacred feet the naked earth.

Never had such an incident happened before. Full of mortification, shame and despondence, and not knowing how to walk, the ladies fell into the dirt.

"Must I go on foot," said one.

"Must I wet my feet," cried another.

"Must I soil my dress," asked a third.

"Execrable Bababalouk," exclaimed all; "Outcast of hell! what hadst thou to do with torches? Better were it to be eaten by tigers than to fall into our present condition; we are for ever undone. Not a porter is there in the army, nor a currier of camels but hath seen some part of our bodies, and what is worse, our very faces!"

On saying this, the most bashful amongst them hid their foreheads on the ground, whilst such as had more boldness flew at Bababalouk, but he, well apprised of their humour, and not wanting in shrewdness, betook himself to his heels along with his comrades, all dropping their torches and striking their tymbals.

It was not less light than in the brightest of the dog-days, and the weather was hot in proportion; but how degrading was the spectacle, to behold the Caliph bespattered like an ordinary mortal! As the exercise of his faculties seemed to be suspended, one of his Ethiopian wives (for he delighted in variety) clasped him in her arms, threw him upon her shoulder like a sack of dates, and finding that the fire was hemming them in, set off with no small expedition, considering the weight of her burden. The other ladies who had just learned the use of their feet followed her; their guards galloped after; and the camel drivers brought up the rear as fast as their charge would permit.

They soon reached the spot where the wild beasts had commenced the carnage, and which they had too much spirit to leave, notwithstanding the approaching tumult, and the luxurious supper they had made. Bababalouk nevertheless seized on a few of the plumpest, which were unable to budge from the place, and began to flay them with admirable adroitness. The cavalcade being got so far from the conflagration as that the heat felt rather grateful than violent, it was immediately resolved on to halt. The tattered chintzes were picked up; the scraps left by the wolves and tigers interred; and vengeance was taken on some dozens of vultures that were too much glutted to rise on the wing. The camels which had been left unmolested to make sal-ammoniac being numbered, and the ladies once more inclosed in their cages, the imperial tent was pitched on the levellest ground they could find.

Vathek, reposing upon a matress of down, and tolerably recovered from the jolting of the Ethiopian, who, to his feelings seemed the roughest trotting jade he had hitherto mounted, called out for something to eat; but alas! those delicate cakes which had been baked in silver ovens for his royal mouth, those rich manchets, amber comfits, flaggons of Schiraz wine, porcelain vases of snow, and grapes from the banks of the Tigris, were all irremediably lost; and nothing had Bababalouk to present in their stead, but a roasted wolf, vultures à la daube, aromatic herbs of the most acrid poignancy, rotten truffles, boiled thistles, and such other wild plants as must ulcerate the throat and parch up the tongue. Nor was he better provided in the article of drink, for he could procure nothing to accompany these irritating viands but a few phials of abominable brandy, which had been secreted by the scullions in their slippers.

Vathek made wry faces at so savage a repast, and Bababalouk answered them with shrugs and contortions. The Caliph however ate with tolerable appetite, and fell into a nap that lasted six hours. The splendour of the sun, reflected from the white cliffs of the mountains in spite of the curtains that inclosed him, at length disturbed his repose. He awoke terrified, and stung to the quick by those wormwood-coloured flies which emit from their wings a suffocating stench. The miserable monarch was perplexed how to act, though his wits were not idle in seeking expedients, whilst Bababalouk lay snoring amidst a swarm of those insects, that busily thronged to pay court to his nose. The little pages, famished with hunger, had dropped their fans on the ground, and exerted their dying voices in bitter reproaches on the Caliph, who now for the first time heard the language of truth.

Thus stimulated, he renewed his imprecations against the Giaour, and bestowed upon Mahomet some soothing expressions.

"Where am I?" cried he; "What are these dreadful rocks; these valleys of darkness? Are we arrived at the horrible Kaf? Is the Simurgh coming to pluck out my eyes as a punishment for undertaking this impious enterprise?"

Having said this, he bellowed like a calf, and turned himself towards an outlet in the side of his pavilion. But alas! what objects occurred to his view! on one side a plain of black sand that appeared to be unbounded, and on the other perpendicular crags bristled over with those abominable thistles which had so severely lacerated his tongue. He fancied, however, that he perceived amongst the brambles and briars some gigantic flowers, but was mistaken, for these were only the dangling palampores and variegated tatters of his gay retinue. As there were several clefts in the rock from whence water seemed to have flowed, Vathek applied his ear with the hope of catching the sound of some latent runnel, but could only distinguish the low murmurs of his people, who were repining at their journey, and complaining for the want of water.

"To what purpose," asked they, "have we been brought hither? Hath our Caliph another tower to build? or have the relentless Afrits whom Carathis so much loves, fixed in this place their abode?"

At the name of Carathis, Vathek recollected the tablets he had received from his mother, who assured him they were fraught with preternatural qualities, and advised him to consult them as emergencies might require. Whilst he was engaged in turning them over, he heard a shout of joy, and a loud clapping of hands. The curtains of his pavilion were soon drawn back, and he beheld Bababalouk, followed by a troop of his favourites, conducting two dwarfs, each a cubit high, who brought between them a large basket of melons, oranges, and pomegranites. They were singing in the sweetest tones the words that follow:

"We dwell on the top of these rocks, in a cabin of rushes and canes; the eagles envy us our nest; a small spring supplies us with abdest, and we daily repeat prayers which the prophet approves. We love you, O commander of the faithful! our master, the good emir Fakreddin, loves you also; he reveres in your person the vicegerent of Mahomet. Little as we are, in us he confides; he knows our hearts to be good, as our bodies are contemptible, and hath placed us here to aid those who are bewildered on these dreary mountains. Last night, whilst we were occupied within our cell in reading the holy koran, a sudden hurricane blew out our lights and rocked our habitation. For two whole hours a palpable darkness prevailed: but we heard sounds at a distance which we conjectured to proceed from the bells of a cafila, passing over the rocks. Our ears were soon filled with deplorable shrieks, frightful roarings, and the sound of tymbals. Chilled with terror, we concluded that the Deggial with his exterminating angels had sent forth their plagues on the earth. In the midst of these melancholy reflections, we perceived flames of the deepest red glow in the horizon, and found ourselves in a few moments covered with flakes of fire. Amazed at so strange an appearance, we took up the volume dictated by the blessed intelligence, and kneeling by the light of the fire that surrounded us, we recited the verse which says: 'Put no trust in any thing but the mercy of heaven; there is no help save in the holy prophet; the mountain of Kaf itself may tremble; it is the power of Alla only that cannot be moved.' After having pronounced these words, we felt consolation, and our minds were hushed into a sacred repose. Silence ensued, and our ears clearly distinguished a voice in the air, saying: 'Servants of my faithful servant, go down to the happy valley of Fakreddin; tell him that an illustrious opportunity now offers to satiate the thirst of his hospitable heart. The commander of true believers is this day bewildered amongst these mountains, and stands in need of thy aid.' We obeyed with joy the angelic mission, and our master, filled with pious zeal, hath culled with his own hands these melons, oranges, and pomegranites. He is following us with a hundred dromedaries laden with the purest waters of his fountains, and is coming to kiss the fringe of your consecrated robe, and implore you to enter his humble habitation, which, placed amidst these barren wilds, resembles an emerald set in lead."

The dwarfs having ended their address, remained still standing, and with hands crossed upon their bosoms, preserved a respectful silence.

Vathek, in the midst of this curious harangue seized the basket, and long before it was finished, the fruits had dissolved in his mouth. As he continued to eat, his piety increased, and in the same breath which recited his prayers, he called for the koran and sugar.

Such was the state of his mind when the tablets, which were thrown by at the approach of the dwarfs, again attracted his eye. He took them up, but was ready to drop on the ground when he beheld, in large red characters, these words inscribed by Carathis, which were indeed enough to make him tremble.

"Beware of thy old doctors, and their puny messengers of but one cubit high; distrust their pious frauds; and instead of eating their melons, impale on a spit the bearers of them. Shouldst thou be such a fool as to visit them, the portal of the subterranean palace will be shut in thy face, and with such force as shall shake thee asunder; thy body shall be spit upon, and bats will engender in thy belly."

"To what tends this ominous rhapsody?" cries the Caliph; "and must I then perish in these deserts with thirst, whilst I may refresh myself in the valley of melons and cucumbers? Accursed be the Giaour with his portal of ebony! he hath made me dance attendance too long already. Besides, who shall prescribe laws to me? I, forsooth, must not enter any one's habitation! Be it so, but what one can I enter that is not my own."

Bababalouk, who lost not a syllable of this soliloquy, applauded it with all his heart; and the ladies, for the first time, agreed with him in opinion. The dwarfs were entertained, caressed, and seated with great ceremony on little cushions of satin. The symmetry of their persons was the subject of criticism; not an inch of them was suffered to pass unexamined. Nick-nacks and dainties were offered in profusion, but all were declined with respectful gravity. They clambered up the sides of the Caliph's seat, and placing themselves each on one of his shoulders, began to whisper prayers in his ears. Their tongues quivered like the leaves of a poplar, and the patience of Vathek was almost exhausted, when the acclamations of the troops announced the approach of Fakreddin, who was come with a hundred old grey-beards, and as many korans and dromedaries. They instantly set about their ablutions, and began to repeat the Bismillah. Vathek, to get rid of these officious monitors, followed their example, for his hands were burning.

The good Emir, who was punctiliously religious, and likewise a great dealer in compliments, made an harangue five times more prolix and insipid than his harbingers had already delivered. The Caliph, unable any longer to refrain, exclaimed:

"For the love of Mahomet, my dear Fakreddin, have done! let us proceed to your valley, and enjoy the fruits that heaven hath vouchsafed you." The hint of proceeding put all into motion. The venerable attendants of the emir set forward somewhat slowly, but Vathek having ordered his little pages, in private, to goad on the dromedaries, loud fits of laughter broke forth from the cages, for the unwieldy curvetting of these poor beasts, and the ridiculous distress of their superannuated riders afforded the ladies no small entertainment.

They descended, however, unhurt into the valley, by the large steps which the emir had cut in the rock; and already the murmuring of streams and the rustling of leaves began to catch their attention. The cavalcade soon entered a path, which was skirted by flowering shrubs, and extended to a vast wood of palm-trees whose branches overspread a building of hewn stone. This edifice was crowned with nine domes, and adorned with as many portals of bronze, on which was engraven the following inscription:

"This is the asylum of pilgrims, the refuge of travellers, and the depository of secrets for all parts of the world."

Nine pages beautiful as the day, and clothed in robes of Egyptian linen, very long and very modest, were standing at each door. They received the whole retinue with an easy and inviting air. Four of the most amiable placed the Caliph on a magnificent taktrevan; four others, somewhat less graceful, took charge of Bababalouk, who capered for joy at the snug little cabin that fell to his share; the pages that remained, waited on the rest of the train.

When every thing masculine was gone out of sight, the gate of a large inclosure on the right turned on its harmonious hinges, and a young female of a slender form came forth. Her light brown hair floated in the hazy breeze of the twilight. A troop of young maidens, like the Pleiades, attended her on tip-toe. They hastened to the pavilions that contained the sultanas; and the young lady gracefully bending said to them:

"Charming princesses, every thing is ready; we have prepared beds for your repose, and strewed your apartments with jasamine; no insects will keep off slumber from visiting your eyelids; we will dispel them with a thousand plumes. Come then, amiable ladies! refresh your delicate feet and your ivory limbs in baths of rose water, and by the light of perfumed lamps your servants will amuse you with tales."

The sultanas accepted with pleasure these obliging offers, and followed the young lady to the emir's harem, where we must for a moment leave them and return to the Caliph.

Vathek found himself beneath a vast dome illuminated by a thousand lamps of rock crystal, as many vases of the same material filled with excellent sherbet sparkled on a large table, where a profusion of viands were spread. Amongst others were sweetbreads stewed in milk of almonds, saffron soups, and lamb à la crême, of all of which the Caliph was amazingly fond. He took of each as much as he was able; testified his sense of the emir's friendship by the gaiety of his heart; and made the dwarfs dance against their will; for these little devotees durst not refuse the commander of the faithful. At last he spread himself on the sofa and slept sounder than he had ever before.

Beneath this dome a general silence prevailed, for there was nothing to disturb it but the jaws of Bababalouk, who had untrussed himself to eat with greater advantage, being anxious to make amends for his fast in the mountains. As his spirits were too high to admit of his sleeping, and not loving to be idle, he proposed with himself to visit the harem, and repair to his charge of the ladies, to examine if they had been properly lubricated with the balm of Mecca, if their eye-brows and tresses were in order, and in a word, to perform all the little offices they might need. He sought for a long time together, but without being able to find out the door. He durst not speak aloud for fear of disturbing the Caliph, and not a soul was stirring in the precincts of the palace. He almost despaired of effecting his purpose, when a low whispering just reached his ear: it came from the dwarfs, who were returned to their old occupation, and for the nine hundred and ninety-ninth time in their lives were reading over the koran. They very politely invited Bababalouk to be of their party, but his head was full of other concerns. The dwarfs, though scandalized at his dissolute morals, directed him to the apartments he wanted to find.

His way thither lay through a hundred dark corridors, along which he groped as he went, and at last began to catch, from the extremity of a passage, the charming gossiping of women, which not a little delighted his heart.

"Ah, ah! what not yet asleep?" cried he, and taking long strides as he spoke, "did you not suspect me of abjuring my charge? I stayed but to finish what my master had left."

Two of the black eunuchs on hearing a voice so loud detached a party in haste, sabre in hand, to discover the cause, but presently was repeated on all sides:

"'Tis only Bababalouk, no one but Bababalouk!"

This circumspect guardian having gone up to a thin veil of carnation colour silk that hung before the doorway, distinguished by means of a softened splendour that shone through it, an oval bath of dark porphyry surrounded by curtains festooned in large folds. Through the apertures between them, as they were not drawn close, groups of young slaves were visible, amongst whom Bababalouk perceived his pupils indulgingly expanding their arms, as if to embrace the perfumed water, and refresh themselves after their fatigues. The looks of tender languor, their confidential whispers, and the enchanting smiles with which they were imparted, the exquisite fragrance of the roses, all combined to inspire a voluptuousness which even Bababalouk himself was scarce able to withstand.

He summoned up, however, his usual solemnity, and in the peremptory tone of authority commanded the ladies instantly to leave the bath. Whilst he was issuing these mandates, the young Nouronihar, daughter of the emir, who was sprightly as an antelope, and full of wanton gaiety, beckoned one of her slaves to let down the great swing, which was suspended to the ceiling by cords of silk, and whilst this was doing winked to her companions in the bath, who chagrined to be forced from so soothing a state of indolence, began to twist it round Bababalouk, and teaze him with a thousand vagaries.

When Nouronihar perceived that he was exhausted with fatigue, she accosted him with an arch air of respectful concern, and said:

"My lord, it is not by any means decent that the chief eunuch of the Caliph our sovereign should thus continue standing, deign but to recline your graceful person upon this sofa, which will burst with vexation if it have not the honour to receive you."

Caught by these flattering accents, Bababalouk gallantly replied:

"Delight of the apple of my eye! I accept the invitation of thy honied lips, and to say truth, my senses are dazzled with the radiance that beams from thy charms."

"Repose, then, at your ease," replied the beauty, and placed him on the pretended sofa, which, quicker than lightning, gave way all at once. The rest of the women having aptly conceived her design, sprang naked from the bath and plied the swing with such unmerciful jerks, that it swept through the whole compass of a very lofty dome, and took from the poor victim all power of respiration. Sometimes his feet rased the surface of the water, and at others the skylight almost flattened his nose. In vain did he pierce the air with the cries of a voice that resembled the ringing of a cracked basin, for their peals of laughter were still more predominant.

Nouronihar in the inebriety of youthful spirits being used only to eunuchs of ordinary harems, and having never seen any thing so royal and disgusting, was far more diverted than all of the rest. She began to parody some Persian verses, and sung with an accent most demurely piquant:

"O gentle white dove as thou soar'st through the air,
Vouchsafe one kind glance on the mate of thy love:
Melodious Philomel I am thy rose;
Warble some couplet to ravish my heart!"

The sultanas and their slaves stimulated by these pleasantries persevered at the swing with such unremitted assiduity, that at length the cord which had secured it snapped suddenly asunder, and Bababalouk fell floundering like a turtle to the bottom of the bath. This accident occasioned a universal shout. Twelve little doors till now unobserved flew open at once, and the ladies in an instant made their escape, after throwing all the towels on his head, and putting out the lights that remained.

The deplorable animal, in water to the chin, overwhelmed with darkness, and unable to extricate himself from the warp that embarrassed him, was still doomed to hear for his further consolation, the fresh bursts of merriment his disaster occasioned. He bustled but in vain to get from the bath, for the margin was become so slippery with the oil spilt in breaking the lamps, that at every effort he slid back with a plunge, which resounded aloud through the hollow of the dome. These cursed peals of laughter at every relapse were redoubled, and he, who thought the place infested rather by devils than women, resolved to cease groping, and abide in the bath, where he amused himself with soliloquies interspersed with imprecations, of which his malicious neighbours, reclining on down, suffered not an accent to escape. In this delectable plight the morning surprised him. The Caliph, wondering at his absence, had caused him to be everywhere sought for. At last he was drawn forth almost smothered from the whisp of linen, and wet even to the marrow. Limping, and chattering his teeth, he appeared before his master, who inquired what was the matter, and how he came soused in so strange a pickle.

"And why did you enter this cursed lodge?" answered Bababalouk, gruffly. "Ought a monarch like you to visit with his harem the abode of a grey bearded emir who knows nothing of life? And with what gracious damsels does the place too abound! Fancy to yourself how they have soaked me like a burnt crust, and made me dance like a jack-pudding the live-long night through on their damnable swing. What an excellent lesson for your sultanas to follow, into whom I have instilled such reserve and decorum!"

Vathek, comprehending not a syllable of all this invective, obliged him to relate minutely the transaction; but instead of sympathising with the miserable sufferer, he laughed immoderately at the device of the swing, and the figure of Bababalouk mounting upon it. The stung eunuch could scarcely preserve the semblance of respect.

"Aye, laugh my lord! laugh," said he, "but I wish this Nouronihar would play some trick on you; she is too wicked to spare even majesty itself."

These words made for the present but a slight impression on the Caliph, but they not long after recurred to his mind.

This conversation was cut short by Fakreddin, who came to request that Vathek would join in the prayers and ablutions to be solemnized on a spacious meadow, watered by innumerable streams. The Caliph found the waters refreshing, but the prayers abominably irksome. He diverted himself however with the multitude of Calenders, Santons, and Dervises who were continually coming and going, but especially with the Brahmins, Faquirs, and other enthusiasts, who had travelled from the heart of India, and halted on their way with the emir. These latter had each of them some mummery peculiar to himself. One dragged a huge chain where ever he went, another an ourang-outang, whilst a third was furnished with scourges, and all performed to a charm. Some clambered up trees, holding one foot in the air; others poised themselves over a fire, and without mercy fillipped their noses. There were some amongst them that cherished vermin, which were not ungrateful in requiting their caresses. These rambling fanatics revolted the hearts of the Dervises, the Calenders, and Santons; however the vehemence of their aversion soon subsided under the hope that the presence of the Caliph would cure their folly, and convert them to the Mussulman faith. But alas! how great was their disappointment! for Vathek, instead of preaching to them, treated them as buffoons; bade them present his compliments to Visnow and Ixhora, and discovered a predilection for a squat old man from the Isle of Serendib, who was more ridiculous than any of the rest.

"Come," said he, "for the love of your gods, bestow a few slaps on your chops to amuse me."

The old fellow offended at such an address began loudly to weep; but as he betrayed a villainous drivelling in his tears, the Caliph turned his back and listened to Bababalouk, who whispered, whilst he held the umbrella over him:

"Your majesty should be cautious of this odd assembly, which hath been collected I know not for what. Is it necessary to exhibit such spectacles to a mighty potentate, with interludes of talapoins more mangy than dogs? Were I you, I would command a fire to be kindled, and at once purge the earth of the emir, his harem, and all his menagery."

"Tush, dolt," answered Vathek, "and know that all this infinitely charms me. Nor shall I leave the meadow till I have visited every hive of these pious mendicants."

Where ever the Caliph directed his course, objects of pity were sure to swarm round him: the blind, the purblind, smarts without noses, damsels without ears, each to extol the munificence of Fakreddin, who, as well as his attendant grey-beards, dealt about gratis plasters and cataplasms to all that applied. At noon a superb corps of cripples made its appearance; and soon after advanced by platoons on the plain the completest association of invalids that had ever been embodied till then. The blind went groping with the blind; the lame limped on together; and the maimed made gestures to each other with the only arm that remained. The sides of a considerable waterfall were crowded by the deaf, amongst whom were some from Pegu, with ears uncommonly handsome and large, but were still less able to hear than the rest. Nor were there wanting others in abundance with hump backs, wenny necks, and even horns of an exquisite polish.

The emir, to aggrandize the solemnity of the festival in honour of his illustrious visitant, ordered the turf to be spread on all sides with skins and table cloths, upon which were served up for the good mussulmans pilaus of every hue, with other orthodox dishes, and by the express order of Vathek, who was shamefully tolerant, small plates of abominations for regaling the rest. This prince on seeing so many mouths put in motion began to think it time for employing his own. In spite, therefore, of every remonstrance from the chief of his eunuchs, he resolved to have a dinner dressed on the spot. The complaisant emir immediately gave orders for a table to be placed in the shade of the willows. The first service consisted of fish, which they drew from a river flowing over sands of gold, at the foot of a lofty hill: these were broiled as fast as taken, and served up with a sauce of vinegar and small herbs that grew on Mount Sinai; for everything with the emir was excellent and pious.

The dessert was not quite set on when the sound of lutes from the hill was repeated by the echoes of the neighbouring mountains. The Caliph with an emotion of pleasure and surprise, had no sooner raised up his head than a handful of jasamine dropped on his face. An abundance of tittering succeeded this frolic, and instantly appeared through the bushes the elegant forms of several young females, skipping and bounding like roes. The fragrance diffused from their hair struck the sense of Vathek, who in an ecstasy, suspending his repast, said to Bababalouk:

"Are the Peries come down from their spheres? Note her in particular whose form is so perfect, venturously running on the brink of the precipice, and turning back her head as regardless of nothing but the graceful flow of her robe. With what captivating impatience doth she contend with the bushes for her veil? Could it be she who threw the jasamine at me?"

"Aye, she it was; and you too would she throw from the top of the rock," answered Bababalouk, "for that is my good friend Nouronihar, who so kindly lent me her swing. My dear lord and master," added he, twisting a twig that hung by the rind from a willow, "let me correct her for her want of respect: the emir will have no reason to complain, since (bating what I owe to his piety) he is much to be censured for keeping a troop of girls on the mountains, whose sharp air gives their blood too brisk a circulation."

"Peace, blasphemer!" said the Caliph: "speak not thus of her who over her mountains leads my heart a willing captive. Contrive, rather, that my eyes may be fixed upon hers—that I may respire her sweet breath, as she bounds panting along these delightful wilds!"

On saying these words, Vathek extended his arms towards the hill, and directing his eyes with an anxiety unknown to him before, endeavoured to keep within view the object that enthralled his soul; but her course was as difficult to follow as the flight of one of those beautiful blue butterflies of Cachmere, which are at once so volatile and rare.

The Caliph, not satisfied with seeing, wished also to hear Nouronihar, and eagerly turned to catch the sound of her voice. At last he distinguished her whispering to one of her companions behind the thicket from whence she had thrown the jasamine:

"A Caliph, it must be owned, is a fine thing to see, but my little Gulchenrouz is much more amiable; one lock of his hair is of more value to me than the richest embroidery of the Indies. I had rather that his teeth should mischievously press my finger, than the richest ring of the imperial treasure. Where have you left him, Sutlememe? and why is he now not here?"

The agitated Caliph still wished to hear more, but she immediately retired with all her attendants. The fond monarch pursued her with his eyes till she was gone out of sight, and then continued like a bewildered and benighted traveller, from whom the clouds had obscured the constellation that guided his way. The curtain of night seemed dropped before him—everything appeared discoloured. The falling waters filled his soul with dejection, and his tears trickled down the jasamines he had caught from Nouronihar, and placed in his inflamed bosom. He snatched up a shining pebble to remind him of the scene where he felt the first tumults of love. Two hours were elapsed, and evening drew on before he could resolve to depart from the place. He often, but in vain, attempted to go: a soft languor enervated the powers of his mind. Extending himself on the brink of the stream, he turned his eyes towards the blue summits of the mountain, and exclaimed:

"What concealest thou behind thee? what is passing in thy solitudes? Whither is she gone? O heaven! perhaps she is now wandering in the grottoes with her happy Gulchenrouz!"

In the meantime the damps began to descend, and the emir, solicitous for the health of the Caliph, ordered the imperial litter to be brought. Vathek, absorbed in his reveries, was imperceptibly removed and conveyed back to the saloon that received him the evening before.

But let us leave the Caliph immersed in his new passion, and attend Nouronihar beyond the rocks, where she had again joined her beloved Gulchenrouz. This Gulchenrouz was the son of Ali Hassan, brother to the emir, and the most delicate and lovely creature in the world. Ali Hassan, who had been absent ten years on a voyage to the unknown seas, committed at his departure this child, the only survivor of many, to the care and protection of his brother. Gulchenrouz could write in various characters with precision, and paint upon vellum the most elegant arabesques that fancy could devise. His sweet voice accompanied the lute in the most enchanting manner; and when he sung the loves of Megnoun and Leileh, or some unfortunate lovers of ancient days, tears insensibly overflowed the cheeks of his auditors. The verses he composed (for like Megnoun, he too was a poet) inspired that unresisting languor so frequently fatal to the female heart. The women all doated upon him, for though he had passed his thirteenth year, they still detained him in the harem. His dancing was light as the gossamer waved by the zephyrs of spring; but his arms which twined so gracefully with those of the young girls in the dance, could neither dart the lance in the chase, nor curb the steeds that pastured his uncle's domains. The bow, however, he drew with a certain aim, and would have excelled his competitors in the race, could he have broken the ties that bound him to Nouronihar.

The two brothers had mutually engaged their children to each other; and Nouronihar loved her cousin more than her eyes. Both had the same tastes and amusements; the same long languishing looks; the same tresses; the same fair complexions; and when Gulchenrouz appeared in the dress of his cousin, he seemed to be more feminine than even herself. If at any time he left the harem to visit Fakreddin, it was with all the bashfulness of a fawn that consciously ventures from the lair of its dam; he was however wanton enough to mock the solemn old grey-beards to whom he was subject, though sure to be rated without mercy in return. Whenever this happened, he would plunge into the recesses of the harem, and sobbing take refuge in the arms of Nouronihar, who loved even his faults beyond the virtues of others.

It fell out this evening that after leaving the Caliph in the meadow, she ran with Gulchenrouz over the green sward of the mountain that sheltered the vale, where Fakreddin had chosen to reside. The sun was dilated on the edge of the horizon; and the young people, whose fancies were lively and inventive, imagined they beheld in the gorgeous clouds of the west the domes of Shadukiam and Ambreabad, where the Peries have fixed their abode. Nouronihar, sitting on the slope of the hill, supported on her knees the perfumed head of Gulchenrouz. The air was calm, and no sound stirred but the voices of other young girls who were drawing cool water from the streams below. The unexpected arrival of the Caliph, and the splendour that marked his appearance, had already filled with emotion the ardent soul of Nouronihar. Her vanity irresistibly prompted her to pique the prince's attention, and this she before took good care to effect whilst he picked up the jasamine she had thrown upon him. But when Gulchenrouz asked after the flowers he had culled for her bosom, Nouronihar was all in confusion. She hastily kissed his forehead, arose in a flutter, and walked with unequal steps on the border of the precipice. Night advanced, and the pure gold of the setting sun had yielded to a sanguine red, the glow of which, like the reflection of a burning furnace, flushed Nouronihar's animated countenance. Gulchenrouz alarmed at the agitation of his cousin, said to her with a supplicating accent:

"Let us be gone; the sky looks portentious: the tamarisks tremble more than common; and the raw wind chills my very heart. Come, let us be gone, 'tis a melancholy night."

Then taking hold of her hand he drew it towards the path he besought her to go. Nouronihar unconsciously followed the attraction, for a thousand strange imaginations occupied her spirit. She passed the large round of honeysuckles, her favourite resort, without ever vouchsafing it a glance, yet Gulchenrouz could not help snatching off a few shoots in his way, though he ran as if a wild beast were behind.

The young females seeing him approach in such haste, and according to custom expecting a dance, instantly assembled in a circle and took each other by the hand, but Gulchenrouz coming up out of breath, fell down at once on the grass. This accident struck with consternation the whole of this frolicsome party, whilst Nouronihar, half distracted, and overcome both by the violence of her exercise and the tumult of her thoughts, sunk feebly down at his side, cherished his cold hands in her bosom, and chafed his temples with a fragrant unguent. At length he came to himself, and wrapping up his head in the robe of his cousin, entreated that she would not return to the harem. He was afraid of being snapped at by Shaban his tutor, a wrinkled old eunuch of a surly disposition, for having interrupted the stated walk of Nouronihar, he dreaded lest the churl should take it amiss. The whole of this sprightly group, sitting round upon a mossy knole, began to entertain themselves with various pastimes, whilst their superintendents the eunuchs were gravely conversing at a distance. The nurse of the emir's daughter observing her pupil sit ruminating with her eyes on the ground, endeavoured to amuse her with diverting tales, to which Gulchenrouz, who had already forgotten his inquietudes, listened with a breathless attention. He laughed; he clapped his hands; and passed a hundred little tricks on the whole of the company, without omitting the eunuchs, whom he provoked to run after him, in spite of their age and decrepitude.

During these occurrences the moon arose, the wind subsided, and the evening became so serene and inviting that a resolution was taken to sup on the spot. Sutlememe, who excelled in dressing a salad, having filled large bowls of porcelain with eggs of small birds, curds turned with citron juice, slices of cucumber, and the inmost leaves of delicate herbs, handed it round from one to another, and gave each their shares in a large spoon of cocknos. Gulchenrouz nestling as usual in the bosom of Nouronihar, pouted out his vermillion little lips against the offer of Sutlememe, and would take it only from the hand of his cousin, on whose mouth he hung like a bee inebriated with the quintessence of flowers. One of the eunuchs ran to fetch melons, whilst others were employed in showering down almonds from the branches that overhung this amiable party.

In the midst of this festive scene there appeared a light on the top of the highest mountain, which attracted the notice of every eye. This light was not less bright than the moon when at full, and might have been taken for her had it not been that the moon was already risen. The phenomenon occasioned a general surprise, and no one could conjecture the cause. It could not be a fire, for the light was clear and bluish; nor had meteors ever been seen of that magnitude or splendour. This strange light faded for a moment, and immediately renewed its brightness. It first appeared motionless at the foot of the rock, whence it darted in an instant to sparkle in a thicket of palm trees, from thence it glided along the torrent, and at last fixed in a glen that was narrow and dark. The moment it had taken its direction, Gulchenrouz, whose heart always trembled at any thing sudden or rare, drew Nouronihar by the robe, and anxiously requested her to return to the harem. The women were importunate in seconding the entreaty, but the curiosity of the emir's daughter prevailed. She not only refused to go back, but resolved at all hazards to pursue the appearance. Whilst they were debating what was best to be done, the light shot forth so dazzling a blaze that they all fled away shrieking. Nouronihar followed them a few steps, but coming to the turn of a little bye path stopped, and went back alone. As she ran with an alertness peculiar to herself, it was not long before she came to the place where they had just been supping. The globe of fire now appeared stationary in the glen, and burned in majestic stillness. Nouronihar compressing her hands upon her bosom, hesitated for some moments to advance. The solitude of her situation was new; the silence of the night awful; and every object inspired sensations which till then she never had felt. The affright of Gulchenrouz recurred to her mind; and she a thousand times turned to go back, but this luminous appearance was always before her. Urged on by an irresistible impulse, she continued to approach it in defiance of every obstacle that opposed her progress.

At length she arrived at the opening of the glen, but instead of coming up to the light, she found herself surrounded by darkness, except that at a considerable distance a faint spark glimmered by fits. She stopped a second time: the sound of waterfalls mingling their murmurs, the hollow rustlings amongst the palm branches, and the funereal screams of the birds from their rifted trunks, all conspired to fill her with terror. She imagined every moment that she trod on some venomous reptile. All the stories of malignant Dives, and dismal Goules thronged into her memory, but her curiosity was notwithstanding more predominant than her fears. She therefore firmly entered a winding track that led towards the spark, but being a stranger to the path, she had not gone far till she began to repent of her rashness.

"Alas!" said she, "that I were but in those secure and illuminated apartments where my evenings glided on with Gulchenrouz! Dear child, how would thy heart flutter with terror wert thou wandering in these wild solitudes like me."

At the close of this apostrophe she regained her road, and coming to steps hewn out in the rock ascended them undismayed. The light, which was now gradually enlarging, appeared above her on the summit of the mountain. At length she distinguished a plaintive and melodious union of voices proceeding from a sort of cavern, that resembled the dirges which are sung over tombs. A sound likewise like that which arises from the filling of baths, at the same time struck her ear. She continued ascending, and discovered large wax torches in full blaze planted here and there in the fissures of the rock. This preparation filled her with fear, whilst the subtle and potent odour which the torches exhaled caused her to sink almost lifeless at the entrance of the grot.

Casting her eyes within in this kind of trance, she beheld a large cistern of gold filled with a water, whose vapour distilled on her face a dew of the essence of roses. A soft symphony resounded through the grot. On the sides of the cistern she noticed appendages of royalty; diadems and feathers of the heron, all sparkling with carbuncles. Whilst her attention was fixed on this display of magnificence, the music ceased, and a voice instantly demanded:

"For what monarch were these torches kindled, this bath prepared, and these habiliments? which belong not only to the sovereigns of the earth, but even to the talismanic powers!"

To which a second voice answered:

"They are for the charming daughter of the emir Fakreddin."

"What," replied the first, "for that trifler who consumes her time with a giddy child, immersed in softness, and who at best can make but an enervated husband?"

"And can she," rejoined the other voice, "be amused with such empty trifles, whilst the Caliph, the sovereign of the world, he who is destined to enjoy the treasures of the preadimite sultans, a prince six feet high, and whose eyes pervade the inmost soul of a female, is inflamed with the love of her? no, she will be wise enough to answer that passion alone that can aggrandize her glory. No doubt she will, and despise the puppet of her fancy; then all the riches this place contains, as well as the carbuncle of Giamschid shall be hers."

"You judge right," returned the first voice, "and I haste to Istakar to prepare the palace of subterranean fire for the reception of the bridal pair."

The voices ceased, the torches were extinguished, the most entire darkness succeeded, and Nouronihar recovering with a start, found herself reclined on a sofa in the harem of her father. She clapped her hands, and immediately came together Gulchenrouz and her women, who, in despair at having lost her, had despatched eunuchs to seek her in every direction.

Shaban appeared with the rest, and began to reprimand her with an air of consequence:

"Little impertinent," said he, "whence got you false keys? or are you beloved of some genius that hath given you a picklock? I will try the extent of your power; come, to your chamber! through the two sky-lights, and expect not the company of Gulchenrouz. Be expeditious! I will shut you up in the double tower."

At these menaces Nouronihar indignantly raised her head, opened on Shaban her black eyes, which since the important dialogue of the enchanted grot were considerably enlarged, and said:

"Go, speak thus to slaves! but learn to reverence her who is born to give laws, and subject all to her power."

She was proceeding in the same style, but was interrupted by a sudden exclamation of,

"The Caliph! the Caliph!"

The curtains at once were thrown open, and the slaves prostrate in double rows, whilst poor little Gulchenrouz hid himself beneath the elevation of a sofa. At first appeared a file of black eunuchs trailing after them long trains of muslin embroidered with gold, and holding in their hands censers, which dispensed as they passed the grateful perfume of the wood of aloes. Next marched Bababalouk with a solemn strut, and tossing his head as not over pleased at the visit. Vathek came close after superbly robed; his gait was unembarrassed and noble, and his presence would have engaged admiration, though he had not been the sovereign of the world. He approached Nouronihar with a throbbing heart, and seemed enraptured at the full effulgence of her radiant eyes, of which he had before caught but a few glimpses; but she instantly depressed them, and her confusion augmented her beauty.

Bababalouk, who was a thorough adept in coincidences of this nature, and knew that the worst game should be played with the best face, immediately made a signal for all to retire, and no sooner did he perceive beneath the sofa the little one's feet, than he drew him forth without ceremony, set him upon his shoulders, and lavished on him as he went off a thousand odious caresses. Gulchenrouz cried out, and resisted till his cheeks became the colour of the blossom of the pomegranite, and the tears that started into his eyes shot forth a gleam of indignation. He cast a significant glance at Nouronihar, which the Caliph noticing, asked:

"Is that then your Gulchenrouz?"

"Sovereign of the world," answered she, "spare my cousin, whose innocence and gentleness deserve not your anger!"

"Take comfort," said Vathek with a smile, "he is in good hands. Bababalouk is fond of children, and never goes without sweetmeats and comfits."

The daughter of Fakreddin was abashed; and suffered Gulchenrouz to be borne away without adding a word. The tumult of her bosom betrayed her confusion; and Vathek becoming still more impassioned, gave a loose to his frenzy, which had only not subdued the last faint strugglings of reluctance, when the emir suddenly bursting in, threw his face upon the ground at the feet of the Caliph, and said:

"Commander of the faithful, abase not yourself to the meanness of your slave."

"No, emir," replied Vathek, "I raise her to an equality with myself; I declare her my wife; and the glory of your race shall extend from one generation to another."

"Alas! my lord," said Fakreddin, as he plucked off the honours of his beard, "cut short the days of your faithful servant rather than force him to depart from his word. Nouronihar, as her hands evince, is solemnly promised to Gulchenrouz, the son of my bother, Ali Hassan; they are united also in heart; their faith is mutually plighted; and affiances so sacred cannot be broken."

"What, then," replied the Caliph bluntly, "would you surrender this divine beauty to a husband more womanish than herself? And can you imagine that I will suffer her charms to decay in hands so inefficient and nerveless? No! she is destined to live out her life within my embraces: such is my will: retire, and disturb not the night I devote to the homage of her charms."

The irritated emir drew forth his sabre, presented it to Vathek, and stretching out his neck, said in a firm tone of voice:

"Strike your unhappy host my lord! he has lived long enough, since he hath seen the prophet's vicegerent violate the rights of hospitality."

At his uttering these words, Nouronihar unable to support any longer the conflict of her passions, sunk down in a swoon. Vathek, both terrified for her life, and furious at an opposition to his will, bade Fakreddin assist his daughter, and withdrew, darting his terrible look at the unfortunate emir, who suddenly fell backward bathed in a sweat, cold as the damp of death.

Gulchenrouz, who had escaped from the hands of Bababalouk, and was that instant returned, called out for help as loudly as he could, not having strength to afford it himself. Pale and panting, the poor child attempted to revive Nouronihar by caresses, and it happened that the thrilling warmth of his lips restored her to life. Fakreddin beginning also to recover from the look of the Caliph, with difficulty tottered to a seat, and after warily casting round his eye to see if this dangerous prince were gone, sent for Shaban and Sutlememe, and said to them apart—

"My friends, violent evils require as violent remedies; the Caliph has brought desolation and horror into my family, and how shall we resist his power? Another of his looks will send me to my grave. Fetch then that narcotic powder which the Dervise brought me from Aracan. A dose of it, the effect of which will continue three days, must be administered to each of these children. The Caliph will believe them to be dead, for they will have all the appearance of death. We shall go as if to inter them in the cave of Meimoune, at the entrance of the great desert of sand, and near the cabin of my dwarfs. When all the spectators shall be withdrawn, you, Shaban, and four select eunuchs shall convey them to the lake, where provision shall be ready to support them a month; for, one day allotted to the surprise this event will occasion, five to the tears, a fortnight to reflection, and the rest to prepare for renewing his progress, will, according to my calculation, fill up the whole time that Vathek will tarry, and I shall then be freed from his intrusion."

"Your plan," said Sutlememe, "is a good one, if it can but be effected. I have remarked that Nouronihar is well able to support the glances of the Caliph, and that he is far from being sparing of them to her; be assured therefore, notwithstanding her fondness for Gulchenrouz, she will never remain quiet while she knows him to be here, unless we can persuade her that both herself and Gulchenrouz are really dead, and that they were conveyed to those rocks for a limited season to expiate the little faults of which their love was the cause. We will add that we killed ourselves in despair, and that your dwarfs whom they never yet saw will preach to them delectable sermons. I will engage that every thing shall succeed to the bent of your wishes."

"Be it so," said Fakreddin; "I approve your proposal; let us lose not a moment to give it effect." They forthwith hastened to seek for the powder, which being mixed in a sherbet was immediately drunk by Gulchenrouz and Nouronihar. Within the space of an hour both were seized with violent palpitations, and a general numbness gradually ensued. They arose from the floor, where they had remained ever since the Caliph's departure, and ascending to the sofa, reclined themselves at full length upon it, clasped in each other's embraces.

"Cherish me, my dear Nouronihar," said Gulchenrouz; "put thy hand upon my heart, for it feels as if it were frozen. Alas!

thou art as cold as myself! hath the Caliph murdered us both with his terrible look?"

"I am dying," cried she in a faltering voice; "press me closer, I am ready to expire!"

"Let us die then together," answered the little Gulchenrouz, whilst his breast laboured with a convulsive sigh; "let me at least breathe forth my soul on thy lips."

They spoke no more, and became as dead.

Immediately the most piercing cries were heard through the harem, whilst Shaban and Sutlememe personated with great adroitness the parts of persons in despair. The emir, who was sufficiently mortified to be forced into such untoward expedients, and had now for the first time made a trial of his powder, was under no necessity of counterfeiting grief. The slaves, who had flocked together from all quarters, stood motionless at the spectacle before them. All lights were extinguished save two lamps, which shed a wan glimmering over the faces of these lovely flowers, that seemed to be faded in the spring-time of life. Funeral vestments were prepared; their bodies were washed with rose water; their beautiful tresses were braided and incensed; and they were wrapped in symars whiter than alabaster. At the moment that their attendants were placing two wreaths of their favourite jasamines on their brows, the Caliph, who had just heard the tragical catastrophe, arrived. He looked not less pale and haggard than the goules that wander at night among graves. Forgetful of himself and every one else, he broke through the midst of the slaves, fell prostrate at the foot of the sofa, beat his bosom, called himself "atrocious murderer," and invoked upon his head a thousand imprecations. With a trembling hand he raised the veil that covered the countenance of Nouronihar, and uttering a loud shriek fell lifeless on the floor. The chief of the eunuchs dragged him off with horrible grimaces, and repeated as he went:

"Aye, I foresaw she would play you some ungracious turn."

No sooner was the Caliph gone than the emir commanded biers to be brought, and forbade that any one should enter the harem. Every window was fastened; all instruments of music were broken; and the Imams began to recite their prayers. Towards the close of this melancholy day Vathek sobbed in silence, for they had been forced to compose with anodynes his convulsions of rage and desperation.

At the dawn of the succeeding morning the wide folding doors of the palace were set open, and the funeral procession moved forward for the mountain. The wailful cries of "La Ilah illa Alla," reached to the Caliph, who was eager to cicatrize himself and attend the ceremonial; nor could he have been dissuaded, had not his excessive weakness disabled him from walking. At the few first steps he fell on the ground, and his people were obliged to lay him on a bed, where he remained many days in such a state of insensibility as excited compassion in the emir himself.

When the procession was arrived at the grot of Meimoune, Shaban and Sutlememe dismissed the whole of the train excepting the four confidential eunuchs who were appointed to remain. After resting some moments near the biers which had been left in the open air, they caused them to be carried to the brink of a small lake whose banks were overgrown with a hoary moss. This was the great resort of herons and storks, which preyed continually on little blue fishes. The dwarfs, instructed by the emir, soon repaired thither, and with the help of the eunuchs began to construct cabins of rushes and reeds, a work in which they had admirable skill. A magazine also was contrived for provisions, with a small oratory for themselves, and a pyramid of wood neatly piled, to furnish the necessary fuel, for the air was bleak in the hollows of the mountains.

At evening two fires were kindled on the brink of the lake, and the two lovely bodies taken from their biers were carefully deposited upon a bed of dried leaves within the same cabin. The dwarfs began to recite the koran with their clear shrill voices, and Shaban and Sutlememe stood at some distance anxiously waiting the effects of the powder. At length Nouronihar and Gulchenrouz faintly stretched out their arms, and gradually opening their eyes began to survey with looks of increasing amazement every object around them. They even attempted to rise, but for want of strength fell back again. Sutlememe on this administered a cordial which the emir had taken care to provide.

Gulchenrouz thoroughly aroused sneezed out aloud, and raising himself with an effort that expressed his surprise, left the cabin, and inhaled the fresh air with the greatest avidity.

"Yes," said he, "I breathe again! again do I exist! I hear sounds! I behold a firmament spangled over with stars!"

Nouronihar catching these beloved accents extricated herself from the leaves, and ran to clasp Gulchenrouz to her bosom. The first objects she remarked were their long symars, their garlands of flowers, and their naked feet: she hid her face in her hands to reflect. The vision of the enchanted bath, the despair of her father, and more vividly than both, the majestic figure of Vathek recurred to her memory. She recollected also, that herself and Gulchenrouz had been sick and dying; but all these images bewildered her mind. Not knowing where she was, she turned her eyes on all sides, as if to recognise the surrounding scene. This singular lake, those flames reflected from its glassy surface, the pale hues of its banks, the romantic cabins, the bull-rushes that sadly waved their drooping heads, the storks whose melancholy cries blended with the shrill voices of the dwarfs, every thing conspired to persuade them that the angel of death had opened the portal of some other world.

Gulchenrouz on his part, lost in wonder, clung to the neck of his cousin. He believed himself in the region of phantoms, and was terrified at the silence she preserved. At length addressing her:

"Speak," said he; "where are we! do you not see those spectres that are stirring the burning coals? Are they the Monker and Nakir, come to throw us into them? Does the fatal bridge cross this lake, whose solemn stillness perhaps conceals from us an abyss, in which for whole ages we shall be doomed incessantly to sink?"

"No my children," said Sutlememe going towards them; "take comfort, the exterminating angel who conducted our souls hither after yours, hath assured us that the chastisement of your indolent and voluptuous life shall be restricted to a certain series of years, which you must pass in this dreary abode, where the sun is scarcely visible, and where the soil yields neither fruits nor flowers. These," continued she, pointing to the dwarfs, "will provide for our wants; for souls so mundane as ours retain too strong a tincture of their earthly extraction. Instead of meats, your food will be nothing but rice, and your bread shall be moistened in the fogs that brood over the surface of the lake."

At this desolating prospect the poor children burst into tears, and prostrated themselves before the dwarfs, who perfectly supported their characters, and delivered an excellent discourse of a customary length upon the sacred camel, which after a thousand years was to convey them to the paradise of the faithful.

The sermon being ended and ablutions performed, they praised Alla and the prophet, supped very indifferently, and retired to their withered leaves. Nouronihar and her little cousin consoled themselves on finding that, though dead, they yet lay in one cabin. Having slept well before, the remainder of the night was spent in conversation on what had befallen them; and both, from a dread of apparitions, betook themselves for protection to one another's arms.

In the morning, which was lowering and rainy, the dwarfs mounted high poles like minarets, and called them to prayers.

The whole congregation, which consisted of Sutlememe, Shaban, the four eunuchs, and some storks, were already assembled. The two children came forth from their cabin with a slow and dejected pace. As their minds were in a tender and melancholy mood, their devotions were performed with fervour. No sooner were they finished than Gulchenrouz demanded of Sutlememe and the rest, "how they happened to die so opportunely for his cousin and himself."

"We killed ourselves," returned Sutlememe, "in despair at your death."

On this, said Nouronihar, who notwithstanding what was past, had not yet forgotten her vision:

"And the Caliph, is he also dead of his grief? and will he likewise come hither?"

The dwarfs, who were prepared with an answer, most demurely replied:

"Vathek is damned beyond all redemption!"

"I readily believe so," said Gulchenrouz; "and am glad from my heart to hear it, for I am convinced it was his horrible look that sent us hither, to listen to sermons and mess upon rice."

One week passed away on the side of the lake unmarked by any variety; Nouronihar ruminating on the grandeur of which death had deprived her, and Gulchenrouz applying to prayers and to panniers along with the dwarfs, who infinitely pleased him. Whilst this scene of innocence was exhibiting in the mountains, the Caliph presented himself to the emir in a new light. The instant he recovered the use of his senses, with a voice that made Bababalouk quake, he thundered out:

"Perfidious Giaour! I renounce thee for ever! it is thou who hast slain my beloved Nouronihar! and I supplicate the pardon of Mahomet, who would have preserved her to me had I been more wise. Let water be brought to perform my ablutions, and let the pious Fakreddin be called to offer up his prayers with mine, and reconcile me to him. Afterwards we will go together and visit the sepulchre of the unfortunate Nouronihar. I am resolved to become a hermit, and consume the residue of my days on this mountain, in hope of expiating my crimes."

Nouronihar was not altogether so content, for though she felt a fondness for Gulchenrouz, who to augment the attachment, had been left at full liberty with her, yet she still regarded him as but a bauble that bore no competition with the carbuncle of Giamschid. At times she indulged doubts on the mode of her being, and scarcely could believe that the dead had all the wants and the whims of the living. To gain satisfaction, however, on so perplexing a topic, she arose one morning whilst all were asleep with a breathless caution from the side of Gulchenrouz, and after having given him a soft kiss, began to follow the windings of the lake till it terminated with a rock whose top was accessible though lofty. This she clambered up with considerable toil, and having reached the summit, set forward in a run like a doe that unwittingly follows her hunter. Though she skipped along with the alertness of an antelope, yet at intervals she was forced to desist, and rest beneath the tamarisks to recover her breath. Whilst she, thus reclined, was occupied with her little reflections on the apprehension that she had some knowledge of the place, Vathek, who finding himself that morning but ill at ease, had gone forth before the dawn, presented himself on a sudden to her view. Motionless with surprise, he durst not approach the figure before him, which lay shrouded up in a symar extended on the ground, trembling and pale, but yet lovely to behold. At length Nouronihar, with a mixture of pleasure and affliction, raising her fine eyes to him, said:

"My lord, are you come hither to eat rice and hear sermons with me?"

"Beloved phantom!" cried Vathek, "dost thou speak? hast thou the same graceful form? the same radiant features? art thou palpable likewise?" and eagerly embracing her he added, "here are limbs and a bosom animated with a gentle warmth! what can such a prodigy mean?"

Nouronihar with diffidence answered:

"You know my lord that I died on the night you honoured me with your visit; my cousin maintains it was from one of your glances, but I cannot believe him, for to me they seem not so dreadful. Gulchenrouz died with me, and we were both brought into a region of desolation, where we are fed with a wretched diet. If you be dead also, and are come hither to join us, I pity your lot, for you will be stunned with the clang of the dwarfs and the storks. Besides, it is mortifying in the extreme that you as well as myself should have lost the treasures of the subterranean palace."

At the mention of the subterranean palace, the Caliph suspended his caresses, which indeed had proceeded pretty far, to seek from Nouronihar an explanation of her meaning. She then recapitulated her vision—what immediately followed—and the history of her pretended death; adding also a description of the palace of expiation from whence she had fled; and all in a manner that would have extorted his laughter, had not the thoughts of Vathek been too deeply engaged. No sooner, however, had she ended, than he again clasped her to his bosom, and said:

"Light of my eyes! the mystery is unravelled; we both are alive! Your father is a cheat, who for the sake of dividing hath deluded us both; and the Giaour, whose design, as far as I can discover, is that we shall proceed together, seems scarce a whit better. It shall be some time at least before he find us in his palace of fire. Your lovely little person in my estimation is far more precious than all the treasures of the preadimite sultans, and I wish to possess it at pleasure, and in open day for many a moon, before I go to burrow under ground like a mole."

"Forget this little trifler Gulchenrouz, and"—

"Ah, my lord," interposed Nouronihar, "let me entreat that you do him no evil."

"No, no," replied Vathek, "I have already bid you forbear to alarm yourself for him. He has been brought up too much on milk and sugar to stimulate my jealousy. We will leave him with the dwarfs, who by the bye are my old acquaintances; their company will suit him far better than yours. As to other matters, I will return no more to your father's. I want not to have my ears dinned by him and his dotards with the violation of the rights of hospitality; as if it were less an honour for you to espouse the sovereign of the world, than a girl dressed up like a boy."

Nouronihar could find nothing to oppose in a discourse so eloquent. She only wished the amorous monarch had discovered more ardour for the carbuncle of Giamschid; but flattered herself it would gradually increase, and therefore yielded to his will with the most bewitching submission.

When the Caliph judged it proper he called for Bababalouk, who was asleep in the cave of Meimoune, and dreaming that the phantom of Nouronihar having mounted him once more on her swing, had just given him such a jerk that he one moment soared above the mountains, and the next sunk into the abyss. Starting from his sleep at the voice of his master, he ran gasping for breath, and had nearly fallen backward at the sight, as he believed, of the spectre, by whom he had so lately been haunted in his dream.

"Ah my lord," cried he, recoiling ten steps, and covering his eyes with both hands, "do you then perform the office of a goule? 'Tis true you have dug up the dead, yet hope not to make her your prey; for after all she hath caused me to suffer, she is even wicked enough to prey upon you."

"Cease thy folly," said Vathek, "and thou shalt soon be convinced that it is Nouronihar herself, alive and well, whom I clasp to my breast. Go only, and pitch my tents in the neighbouring valley. There will I fix my abode with this beautiful tulip, whose colours I soon shall restore. There exert thy best endeavours to procure whatever can augment the enjoyments of life, till I shall disclose to thee more of my will."

The news of so unlucky an event soon reached the ears of the emir, who abandoned himself to grief and despair, and began, as did all his old greybeards, to begrime his visage with ashes. A total supineness ensued; travellers were no longer entertained, no more plasters were spread, and instead of the charitable activity that had distinguished this asylum, the whole of its inhabitants exhibited only faces of a half cubit long, and uttered groans that accorded with their forlorn situation.

Though Fakreddin bewailed his daughter as lost to him for ever, yet Gulchenrouz was not forgotten. He despatched immediate instruction to Sutlememe, Shaban, and the dwarfs, enjoining them not to undeceive the child in respect to his state, but under some pretence to convey him far from the lofty rock at the extremity of the lake, to a place which he should appoint, as safer from danger; for he suspected that Vathek intended him evil.

Gulchenrouz in the mean while was filled with amazement at not finding his cousin; nor were the dwarfs at all less surprised; but Sutlememe, who had more penetration, immediately guessed what had happened. Gulchenrouz was amused with the delusive hope of once more embracing Nouronihar in the interior recesses of the mountains, where the ground, strewed over with orange blossoms and jasamines, offered beds much more inviting than the withered leaves in their cabin, where they might accompany with their voices the sounds of their lutes, and chase butterflies in concert. Sutlememe was far gone in this sort of description when one of the four eunuchs beckoned her aside to apprise her of the arrival of a messenger from their fraternity, who had explained the secret of the flight of Nouronihar, and brought the commands of the emir. A council with Shaban and the dwarfs was immediately held. Their baggage being stowed in consequence of it, they embarked in a shallop and quietly sailed with the little one, who acquiesced in all their proposals. Their voyage proceeded in the same manner, till they came to the place where the lake sinks beneath the hollow of the rock, but as soon as the bark had entered it, and Gulchenrouz found himself surrounded with darkness, he was seized with a dreadful consternation, and incessantly uttered the most piercing outcries; for he now was persuaded he should actually be damned for having taken too many little freedoms in his life-time with his cousin.

But let us return to the Caliph, and her who ruled over his heart. Bababalouk had pitched the tents, and closed up the extremities of the valley with magnificent screens of India cloth, which were guarded by Ethiopian slaves with their drawn sabres. To preserve the verdure of this beautiful enclosure in its natural freshness, the white eunuchs went continually round it with their red water vessels. The waving of fans was heard near the imperial pavilion, where by the voluptuous light that glowed through the muslins, the Caliph enjoyed at full view all the attractions of Nouronihar. Inebriated with delight, he was all ear to her charming voice which accompanied the lute; while she was not less captivated with his descriptions of Samarah and the tower full of wonders, but especially with his relation of the adventure of the ball, and the chasm of the Giaour with its ebony portal.

In this manner they conversed for a day and a night; they bathed together in a basin of black marble, which admirably relieved the fairness of Nouronihar. Bababalouk, whose good graces this beauty had regained, spared no attention that their repasts might be served up with the minutest exactness: some exquisite rariety was ever placed before them; and he sent even to Schiraz for that fragrant and delicious wine which had been hoarded up in bottles prior to the birth of Mahomet. He had excavated little ovens in the rock to bake the nice manchets which were prepared by the hands of Nouronihar, from whence they had derived a flavour so grateful to Vathek, that he regarded the ragouts of his other wives as entirely maukish; whilst they would have died at the emir's of chagrin at finding themselves so neglected, if Fakreddin, notwithstanding his resentment, had not taken pity upon them.

The sultana Dilara, who till then had been the favourite, took this dereliction of the Caliph to heart with a vehemence natural to her character; for during her continuance in favour she had imbibed from Vathek many of his extravagant fancies, and was fired with impatience to behold the superb tombs of Istakar, and the palace of forty columns; besides, having been brought up amongst the magi, she had fondly cherished the idea of the Caliph's devoting himself to the worship of fire; thus his voluptuous and desultory life with her rival was to her a double source of affliction. The transient piety of Vathek had occasioned her some serious alarms, but the present was an evil of far greater magnitude. She resolved therefore without hesitation to write to Carathis, and acquaint her that all things went ill; that they had eaten, slept, and revelled at an old emir's, whose sanctity was very formidable, and that after all the prospect of possessing the treasures of the preadimite sultans was no less remote than before. This letter was entrusted to the care of two woodmen who were at work on one of the great forests of the mountains, and being acquainted with the shortest cuts, arrived in ten days at Samarah.

The princess Carathis was engaged at chess with Morakanabad, when the arrival of these wood-fellers was announced. She, after some weeks of Vathek's absence, had forsaken the upper regions of her tower, because everything appeared in confusion among the stars, whom she consulted relative to the fate of her son. In vain did she renew her fumigations, and extend herself on the roof to obtain mystic visions, nothing more could she see in her dreams than pieces of brocade, nosegays of flowers, and other unmeaning gewgaws. These disappointments had thrown her into a state of dejection which no drug in her power was sufficient to remove. Her only resource was in Morakanabad, who was a good man, and endowed with a decent share of confidence, yet whilst in her company he never thought himself on roses.

No person knew aught of Vathek, and a thousand ridiculous stories were propagated at his expense. The eagerness of Carathis may be easily guessed at receiving the letter, as well as her rage at reading the dissolute conduct of her son.

"Is it so," said she; "either I will perish, or Vathek shall enter the palace of fire. Let me expire in flames, provided he may reign on the throne of Soliman!"

Having said this, and whirled herself round in a magical manner, which struck Morakanabad with such terror as caused him to recoil, she ordered her great camel Alboufaki to be brought, and the hideous Nerkes with the unrelenting Cafour to attend.

"I require no other retinue," said she to Morakanabad: "I am going on affairs of emergency, a truce therefore to parade! Take you care of the people, fleece them well in my absence, for we shall expend large sums, and one knows not what may betide."

The night was uncommonly dark, and a pestilential blast ravaged the plain of Catoul that would have deterred any other traveller however urgent the call; but Carathis enjoyed most whatever filled others with dread. Nerkes concurred in opinion with her, and Cafour had a particular predilection for a pestilence. In the morning this accomplished caravan, with the wood-fellers who directed their route, halted on the edge of an extensive marsh, from whence so noxious a vapour arose as would have destroyed any animal but Alboufaki, who naturally inhaled these malignant fogs. The peasants entreated their convoy not to sleep in this place.

"To sleep," cried Carathis, "what an excellent thought! I never sleep but for visions; and as to my attendants, their occupations are too many to close the only eye they each have."

The poor peasants, who were not over pleased with their party, remained open-mouthed with surprise.

Carathis alighted as well as her negresses, and severally stripping off their outer garments, they all ran in their drawers to cull from those spots where the sun shone fiercest, the venomous plants that grew on the marsh. This provision was made for the family of the emir, and whoever might retard the expedition to Istakar. The woodmen were overcome with fear when they beheld these three horrible phantoms run, and not much relishing the company of Alboufaki, stood aghast at the command of Carathis to set forward, notwithstanding it was noon, and the heat fierce enough to calcine even rocks. In spite, however, of every remonstrance, they were forced implicitly to submit.

Alboufaki, who delighted in solitude, constantly snorted whenever he perceived himself near a habitation, and Carathis, who was apt to spoil him with indulgence, as constantly turned him aside; so that the peasants were precluded from procuring subsistence; for the milch goats and ewes which Providence had sent towards the district they traversed, to refresh travellers with their milk, all fled at the sight of the hideous animal and his strange riders. As to Carathis, she needed no common aliment; for her invention had previously furnished her with an opiate to stay her stomach, some of which she imparted to her mutes.

At the fall of night Alboufaki making a sudden stop, stamped with his foot, which to Carathis, who understood his paces, was a certain indication that she was near the confines of some cemetery. The moon shed a bright light on the spot, which served to discover a long wall with a large door in it standing ajar, and so high that Alboufaki might easily enter. The miserable guides, who perceived their end approaching, humbly implored Carathis, as she had now so good an opportunity, to inter them, and immediately gave up the ghost. Nerkes and Cafour, whose wit was of a style peculiar to themselves, were by no means parsimonious of it on the folly of these poor people, nor could any thing have been found more suited to their taste than the site of the burying ground, and the sepulchres which its precincts contained. There were at least two thousand of them on the declivity of a hill; some in the form of pyramids, others like columns, and in short the variety of their shapes was endless. Carathis was too much immersed in her sublime contemplations to stop at the view, charming as it appeared in her eyes. Pondering the advantages that might accrue from her present situation, she could not forbear to exclaim:

"So beautiful a cemetery must be haunted by Gouls, and they want not for intelligence! having heedlessly suffered my guides to expire, I will apply for directions to them, and as an inducement, will invite them to regale on these fresh corpses."

After this short soliloquy, she beckoned to Nerkes and Cafour, and made signs with her fingers, as much as to say:

"Go, knock against the sides of the tombs, and strike up your delightful warblings, that are so like to those of the guests whose company I wish to obtain."

The negresses, full of joy at the behests of their mistress, and promising themselves much pleasure from the society of the Gouls, went with an air of conquest, and began their knockings at the tombs. As their strokes were repeated, a hollow noise was heard in the earth, the surface hove up into heaps, and the Gouls on all sides protruded their noses to inhale the effluvia which the carcasses of the woodmen began to emit.

They assembled before a sarcophagus of white marble, where Carathis was seated between the bodies of her miserable guides. The princess received her visitants with distinguished politeness, and when supper was ended, proceeded with them to business. Having soon learnt from them every thing she wished to discover, it was her intention to set forward forthwith on her journey, but her negresses, who were forming tender connections with the Gouls, importuned her with all their fingers to wait, at least till the dawn. Carathis, however, being chastity in the abstract, and an implacable enemy to love and repose, at once rejected their prayer, mounted Alboufaki, and commanded them to take their seats in a moment. Four days and four nights she continued her route, without turning to the right hand or left; on the fifth she traversed the mountains and half-burnt forests, and arrived on the sixth before the beautiful screens which concealed from all eyes the voluptuous wanderings of her son.

It was day-break, and the guards were snoring on their posts in careless security, when the rough trot of Alboufaki awoke them in consternation. Imagining that a group of spectres ascended from the abyss was approaching, they all without ceremony took to their heels. Vathek was at that instant with Nouronihar in the bath, hearing tales and laughing at Bababalouk who related them; but no sooner did the outcry of his guards reach him, than he flounced from the water like a carp, and as soon threw himself back at the sight of Carathis, who advancing with her negresses upon Alboufaki, broke through the muslin awnings and veils of the pavilion. At this sudden apparition Nouronihar (for she was not at all times free from remorse) fancied that the moment of celestial vengeance was come, and clung about the Caliph in amorous despondence.

Carathis, still seated on her camel, foamed with indignation at the spectacle which obtruded itself on her chaste view. She thundered forth without check or mercy:

"Thou double-headed and four legged monster! what means all this winding and writhing? art thou not ashamed to be seen grasping this limber sapling, in preference to the sceptre of the preadimite sultans? Is it then for this paltry doxy that thou hast violated the conditions in the parchment of our Giaour? Is it on her thou hast lavished thy precious moments? Is this the fruit of the knowledge I have taught thee? Is this the end of thy journey? Tear thyself from the arms of this little simpleton; drown her in the water before me, and instantly follow my guidance."

In the first ebullition of his fury, Vathek resolved to make a skeleton of Alboufaki, and to stuff the skins of Carathis and her blacks; but the ideas of the Giaour, the palace of Istakar, the sabres, and the talismans, flashing before his imagination with the simultaneousness of lightning, he became more moderate, and said to his mother in a civil but decisive tone:

"Dread lady, you shall be obeyed; but I will not drown Nouronihar; she is sweeter to me than a Myrabolan comfit, and is enamoured of carbuncles, especially that of Giamschid, which hath also been promised to be conferred upon her; she therefore shall go along with us, for I intend to repose with her beneath the canopies of Soliman; I can sleep no more without her."

"Be it so," replied Carathis alighting, and at the same time committing Alboufaki to the charge of her women.

Nouronihar, who had not yet quitted her hold, began to take courage, and said with an accent of fondness to the Caliph:

"Dear sovereign of my soul! I will follow thee, if it be thy will beyond the Kaf, in the land of the Afrits. I will not hesitate to climb for thee the nest of the Simurgh, who, this lady excepted, is the most awful of created existences."

"We have here then," subjoined Carathis, "a girl both of courage and science."

Nouronihar had certainly both; but notwithstanding all her firmness, she could not help casting back a look of regret upon the graces of her little Gulchenrouz, and the days of tenderness she had participated with him. She even dropped a few tears, which Carathis observed, and inadvertently breathed out with a sigh:

"Alas! my gentle cousin, what will become of him!"

Vathek at this apostrophe knitted up his brows, and Carathis enquired what it could mean.

"She is preposterously sighing after a stripling with languishing eyes and soft hair who loves her," said the Caliph.

"Where is he?" asked Carathis. "I must be acquainted with this pretty child; for," added she, lowering her voice, "I design before I depart to regain the favour of the Giaour. There is nothing so delicious in his estimation as the heart of a delicate boy, palpitating with the first tumults of love."

Vathek as he came from the bath commanded Bababalouk to collect the women and other moveables of his harem, embody his troops, and hold himself in readiness to march in three days; whilst Carathis retired alone to a tent, where the Giaour solaced her with encouraging visions; but at length waking, she found at her feet Nerkes and Cafour, who informed her by their signs, that having led Alboufaki to the borders of a lake, to browse on some moss that looked tolerably venomous, they had discovered certain blue fishes of the same kind with those in the reservoir on the top of the tower.

"Ah, ah," said she, "I will go thither to them. These fish are past doubt of a species that by a small operation I can render oracular. They may tell me where this little Gulchenrouz is, whom I am bent upon sacrificing."

Having thus spoken, she immediately set out with her swarthy retinue.

It being but seldom that time is lost in the accomplishment of a wicked enterprise, Carathis and her negresses soon arrived at the lake, where, after burning the magical drugs with which they were always provided, they, stripping themselves naked, waded to their chins, Nerkes and Cafour waving torches around them, and Carathis pronouncing her barbarous incantations. The fishes with one accord thrust forth their heads from the water, which was violently rippled by the flutter of their fins, and at length finding themselves constrained by the potency of the charm, they opened their piteous mouths, said:

"From gills to tail we are yours; what seek ye to know?"

"Fishes," answered she, "I conjure you by your glittering scales, tell me where now is Gulchenrouz?"

"Beyond the rock," replied the shoal in full chorus: "will this content you? for we do not delight in expanding our mouths."

"It will," returned the princess: "I am not to learn that you like not long conversations; I will leave you therefore to repose, though I had other questions to propound."

The instant she had spoken the water became smooth, and the fishes at once disappeared.

Carathis, inflated with the venom of her projects, strode hastily over the rock, and found the amiable Gulchenrouz asleep in an arbour, whilst the two dwarfs were watching at his side, and ruminating their accustomed prayers. These diminutive personages possessed the gift of divining whenever an enemy to good Mussulmans approached; thus they anticipated the arrival of Carathis, who stopping short, said to herself:

"How placidly doth he recline his lovely little head! how pale and languishing are his looks! it is just the very child of my wishes!"

The dwarfs interrupted this delectable soliloquy by leaping instantly upon her, and scratching her face with their utmost zeal. But Nerkes and Cafour betaking themselves to the succour of their mistress, pinched the dwarfs so severely in return, that they both gave up the ghost, imploring Mahomet to inflict his sorest vengeance upon this wicked woman and all her houschold.

At the noise which this strange conflict occasioned in the valley, Gulchenrouz awoke, and bewildered with terror sprung impetuously upon an old fig-tree that rose against the acclivity of the rocks, from thence gained their summits, and ran for two hours without once looking back. At last, exhausted with fatigue, he fell as if dead into the arms of a good old Genius, whose fondness for the company of children had made it his sole occupation to protect them, and who, whilst performing his wonted rounds through the air, happening on the cruel Giaour at the instant of his growling in the horrible chasm, rescued the fifty little victims which the impiety of Vathek had devoted to his maw. These the Genius brought up in nests still higher than the clouds, and himself fixed his abode in a nest more capacious than the rest, from which he had expelled the possessors that had built it.

These inviolable asylums were defended against the Dives and the Afrits by waving streamers, on which were inscribed in characters of gold that flashed like lightning, the names of Alla and the prophet. It was there that Gulchenrouz, who as yet remained undeceived with respect to his pretended death, thought himself in the mansions of eternal peace. He admitted without fear the congratulations of his little friends, who were all assembled in the nest of the venerable Genius, and vied with each other in kissing his serene forehead and beautiful eye-lids. This he found to be the state congenial to his soul—remote from the inquietudes of earth—the impertinence of harems—the brutality of eunuchs—and the lubricity of women. In this peaceable society his days, months, and years glided on, nor was he less happy than the rest of his companions, for the Genius, instead of burdening his pupils with perishable riches, and the vain sciences of the world, conferred upon them the boon of perpetual childhood.

Carathis, unaccustomed to the loss of her prey, vented a thousand execrations on her negresses for not seizing the child, instead of amusing themselves with pinching to death the dwarfs, from which they could gain no advantage. She returned into the valley murmuring, and finding that her son was not risen from the arms of Nouronihar, discharged her ill-humour upon both. The idea, however, of departing next day for Istakar, and cultivating, through the good offices of the Giaour, an intimacy with Eblis himself, at length consoled her chagrin: but fate had ordained it otherwise.

In the evening, as Carathis was conversing with Dilara, who through her contrivance had become of the party, and whose taste resembled her own, Bababalouk came to acquaint her "that the sky towards Samarah looked of a fiery red, and seemed to portend some alarming disaster." Immediately recurring to her astrolabes and instruments of magic, she took the altitude of the planets, and discovered by her calculations, to her great mortification, that a formidable revolt had taken place at Samarah; that Motavakel, availing himself of the disgust which was inveterate against his brother had incited commotions amongst the populace, made himself master of the palace, and actually invested the great tower, to which Morakanabad had retired with a handful of the few that still remained faithful to Vathek.

"What," exclaimed she, "must I lose then my tower, my mutes, my negresses, my mummies, and worse than all, the laboratory, in which I have spent so many a night, without knowing, at least, if my hair-brained son will complete his adventure? No! I will not be the dupe! Immediately will I speed to support Morakanabad. By my formidable art the clouds shall sleet hail-stones in the faces of the assailants, and shafts of red-hot iron on their heads. I will spring mines of serpents and torpedoes from beneath them, and we shall soon see the stand they will make against such an explosion!"

Having thus spoken, Carathis hasted to her son, who was tranquilly banqueting with Nouronihar in his superb carnation coloured tent.

"Glutton that thou art," cried she, "were it not for me, thou wouldst soon find thyself the commander only of pies. Thy faithful subjects have abjured the faith they swore to thee.

Motavakel thy brother now reigns on the hill of pied horses; and had I not some slight resources in the tower, would not be easily persuaded to abdicate. But that time may not be lost, I shall only add four words: strike tent tonight; set forward; and beware how thou loiterest again by the way. Though thou hast forfeited the conditions of the parchment, I am not yet without hope; for it cannot be denied that thou hast violated to admiration the laws of hospitality by seducing the daughter of the emir, after having partaken of his bread and his salt. Such a conduct cannot but be delightful to the Giaour; and if on thy march thou canst signalize thyself by an additional crime, all will still go well, and thou shalt enter the palace of Soliman in triumph. Adieu! Alboufaki and my negresses are waiting."

The Caliph had nothing to offer in reply: he wished his mother a prosperous journey, and eat on till he had finished his supper. At midnight the camp broke up, amidst the flourishing of trumpets and other martial instruments; but loud indeed must have been the sound of the tymbals, to overpower the blubbering of the emir and his long-beards, who by an excessive profusion of tears had so far exhausted the radical moisture, that their eyes shrivelled up in their sockets, and their hairs dropped off by the roots. Nouronihar, to whom such a symphony was painful, did not grieve to get out of hearing. She accompanied the Caliph in the imperial litter, where they amused themselves with imagining the splendour which was soon to surround them. The other women, overcome with dejection, were dolefully rocked in their cages, whilst Dilara consoled herself with anticipating the joy of celebrating the rites of fire on the stately terraces of Istakar.

In four days they reached the spacious valley of Rocnabad. The season of spring was in all its vigour, and the grotesque branches of the almond trees in full blossom fantastically chequered the clear blue sky. The earth, variegated with hyacinths and jonquils, breathed forth a fragrance which diffused through the soul a divine repose. Myriads of bees, and scarce fewer of Santons had there taken up their abode. On the banks of the stream hives and oratories were alternately ranged, and their neatness and whiteness were set off by the deep green of the cypresses that spired up amongst them. These pious personages amused themselves with cultivating little gardens that abounded with flowers and fruits, especially musk-melons of the best flavour that Persia could boast. Sometimes dispersed over the meadow they entertained themselves with feeding peacocks whiter than snow, and turtles more blue than the sapphire. In this manner were they occupied when the harbingers of the imperial procession began to proclaim:

"Inhabitants of Rocnabad, prostrate yourselves on the brink of your pure waters, and tender your thanksgivings to heaven that vouchsafeth to shew you a ray of its glory; for lo! the commander of the faithful draws near."

The poor Santons, filled with holy energy, having bustled to light up wax torches in their oratories, and expand the koran on their ebony desks, went forth to meet the Caliph with baskets of honeycomb, dates, and melons. But whilst they were advancing in solemn procession and with measured steps, the horses, camels, and guards wantoned over their tulips and other flowers, and made a terrible havoc amongst them. The Santons could not help casting from one eye a look of pity on the ravages committing around them, whilst the other was fixed upon the Caliph and heaven. Nouronihar, enraptured with the scenery of a place which brought back to her remembrance the pleasing solitudes where her infancy had passed, entreated Vathek to stop, but he, suspecting that each oratory might be deemed by the Giaour a distinct habitation, commanded his pioneers to level them all. The Santons stood motionless with horror at the barbarous mandate, and at last broke out into lamentations, but these were uttered with so ill a grace, that Vathek bade his eunuchs to kick them from his presence.

He then descended from the litter with Nouronihar. They sauntered together in the meadow, and amused themselves with culling flowers, and passing a thousand pleasantries on each other. But the bees, who were staunch Mussulmans, thinking it their duty to revenge the insult on their dear masters the Santons, assembled so zealously to do it with effect, that the Caliph and Nouronihar were glad to find their tents prepared to receive them.

Bababalouk, who in capacity of purveyor, had acquitted himself with applause, as to peacocks and turtles, lost no time in consigning some dozens to the spit, and as many more to be fricasseed. Whilst they were feasting, laughing, carousing, and blaspheming at pleasure on the banquet so liberally furnished, the Moullahs, the Sheiks, the Cadis, and Imans of Schiraz (who seemed not to have met the Santons) arrived, leading by bridles of ribband, inscribed from the koran, a train of asses which were loaded with the choicest fruits the country could boast. Having presented their offerings to the Caliph, they petitioned him to honour their city and mosques with his presence.

"Fancy not," said Vathek, "that you can detain me. Your presents I condescend to accept, but beg you will let me be quiet, for I am not over fond of resisting temptation. Retire then. Yet, as it is not decent for personages so reverend to return on foot, and as you have not the appearance of expert riders, my eunuchs shall tie you on your asses with the precaution that your backs be not turned towards me, for they understand etiquette."

In this deputation were some high-stomached Sheiks, who taking Vathek for a fool, scrupled not to speak their opinion. These Bababalouk girded with double cords; and having well disciplined their asses with nettles behind, they all started with a preternatural alertness, plunging, kicking, and running foul of each other in the most ludicrous manner imaginable.

Nouronihar and the Caliph mutually contended who should most enjoy so degrading a sight. They burst out in volleys of laughter to see the old men and their asses fall into the stream. The leg of one was fractured, the shoulder of another dislocated, the teeth of a third dashed out, and the rest suffered still worse.

Two days more, undisturbed by fresh embassies, having been devoted to the pleasures of Rocnabad, the expedition proceeded, leaving Schiraz on the right, and verging towards a large plain, from whence were discernible on the edge of the horizon the dark summits of the mountains of Istakar.

At this prospect the Caliph and Nouronihar were unable to repress their transports. They bounded from their litter to the ground, and broke forth into such wild exclamations as amazed all within hearing. Interrogating each other, they shouted,

"Are we not approaching the radiant palace of light, or gardens more delightful than those of Sheddad?"

Infatuated mortals! they thus indulged delusive conjecture, unable to fathom the decrees of the Most High!

The good Genii who had not totally relinquished the superintendence of Vathek, repairing to Mahomet in the seventh heaven, said:

"Merciful Prophet! stretch forth thy propitious arms towards thy vicegerent, who is ready to fall irretrievably into the snare which his enemies the Dives have prepared to destroy him. The Giaour is awaiting his arrival in the abominable palace of fire, where if he once set his foot his perdition will be inevitable."

Mahomet answered with an air of indignation:

"He hath too well deserved to be resigned to himself; but I permit you to try if one effort more will be effectual to divert him from pursuing his ruin."

One of these beneficent Genii, assuming without delay the exterior of a shepherd, more renowned for his piety than all the Dervises and Santons of the region, took his station near a flock of white sheep on the slope of a hill, and began to pour forth from his flute such airs of pathetic melody, as subdued the very soul; and awakening remorse, drove far from it every frivolous fancy. At these energetic sounds, the sun hid himself beneath a gloomy cloud; and the waters of two little lakes, that were naturally clearer than chrystal, became a colour like blood. The whole of this superb assembly, was involuntarily drawn towards the declivity of the hill. With downcast eyes, they all stood abashed; each upbraiding himself with the evil he had done. The heart of Dilara palpitated; and the chief of the eunuchs, with a sigh of contrition, implored pardon of the women, whom, for his own satisfaction, he had so often tormented.

Vathek and Nouronihar turned pale in their litter; and, regarding each other with haggard looks, reproached themselves—the one with a thousand of the blackest crimes, a thousand projects of impious ambition; the other, with the desolation of her family, and the perdition of the amiable Gulchenrouz. Nouronihar persuaded herself that she heard in the fatal music the groans of her dying father; and Vathek, the sobs of the fifty children he had sacrificed to the Giaour. Amidst these complicated pangs of anguish, they perceived themselves impelled towards the shepherd, whose countenance was so commanding, that Vathek, for the first time, felt overawed; whilst Nouronihar concealed her face with her hands. The music paused, and the Genius, addressing the Caliph, said:

"Deluded Prince! to whom Providence hath confided the care of innumerable subjects, is it thus that thou fulfillest thy mission? Thy crimes are already completed; and, art thou now hastening towards thy punishment? Thou knowest, that beyond these mountains, Eblis and his accursed Dives hold their infernal empire; and seduced by a malignant phantom, thou art proceeding to surrender thyself to them! This moment is the last of grace allowed thee! Abandon thy atrocious purpose. Return. Give back Nouronihar to her father, who still retains a few sparks of life. Destroy thy tower, with all its abominations. Drive Carathis from thy councils. Be just to thy subjects. Respect the ministers of the Prophet. Compensate for thy impieties by an exemplary life; and, instead of squandering thy days in voluptuous indulgence, lament thy crimes on the sepulchres of thy ancestors. Thou beholdest the clouds that obscure the sun; at the instant he recovers his splendour, if thy heart be not changed, the time of mercy assigned thee will be past for ever."

Vathek, depressed with fear, was on the point of prostrating himself at the feet of the shepherd, whom he perceived to be of a nature superior to man, but his pride prevailing, he audaciously lifted his head, and glancing at him one of his terrible looks, said:

"Whoever thou art, withhold thy useless admonitions. Thou wouldst either delude me, or art thyself deceived. If what I have done be so criminal as thou pretendest, there remains not for me a moment of grace. I have traversed a sea of blood, to acquire a power which will make thy equals tremble; deem not that I shall retire when in view of the port; or that I will relinquish her who is dearer to me than either my life or thy mercy. Let the sun appear! Let him illumine my career! It matters not where it may end."

On uttering these words, which made even the Genius shudder, Vathek threw himself into the arms of Nouronihar, and commanded that his horses should be forced back to the road.

There was no difficulty in obeying these orders, for the attraction had ceased, the sun shone forth in all his glory, and the shepherd vanished with a lamentable scream.

The fatal impression of the music of the Genius remained, notwithstanding, in the hearts of Vathek's attendants. They viewed each other with looks of consternation. At the approach of night, almost all of them escaped; and, of this numerous assemblage, there only remained the chief of the eunuchs, some idolatrous slaves, Dilara, and a few other women, who, like herself, were votaries of the religion of the Magi.

The Caliph, fired with the ambition of prescribing laws to the Intelligences of Darkness, was but little embarrassed at this dereliction. The impetuosity of his blood prevented him from sleeping; nor did he encamp any more as before. Nouronihar, whose impatience, if possible, exceeded his own, importuned him to hasten his march, and lavished on him a thousand caresses, to beguile all reflection. She fancied herself already more potent than Balkis; and pictured to her imagination the Genii falling prostrate at the foot of her throne. In this manner they advanced by moonlight, till they came within view of the two towering rocks, that form a kind of portal to the valley, at whose extremity rose the vast ruins of Istakar. Aloft on the mountain, glimmered the fronts of various royal mausoleums, the horror of which was deepened by the shadows of night. They passed through two villages, almost deserted; the only inhabitants remaining being a few feeble old men, who at the sight of horses and litters fell upon their knees, and cried out:

"O heaven! is it then by these phantoms that we have been for six months tormented! Alas! it was from the terror of these spectres, and the noise beneath the mountains, that our people have fled, and left us at the mercy of maleficent spirits!"

The Caliph, to whom these complaints were but unpromising auguries, drove over the bodies of these wretched old men, and at length arrived at the foot of the terrace of black marble. There he descended from his litter, handing down Nouronihar; both, with beating hearts, stared wildly around them, and expected, with an apprehensive shudder, the approach of the Giaour. But nothing as yet announced his appearance.

A deathlike stillness reigned over the mountain, and through the air. The moon dilated, on a vast platform, the shades of the lofty columns, which reached from the terrace almost to the clouds. The gloomy watch-towers, whose number could not be counted, were veiled by no roof: and their capitals, of an architecture unknown in the records of the earth, served as an asylum for the birds of darkness, which, alarmed at the approach of such visitants, fled away croaking.

The chief of the eunuchs, trembling with fear, besought Vathek that a fire might be kindled.

"No!" replied he, "there is no time left to think of such trifles; abide where thou art, and expect my commands."

Having thus spoken, he presented his hand to Nouronihar, and ascending the steps of a vast staircase, reached the terrace, which was flagged with squares of marble, and resembled a smooth expanse of water, upon whose surface not a leaf ever dared to vegetate. On the right rose the watch-towers, ranged before the ruins of an immense palace, whose walls were embossed with various figures. In front stood forth the colossal forms of four creatures, composed of the leopard and the griffin; and though but of stone, inspired emotions of terror. Near these were distinguished by the splendour of the moon, which streamed full on the place, characters like those on the sabres of the Giaour, that possessed the same virtue of changing every moment. These, after vacillating for some time, at last fixed in Arabic letters, and prescribed to the Caliph the following words:

"Vathek! thou hast violated the conditions of my parchment, and deservest to be sent back; but in favour to thy companion, and as the meed for what thou hast done to obtain it, Eblis permitteth that the portal of his palace shall be opened, and the subterranean fire will receive thee into the number of its adorers."

He scarcely had read these words before the mountain, against which the terrace was reared, trembled; and the watch-towers were ready to topple headlong upon them. The rock yawned, and disclosed within it a staircase of polished marble, that seemed to approach the abyss. Upon each stair were planted two large torches, like those Nouronihar had seen in her vision, the camphorated vapour ascending from which gathered into a cloud under the hollow of the vault.

This appearance, instead of terrifying, gave new courage to the daughter of Fakreddin. Scarcely deigning to bid adieu to the moon and the firmament, she abandoned without hesitation the pure atmosphere, to plunge into these infernal exhalations. The gait of those impious personages was haughty and determined. As they descended, by the effulgence of the torches, they gazed on each other with mutual admiration, and both appeared so resplendent, that they already esteemed themselves spiritual intelligences. The only circumstance that perplexed them, was their not arriving at the bottom of the stairs. On hastening their descent, with an ardent impetuosity, they felt their steps accelerated to such a degree, that they seemed not walking, but falling from a precipice. Their progress, however, was at length impeded by a vast portal of ebony, which the Caliph without difficulty recognized. Here the Giaour awaited them, with the key in his hand,

"Ye are welcome!" said he to them, with a ghastly smile, "in spite of Mahomet, and all his dependents. I will now admit you into that palace, where you have so highly merited a place."

Whilst he was uttering these words, he touched the enamelled lock with his key, and the doors at once expanded with a noise still louder than the thunder of mountains, and as suddenly recoiled the moment they had entered.

The Caliph and Nouronihar beheld each other with amazement, at finding themselves in a place which, though roofed with a vaulted ceiling, was so spacious and lofty, that at first they took it for an immeasurable plain. But their eyes at length growing to the grandeur of the objects at hand, they extended their view to those at a distance, and discovered rows of columns and arcades, which gradually diminished, till they terminated in a point, radiant as the sun, when he darts his last beams athwart the ocean. The pavement, strewed over with gold dust and saffron, exhaled so subtile an odour, as almost overpowered them. They, however, went on, and observed an infinity of censers, in which ambergris and the wood of aloes were continually burning. Between the several columns were placed tables, each spread with a profusion of viands, and wines of every species, sparkling in vases of chrystal. A throng of Genii, and other phantastic spirits, of each sex, danced lasciviously in troops, at the sound of music which issued from beneath.

In the midst of this immense hall, a vast multitude was incessantly passing, who severally kept their right hands on their hearts, without once regarding any thing around them. They had all the livid paleness of death. Their eyes, deep sank in their sockets, resembled those phosphoric meteors, that glimmer by night in places of interment. Some stalked slowly on, absorbed in profound reverie; some shrieking with agony, ran furiously about, like tigers wounded with poisoned arrows; whilst others, grinding their teeth in rage, foamed along, more frantic than the wildest maniac. They all avoided each other, and though surrounded by a multitude that no one could number, each wandered at random unheedful of the rest, as if alone on a desert which no foot had trodden.

Vathek and Nouronihar, frozen with terror at a sight so baleful, demanded of the Giaour what these appearances might mean, and why these ambulating spectres never withdrew their hands from their hearts.

"Perplex not yourselves," replied he bluntly, "with so much at once, you will soon be acquainted with all; let us haste and present you to Eblis."

They continued their way through the multitude, but notwithstanding their confidence at first, they were not sufficiently composed to examine with attention the various perspectives of halls, and of galleries, that opened on the right hand and left, which were all illuminated by torches and braziers, whose flames rose in pyramids, to the centre of the vault. At length they came to a place where long curtains, brocaded with crimson and gold, fell from all parts, in striking confusion. Here the choirs and dances were heard no longer. The light which glimmered came from afar.

After some time Vathek and Nouronihar perceived a gleam brightening through the drapery, and entered a vast tabernacle, carpeted with the skins of leopards. An infinity of elders, with streaming beards, and afrits, in complete armour, had prostrated themselves before the ascent of a lofty eminence, on the top of which, upon a globe of fire, sat the formidable Eblis. His person was that of a young man, whose noble and regular features seemed to have been tarnished by malignant vapours. In his large eyes appeared both pride and despair; his flowing hair retained some resemblance to that of an angel of light. In his hand, which thunder had blasted, he swayed the iron sceptre, that causes the monster Ouranabad, the afrits, and all the powers of the abyss to tremble. At his presence the heart of the Caliph sank within him, and, for the first time, he fell prostrate on his face. Nouronihar, however, though greatly dismayed, could not help admiring the person of Eblis, for she expected to have seen some stupendous giant. Eblis, with a voice more mild than might be imagined, but such as transfused through the soul the deepest melancholy, said:

"Creatures of clay, I receive you into mine empire. Ye are numbered amongst my adorers. Enjoy whatever this palace affords—the treasures of the preadimite sultans, their bickering sabres, and those talismans that compel the Dives to open the subterranean expanses of the mountain of Kaf, which communicate with these. There, insatiable as your curiosity may be, shall you find sufficient to gratify it. You shall possess the exclusive privilege of entering the fortress of Aherman, and the halls of Argenk, where are portrayed all creatures endowed with intelligence, and the various animals that inhabited the earth prior to the creation of that contemptible being, whom ye denominate the Father of Mankind."

Vathek and Nouronihar feeling themselves revived and encouraged by this harangue, eagerly said to the Giaour:

"Bring us instantly to the place which contains these precious talismans."

"Come," answered this wicked Dive, with his malignant grin, "come, and possess all that my sovereign hath promised, and more."

He then conducted them into a long aisle adjoining the tabernacle, preceding them with hasty steps, and followed by his disciples with the utmost alacrity. They reached at length a hall of great extent, and covered with a lofty dome, around which appeared fifty portals of bronze, secured with as many fastenings of iron. A funereal gloom prevailed over the whole scene. Here, upon two beds of incorruptible cedar, lay recumbent the fleshless forms of the preadimite kings, who had been monarchs of the whole earth. They still possessed enough of life to be conscious of their deplorable condition. Their eyes retained a melancholy motion; they regarded each other with looks of the deepest dejection, each holding his right hand motionless on his heart. At their feet were inscribed the events of their several reigns, their power, their pride, and their crimes. Soliman Raad, Soliman Daki, and Soliman Di Gian Ben Gian, who, after having chained up the Dives in the dark caverns of Kaf, became so presumptuous, as to doubt of the Supreme Power. All these maintained great state, though not to be compared with the eminence of Soliman Ben Daoud.

This king, so renowned for his wisdom, was on the loftiest elevation, and placed immediately under the dome. He appeared to possess more animation than the rest, though, from time to time, he laboured with profound sighs, and, like his companions, kept his right hand on his heart; yet his countenance was more composed, and he seemed to be listening to the sullen roar of a vast cataract, visible in part through the grated portals. This was the only sound that intruded on the silence of these doleful mansions. A range of brazen vases surrounded the elevation.

"Remove the covers from these cabalistic depositaries," said the Giaour to Vathek, "and avail thyself of the talismans, which will break asunder all these gates of bronze, and not only render thee master of the treasures contained within them, but also of the spirits by which they are guarded."

The Caliph, whom this ominous preliminary had entirely disconcerted, approached the vases with faltering footsteps, and was ready to sink with terror, when he heard the groans of Soliman. As he proceeded, a voice from the livid lips of the prophet articulated these words:

"In my lifetime, I filled a magnificent throne, having on my right hand twelve thousand seats of gold, where the patriarchs and prophets heard my doctrines; on my left the sages and doctors, upon as many thrones of silver, were present at all my decisions. Whilst I thus administered justice to innumerable multitudes, the birds of the air librating over me, served as a canopy from the rays of the sun. My people flourished, and my palace rose to the clouds. I erected a temple to the Most High, which was the wonder of the universe; but I basely suffered myself to be seduced by the love of women, and a curiosity that could not be restrained by sub-lunary things. I listened to the counsels of Aherman, and the daughter of Pharaoh; and adored fire, and the host of heaven. I forsook the holy city, and commanded the Genii to rear the stupendous palace of Istakar, and the terrace of the watch-towers, each of which was consecrated to a star. There for a while I enjoyed myself in the zenith of glory and pleasure. Not only men, but supernatural existences were subject also to my will. I began to think, as these unhappy monarchs around had already thought, that the vengeance of heaven was asleep, when at once the thunder burst my structures asunder, and precipitated me hither; where, however, I do not remain like the other inhabitants totally destitute of hope, for an angel of light hath revealed, that in consideration of the piety of my early youth, my woes shall come to an end when this cataract shall for ever cease to flow. Till then I am in torments, ineffable torments, an unrelenting fire preys on my heart."

Having uttered this exclamation, Soliman raised his hands towards heaven, in token of supplication, and the Caliph discerned through his bosom, which was transparent as crystal, his heart enveloped in flames. At a sight so full of horror, Nouronihar fell back like one petrified, into the arms of Vathek, who cried out with a convulsive sob:

"O Giaour! whither hast thou brought us! Allow us to depart, and I will relinquish all thou hast promised. O Mahomet! remains there no more mercy!"

"None! none!" replied the malicious Dive. "Know, miserable prince, thou art now in the abode of vengeance, and despair. Thy heart, also, will be kindled, like those of the other votaries of Eblis. A few days are allotted thee previous to this fatal period: employ them as thou wilt. Recline on these heaps of gold: command the Infernal Potentates: range at thy pleasure through these immense subterranean domains. No barrier shall be shut against thee. As for me, I have fulfilled my mission. I now leave thee to thyself."

At these words he vanished.

The Caliph and Nouronihar remained in the most abject affliction. Their tears unable to flow, scarcely could they support themselves. At length, taking each other despondingly by the hand, they went faltering from this fatal hall, indifferent which way they turned their steps. Every portal opened at their approach. The Dives fell prostrate before them. Every reservoir of riches was disclosed to their view, but they no longer felt the incentives of curiosity, pride, or avarice. With like apathy they heard the chorus of Genii, and saw the stately banquets prepared to regale them. They went wandering on from chamber to chamber, hall to hall, and gallery to gallery; all without bounds or limit; all distinguishable by the same lowering gloom; all adorned with the same awful grandeur; all traversed by persons in search of repose and consolation, but who sought them in vain, for every one carried within him a heart tormented in flames. Shunned by these various sufferers, who seemed by their looks to be upbraiding the partners of their guilt, they withdrew from them, to wait in direful suspense the moment which should render them to each other the like objects of terror.

"What," exclaimed Nouronihar, "will the time come, when I shall snatch my hand from thine!"

"Ah!" said Vathek, "and shall my eyes ever cease to drink from thine long draughts of enjoyment! Shall the moments of our reciprocal ecstasies be reflected on with horror! It was not thou that broughtest me hither; the principles by which Carathis perverted my youth have been the sole cause of my perdition!"

Having given vent to these painful expressions, he called to an Afrit, who was stirring up one of the braziers, and bade him fetch the Princess Carathis from the palace of Samarah.

After issuing these orders, the Caliph and Nouronihar continued walking amidst the silent crowd, till they heard voices at the end of the gallery. Presuming them to proceed from some unhappy beings, who like themselves were awaiting their final doom, they followed the sound, and found it to come from a small square chamber, where they discovered sitting on sofas, five young men of goodly figure, and a lovely female, who were all holding a melancholy conversation, by the glimmering of a lonely lamp. Each had a gloomy and forlorn air, and two of them were embracing each other with great tenderness. On seeing the Caliph and the daughter of Fakreddin enter they arose, saluted, and gave them place. Then he who had appeared the most considerable of the group, addressed himself thus to Vathek:

"Strangers! who doubtless are in the same state of suspense as ourselves, as you do not yet bear your hand on your heart, if you are come hither to pass the interval allotted previous to the infliction of our common punishment, condescend to relate the adventures that have brought you to this fatal place; and we in return will acquaint you with ours; which deserves but too well to be heard. We will trace back our crimes to their source, though we are not permitted to repent. This is the only employment suited to wretches like us."

The Caliph and Nouronihar assented to the proposal, and Vathek began, not without tears and lamentations, a sincere recital of every circumstance that had passed. When the afflicting narrative was closed, the young man entered on his own. Each person proceeded in order, and when the fourth prince had reached the midst of his adventures, a sudden noise interrupted him, which caused the vault to tremble, and to open.

Immediately a cloud descended, which gradually dissipating, discovered Carathis, on the back of an Afrit, who grievously complained of his burden. She, instantly springing to the ground, advanced towards her son, and said:

"What dost thou here, in this little square chamber? As the Dives are become subject to thy beck, I expected to have found thee on the throne of the preadimite kings."

"Execrable woman!" answered the Caliph; "cursed be the day thou gavest me birth! Go! follow this Afrit; let him conduct thee to the hall of the Prophet Soliman; there thou wilt learn to what these palaces are destined, and how much I ought to abhor the impious knowledge thou hast taught me."

"The height of power to which thou art arrived, has certainly turned thy brain," answered Carathis; "but I ask no more, than permission to show my respect for the prophet. It is, however, proper thou shouldst know, that, as the Afrit has informed me neither of us shall return to Samarah, I requested his permission to arrange my affairs, and he politely consented. Availing myself, therefore, of the few moments allowed me, I set fire to the tower, and consumed in it the mutes, negresses, and serpents, which have rendered me so much good service; nor should I have been less kind to Morakanabad, had he not prevented me, by deserting at last to thy brother. As for Bababalouk, who had the folly to return to Samarah, and all the good brotherhood to provide husbands for thy wives, I undoubtedly would have put them to the torture, could I but have allowed them the time. Being, however, in a hurry, I only hung him, after having caught him in a snare with thy wives; whilst them I buried alive by the help of my negresses, who thus spent their last moments, greatly to their satisfaction. With respect to Dilara, who ever stood high in my favour, she hath evinced the greatness of her mind, by fixing herself near, in the service of one of the Magi, and, I think, will soon be our own."

Vathek, too much cast down to express the indignation excited by such a discourse, ordered the Afrit to remove Carathis from his presence, and continued immersed in thought, which his companions durst not disturb.

Carathis, however, eagerly entered the dome of Soliman, and, without regarding in the least the groans of the Prophet, undauntedly removed the covers of the vases, and violently seized on the talismans. Then, with a voice more loud than had hitherto been heard in these mansions, she compelled the Dives to disclose to her the most secret treasures, the most profound stores, which the Afrit himself had not seen. She passed by rapid descents known only to Eblis and his most favoured Potentates, and thus penetrated the very entrails of the earth, where breathes the Sansar, or icy wind of death. Nothing appalled her dauntless soul. She perceived, however, in all the inmates who bore their hands on their heart, a little singularity not much to her taste. As she was emerging from one of the abysses, Eblis stood forth to her view, but, notwithstanding he displayed the full effulgence of his infernal majesty, she preserved her countenance unaltered, and even paid her compliments with considerable firmness.

This superb monarch thus answered:

"PRINCESS, whose knowledge and whose crimes have merited a conspicuous rank in my empire, thou doest well to employ the leisure that remains, for the flames and torments which are ready to seize on thy heart, will not fail to provide thee with full employment."

He said this, and was lost in the curtains of his tabernacle.

Carathis paused for a moment with surprise, but, resolved to follow the advice of Eblis, she assembled all the choirs of Genii, and all the Dives, to pay her homage. Thus marched she in triumph through a vapour of perfumes, amidst the acclamations of all the malignant spirits; with most of whom she had formed a previous acquaintance. She even attempted to dethrone one of the Solimans, for the purpose of usurping his place, when a voice, proceeding from the Abyss of Death, proclaimed:

"ALL IS ACCOMPLISHED!"

Instantaneously, the haughty forehead of the intrepid princess became corrugated with agony; she uttered a tremendous yell, and fixed—no more to be withdrawn—her right hand upon her heart, which was become a receptacle of eternal fire.

In this delirium, forgetting all ambitious projects, and her thirst for that knowledge which should ever be hidden from mortals, she overturned the offerings of the Genii; and, having execrated the hour she was begotten, and the womb that had borne her, glanced off in a whirl that rendered her invisible, and continued to revolve without intermission.

At almost the same instant, the same voice announced to the Caliph, Nouronihar, the five princes, and the princess, the awful and irrevocable decree. Their hearts immediately took fire, and they at once lost the most precious of the gifts of heaven—HOPE. These unhappy beings recoiled, with looks of the most furious distraction. Vathek beheld in the eyes of Nouronihar nothing but rage and vengeance; nor could she discern ought in his but aversion and despair. The two princes who were friends, and till that moment had preserved their attachment, shrunk back, gnashing their teeth with mutual and unchangeable hatred. Kalilah and his sister made reciprocal gestures of imprecation; whilst the two other princes testified their horror for each other by the most ghastly convulsions, and screams that could not be smothered. All severally plunged themselves into the accursed multitude, there to wander in an eternity of unabating anguish.

Such was, and such should be, the punishment of unrestrained passions, and atrocious actions. Such is, and such should be, the chastisement of blind ambition, that would transgress those bounds which the Creator hath prescribed to human knowledge, and by aiming at discoveries reserved for pure intelligence, acquire that infatuated pride, which perceives not the condition appointed to man is, TO BE IGNORANT AND HUMBLE.

Thus the CALIPH VATHEK who, for the sake of empty pomp and forbidden power, hath sullied himself with a thousand crimes, became a prey to grief without end, and remorse without mitigation; whilst the humble and despised GULCHENROUZ passed whole ages in undisturbed tranquillity, and the pure happiness of childhood.